Critical Praise for Corporate T

Wind|

"Pen Wilkinson is one of the most intriguing new characters on the Minnesota crime scene."

—*St. Paul Pioneer Press*

"Suspenseful . . . a great read."

—*Mystery Sequels*

"A nicely written and taut book, *Windfall* would be a welcome addition to any library for fans of corporate thrillers . . . a fun read."

—*Reading Other People*

"With a fast-moving action-packed plot, this thriller has you jumping at shadows and considering keeping a gun on your nightstand, or better yet, under your pillow. Character driven and well written, you feel like you're in the middle of the action."

—*Sweet Mystery Books*

Downfall

"*Downfall* is an exhilarating, action-packed financial thriller . . ."
—Harriet Klausner, *Mystery Gazette*

". . . a fantastic read . . . an entertaining and engrossing book."
—*Charline Ratcliff Reviews*

"*Downfall* is a very intense thriller. Once I started reading, I couldn't put it down."

—*Mystery Sequels*

"*Downfall* by Brian Lutterman is a well-constructed thriller . . . an excellent read."

—Larry Krantz, *Readers' Favorite Reviews*

". . . replete with suspense made even more dramatic by the protagonist being confined to a wheelchair."

—John A. Broussard, *I Love a Mystery*

Bound to Die

Minnesota Book Award Runner-Up

"...a taut, swift-paced and well-plotted debut thriller by a Minnesota author."

—*St. Paul Pioneer Press*

"...a gripping, twisted, lethal saga, and one that quickly captures the reader's total attention and won't let go until the shocking climax..."

—*Midwest Book Review*

"An inexplicable quadruple murder, a duplicitous presidential adviser and a mysterious and deadly cult called the Bound bear mysterious connections to each other in lawyer Brian Lutterman's debut mystery, *Bound to Die*. Widow Tori McMillan wanders jungles, mountains and the nation's capital as she tries to find her best friend and a group of missing children, as well as to determine what actually happened to her husband."

—*Publishers Weekly*

"...bound to entertain...gets your interest from the get-go."

—Kristofer Upjohn, *Pine Bluff Commercial*

"With the help of an infatuated police officer and the hindrance of an FBI agent, Tori finds herself traveling from the Yucatan jungle into the mountains of Denver to the steps of the White House. Before it is over, Tori will question all that she believes to be good. Tori also puts her life on the line in order to solve the mystery that now threatens her sanity."

—Susan Johnson, *All About Murder*

Poised to Kill

"Author Brian Lutterman has proven himself to be a master storyteller in this masterfully woven tale of tycoons and terrorists. *Poised to Kill* is highly recommended reading, especially for enthusiasts of contemporary action/adventure thrillers."

—*Midwest Book Review*

"Lutterman keeps his readers on the edge of their chairs until the last page. The twists, chases, and shootings by professional terrorists keep occurring with increasing tension. Written in the first person, Lutterman draws his readers into the thriller. Lutterman is the author of **BOUND TO DIE**, another taut, top quality thriller. This is a suspenseful, must read book."

—Marion Cason, *I Love a Mystery*

"…a good, enjoyable read, with satisfying links to today's society. Lutterman should garner wide audiences for this story, and for those to come."

—Carl Brookins, *Reviewing the Evidence*

"Lawyer and author Brian P. Lutterman's latest novel, *Poised to Kill*, is an action-packed suspense thriller that's just simply enjoyable. Lutterman, who packed a punch with his debut novel, *Bound to Die*, proves that he is not just a flash in the pan or a one-book wonder with *Poised to Kill*... Highly recommended."

—*New Mystery Reader Review*

"...tightly plotted and has a fascinating take on an interesting scenario."

—*Books 'n' Bytes*

"Layers of betrayal is the name of the game in *Poised to Kill*. The plot ventures cross country and back around many twists and turns to uncover who might be behind the plan to cripple a nation, a major company, and ruin one man's life. *Poised to Kill* is very intriguing and full of unlikely suspects. It will keep you turning the pages and digging to find out which betrayal is the root, or are they all just pieces of one big plan."

—Joy Spear, *Murder and Mayhem Book Club*

for Doug & Peggy: with warmest best wishes,

Freefall

Brian Lutterman

Brian Lutterman

Conquill Press

This book is a work of fiction. Names, characters, places and incidents either are products of the author's imagination or are used fictitiously. Certain liberties have been taken in portraying actual law enforcement and prosecutorial agencies. This is wholly intentional. Any resemblance to actual events, or to actual persons living or dead, is entirely coincidental. For information about special discounts for bulk purchases, contact conquillpress@comcast.net.

FREEFALL

Cover Design: Rebecca Treadway

Library of Congress Control Number: 2016958094

Lutterman, Brian

Freefall: a novel / by Brian Lutterman – 1st edition

ISBN: 978-0-9908461-8-5

Conquill Press/April 2017

Printed in the United States of America

10 9 8 7 6 5 4 3 2 1

In memory of my mother, Anna Lutterman
(1932-2011)

Also by Brian Lutterman

Windfall

Downfall

Bound to Die

Poised to Kill

Acknowledgments

The author gratefully acknowledges the assistance of the following people in researching topics for this book:

Corporate IT systems and hacking: Don Klabunde, Peter Hilpisch and Greg Gardner

Labor and delivery procedures: Kara Pratt

Banking systems and management: Jeanne Hilpisch

Chapter 1

Kenny Sellars lay in bed with his clothes on, waiting for them to come. Through a slight opening in his window, he listened to the innocuous sounds of the suburban neighborhood — crickets chirping, an unhappy dog a couple of blocks away, the occasional car traversing the quiet street, the hiss of leaves rustling in the gentle June breeze. He had shut the air conditioning off, eliminating the background hum. He had turned on every exterior light. He waited here, waited for them to come, waited for the same depressing reason he seemed to do everything: he didn't know what else to do.

They would come at night—that was just common sense. They would come from the rear, through the neighbor's yard, but he had to assume they would watch the front, too, probably using a clump of bushes near the street as cover. Once they got here, he was less sure how they would get in. He guessed they would either pry open the sliding glass door on the rear deck or force a basement window. They undoubtedly knew he was home alone.

Why on earth was he still here? As long as he stayed, he could hope they wouldn't come—might never come. He could tell himself running would be silly. He was a bit player, hardly worth the effort.

They would come. Some things you just know.

Kenny supposed that someone who had done what he had done, associated with the people he had associated with, should be hardened, street-smart—wise beyond his years. But he felt as oblivious, as confused, as manipulated as the clueless teenager he had been all along. And yet, late at night, when the swirling thoughts and emotions slowed, sorting themselves out, settling like a stone in the pit of his abdomen, the appalling clarity set in: He had sold his soul. Sold it cheaply. Sold it without thinking, for the most shallow, banal, teenage reasons.

He heard something. Or maybe sensed it. He couldn't say, now or later, exactly what caused the change in his environment's equilibrium. He had willed himself not to get up constantly to check the back yard. But now, he got up.

He stood well back from the window, scanning the yard. The movement he sensed came in the form of shadows, of dark, indistinct shapes. He thought there were two.

It was really happening. Incredible, but inevitable. He didn't have time to think about it. He'd been warned that there were at least two: the tall woman—the blonde—and another guy. But there might be more. And what did they want? His friend Liam didn't know.

But Kenny did.

There. One shape scooted along the edge of the yard to the corner of the house. *Showtime,* Kenny thought. He went next door to the master bedroom, picked up the landline on the nightstand, and dialed 911. When the operator picked up, he spoke the words "Home invasion" and set the phone on the table.

Next, he pulled out his cell phone, sent a brief text, and replaced the phone in his pocket. From the off-the-hook phone on the nightstand, he could hear the operator's voice. "Sir? Sir? Are you there? Did you say 'home invasion'?"

He ran back to his bedroom. From downstairs, he heard a muted crack as someone forced open the sliding glass door. He didn't bother looking out toward the front of the house; the intruders would have that covered. Hesitating briefly, he listened, hearing footsteps downstairs. And then, on the staircase.

Kenny grabbed his pre-loaded backpack and ran toward the bathroom at the end of the hallway. Guided by a faint night light, he stepped into the bathtub and pushed open the small window on the wall above it. From down the hallway, he heard shuffling and saw the jerky streaks of flashlights on the walls.

He squeezed through the window and dropped down onto the roof of a metal storage shed a few feet away from the house, as he had practiced earlier in the day. From there, he jumped down to the ground, stumbled, and crawled through the shrubbery shielding his house from the next-door neighbor's. As he emerged in the neighbor's yard, he heard a clatter and a thump behind him. One of the intruders had come out the window after him.

He hadn't expected that.

He ran through the dark, as fast as safety would allow, through the back yard, parallel to the street, to the opposite end of the neighbor's house, to the far side of the yard, vaulting over a chain link fence. He could hear footsteps behind him.

He made it through another back yard, then swerved to his right, to the street, reasoning that the intruders' vehicle probably would have been parked on the street behind his block, rather than out front. He began to turn left, down the street, but headlights, apparently belonging to a large SUV, appeared at the end of the block. He continued across the street, briefly illuminated by the headlights, past a house, and into another back yard. Meanwhile, he heard footsteps behind him, on the street.

Kenny now found himself in uncharted territory. He had planned his route earlier in the day, scouting out obstacles and estimating distances, confident that he'd be able to lose any pursuers. But the unknown followers were forcing him to change the plan. He couldn't follow the street, and now, traversing unfamiliar, dark back yards, he was running as blindly as those who followed. Behind him, a dog barked. He sensed a shape ahead, too late. He ran into a chain link fence, hitting it waisthigh. Letting his momentum carry him, he flipped headfirst over the fence, landing hard on his back on the other side.

Instantly, his pursuer appeared at the fence, vaulting over behind him. When the figure lunged at him, he scuttled off to the side, along the fence, scraping his hand on a large, protruding tree root. He jumped to his feet and took off. Behind him, he heard a muffled thud and a muttered curse. His pursuer had stumbled, probably on the tree root. Kenny ran between two houses toward a lighted street. He emerged at the street and was instantly illuminated by headlights from a large SUV, undoubtedly the same one he'd seen earlier.

He didn't break stride. He shot across the street into another yard and, after negotiating the back yard, found himself in a wooded area. He took a sharp right and thrashed blindly through the woods. Bushes scraped his hands and face, and then he fell hard over a rock. He got up and resumed his flight. He could hear scraping sounds behind him, but he couldn't tell if the woman was on his trail.

The woman. The blonde woman. He'd caught a glimpse of her when she had lunged at him at the base of the fence. She was as Liam had described her—tall, athletic. And Liam . . . Who knew what had happened to him?

And then he was falling. Rolling, tumbling, further and further down a large hill, over branches, bushes, and weeds, finally coming to rest in a bed of rotted leaves. Instinctively, he crawled under the leaves, next to a log, and remained motionless, breathing in the pungent odor of leaves, rotting wood, and dirt. From above came the sounds of thrashing and the jerky zigzags of flashlight beams. After a few minutes there were voices, accompanied by more thrashing and more flashlights. He burrowed deeper into the leaves, deeper into the black hole of primal fear, feeling the ancient, imprinted certainty of the hunted.

If these people found him, he would die.

Chapter 2

My sister hated me. We rarely talked. I had not seen her in more than a year. When she called in the middle of the night, I didn't recognize her voice instantly.

"Marsha, is that you?"

"Pen, I need help."

"Marsha, it's three in the morning," I said, rubbing my eyes.

"Well, it's six here in Tampa."

"So LA is eccentric about the time zone thing."

"I couldn't sleep, Pen. I need help."

"What crisis could make you desperate enough to resort to calling me?"

The crisis, it turned out, was just about the only one that would compel me to respond.

"Kenny's gone, Pen. Vanished."

"Kenny ran away?"

"No. He left."

"There's a difference?"

"Of course there is. Something happened. He's dropped out of contact."

I propped myself on one elbow and adjusted the phone under my chin. Marsha, my older sister, was not having a good life. She had been divorced for six years. Four years ago, she had lost her young daughter in a car accident. Her teenage son, Kenny, was brilliant but unfocused. In her job as a labor and delivery nurse, she worked grueling, irregular night shifts. And now her son had taken off. The gods were piling it on.

5

"When did he leave?" I asked.

"Friday night, I think. That's the last anybody has seen or heard from him."

"Today is . . . Monday. So a little over forty-eight hours. What do you think happened?"

"I don't know. But I'm sure he's in trouble."

"He's in Minnesota, Marsh. So he hasn't been in touch for a couple of days. He's eighteen, right? An adult. Is this really a big deal?"

"Yes, it is a big deal." She bit off the words with exasperated precision. "He doesn't answer my calls or texts. He just disappeared."

"What does Alec say?"

By asking about her ex-husband, I was wading right into the muck. Kenny had left Tampa to join his now-remarried father in Minnesota about a year ago, before his senior year in high school.

"Alec says that Kenny left. And *Alec* doesn't know anything more."

"Have you talked to the Minneapolis police?"

"Yes. A guy called back and asked me some questions. But they say he's eighteen and not a danger to himself or others. They won't even take a missing person's report."

I wasn't surprised. I had encountered the same response from the police in Minneapolis a few months earlier when I had tried to locate a missing witness there.

"You think he's in danger?" I asked.

"What do you think? He's up and disappeared. He doesn't respond. Of course he's in danger. If he's alive."

She was being dramatic, I thought. The situation might be a cause for mild concern. But life and death? "Are you two getting along? Is he mad at you for some reason?"

"We're getting along fine. Better, in fact, since he moved up there. We had a very friendly conversation on Thursday."

"So what do you want me to do?"

A pause. "I need someone to go up there and look for him."

"Isn't Alec looking?"

She didn't respond.

"All right, silly question." Alec was an idiot. "So why me?"

"I don't know who else to turn to, Pen. You're experienced at investigating. And . . ." She hesitated, wondering, I thought, whether to push her entire stake onto the table. She did. "You're family."

Indeed I was. But the observation had little to do with our blood relationship and everything to do with the Elephant in the Room, the subject we never broached. By saying I was family, she really meant that I owed her.

And I did.

"Why don't you go up there yourself?" I asked.

"I will, but I can't get off from work right away. It's really busy, and I can't just take off without finding someone to cover my shifts—not if I want to be employed when I get back. I hope to get up there in the next day or two if he isn't found by then."

I shouldn't have been surprised. Her son was in trouble, but a lot of other mothers, and their babies, needed her, too. "And you're assuming I can just take off from my job?"

"Come on, Pen. You're the high-powered career woman. You don't punch a clock."

It was true that my job as a federal prosecutor was salaried, but that cut both ways. I worked long hours, and in only two weeks, I was starting a major trial. To top it off, I was working for a new boss who didn't like me.

I knew I had to be missing something basic. "What is this about, Marsha? Did he just not get along with Alec? Or Alec's wife?"

"No, that's not it."

"What is Kenny involved in? Drugs?"

"Not drugs," she said without hesitation.

"Then what?"

It took her a long moment to respond. "I have no idea."

*   *   *   *

Clusters of passengers were starting to hover around my departure gate at LAX Airport, poised for the land-rush sprint to claim space for carry-ons in the plane's overhead bins. A gate agent had announced pre-boarding, and I saw another agent heading toward me. Since I'm in a wheelchair, I qualified for pre-boarding, which I appreciated. But right now, I was trying to listen on my phone as my boss shot me down.

"I won't be gone long." I explained the reason for my trip.

"I'm afraid you won't be gone at all," said Wade Hirsch, the new chief of the Public Integrity and Civil Rights Section of the US attorney's office in LA. "I'm sorry about your unfortunate situation, but of course, any time off right now is out of the question."

"Miss?" I looked up. A gate agent—an older woman—stood in front of me, gesturing toward the gate.

I exhaled and adjusted my grip on the phone. "It's important, Wade. A family emergency."

His reply was patient, his voice soft. "No, *Vargas* is important," he said, referring to the upcoming trial of *United States v. Vargas et al*, a case involving two US marshals accused of taking bribes. In my job, I had the unenviable task of prosecuting not the usual criminals, but people who were supposed to be the good guys, people who, in breaking the law, had abused their positions of public trust.

"Miss, you need to board now."

I tried to ignore the agent. I said into the phone, "But my nephew is—"

"Your nephew? I'm afraid the young man will have to resolve his own difficulties." His tone hardened. "This is your job we're talking about. It's *Vargas*. Do you really want to display such a lack of seriousness and commitment?"

The lady from the airline looked like she wanted to rip the phone from my hand. "Miss, you are holding up the boarding process."

"I'll make the trip as short as I can," I told Wade, "and I'll stay in touch and do what I can from Minnesota."

I looked around; other passengers were starting to give me dirty looks.

Hirsch's response was tired and condescending. "Pen, you're not listening to me. I'm telling you this is not acceptable. After the trial you can take a vacation, if you really need one."

"Miss—"

"No, Wade," I said, my voice rising, "I'm afraid you're the one with a hearing problem. This is not a vacation. It's an emergency. I'm getting onto a plane now."

Following a brief, stunned silence, he said, "You propose to go to . . . Minnesota, is it?" He made it sound like a frontier outpost in the Yukon Territory. There were some similarities, I acknowledged to myself, at least in the winter.

"That's right."

A heavy sigh made its way over the line to me. "Make it brief. I will expect daily reports on your preparation. And you'd better win the goddamned case." He hung up.

I replaced my phone, relieved but daunted by the challenge of keeping the balls in the air while I was gone.

I followed the now-angry agent down the ramp, where I transferred to a waiting aisle chair. A flight attendant pushed me carefully onto the plane, where I slid into an aisle seat.

I valued my career a lot. But after only a few months, I'd had just about enough of Wade Hirsch. From the beginning, he'd seemed unaccountably hostile to me. I'd asked around discreetly and finally learned that Hirsch had been heard grousing about the coddling and special treatment I allegedly received because I was female and handicapped. My request for time off just before an important trial fit snugly into that ridiculous but apparently powerful narrative. But I felt sure there was more to it than I knew.

As the rest of the passengers filed past me, I called my co-counsel for the trial, Cassandra Freeman, and filled her in. She was understanding and supportive, but sounded anxious, about both Wade's reaction and the trial. I promised to stay in touch.

I settled back, took a deep breath, and tried to collect my thoughts, feeling out of my depth and under the gun. I reflected on how little I knew about Kenny. I hadn't seen my nephew in four years. He was a young man now, and God only knew what he had gotten himself into. It was starting to become clear, however, what this little jaunt to Minnesota was getting me into.

*   *   *

I woke up as the pilot announced our arrival in Minneapolis. Somehow, I'd fallen asleep during the flight, after spending a couple of hours working on the Vargas case. We pulled up to the gate, and I waited patiently while all the other passengers got off the plane. During the wait, I powered up my phone and checked my voicemail. The only message of consequence was from Cassandra, who had several questions about the trial preparation. I left her a message, answering her questions as best I could. Then I sent Wade Hirsch a brief email, confirming our conversation that morning, apologizing for not completing the proper paperwork for a leave, and asking that the forms be forwarded to me. I didn't know if there was actually a procedure or forms, or, indeed, any provision for a family leave at all. But, being a lawyer, I figured I'd better cover myself.

That done, I put in a quick call to James Carter, the man I'd been dating for more than a year. Our conversation was brief and a little strained. I tried to make the trip sound as routine as possible, but he sounded unconvinced. We agreed to talk again later that night.

After the plane emptied out, a crew member brought an aisle chair to my seat. I transferred over to it and grabbed my carry-on bag and laptop. The man pushed me out to the jetway, where I waited for my wheelchair to be brought up.

The wheelchair. It always came back to the wheelchair, to the ever-present reminder of the moment when so many things, including my relationship with Marsha, had changed forever. In one instant, on a freeway near Tampa, the timelines had diverged, the course permanently altered. The image of the truck veering into my lane still flashed through my mind every day, and I wasn't even sure anymore how much of my recollection was accurate and how much was imagined. But there was no doubt how the moment had ended.

For me, the ability to walk was the moment's first casualty, soon to be followed by my career and my upcoming marriage. For Marsha's six-year-old daughter, Tracy, who had unbuckled her seat belt in the back, it was not only the moment, but her life, that had ended. For Marsha, her feelings toward me, always distant, had dissolved into unacknowledged hatred. My obligation to her could never really be repaid, not by finding Kenny—not even by spending the rest of my life in a wheelchair. But there it was. And here I was.

Chapter 3

"I don't like it," Ian said. He and Brit sat in the surveillance van, watching Alec Sellars's house.

"Suburban neighborhood," Ian continued in his Aussie accent. "In daylight. We're exposed." He rolled his window down further, trying to stay cool in the summer warmth.

"Everything is clean so far," Brit said. "We've been watching for more than an hour." She glanced at her watch. "We'll give it another ten minutes."

After another period of silence Ian said, "Are you sure this is the right time?"

"We can't wait any longer. We've already wasted time trying to track down his friends." She fingered the balaclava and heavy plastic bag in her hand. "I can't believe the little bastard got away. I was only half a minute behind him—it was just rotten luck, getting tripped up by that damned tree root. And then he just vanishes into the woods. I found his hiding place, you know—a little hollow next to a fallen tree. I was searching all over the hill that night, probably within ten feet of him."

"Let's just hope the parents give him up fast. The quicker we get out of here, the better." He picked up the secure walkie-talkie from the seat beside him, clicked it on, and said, "Anything?"

"All quiet," came the response from Oliver, the team member who watched from the street behind the Sellars home.

"Stay cool. We make our move in eight." He clicked off.

"Even if Sellars and his wife don't know where he is, they'll give us the names of a couple of the kid's friends," Brit said. "We'll have what we need in two minutes."

"What if they don't know?"

"They might not know where Kenny is, but why wouldn't they know the names of his friends?"

"Carlin checked social media. Kenny doesn't seem to have much in the way of friends."

"He's found squat."

"No names." Ian agreed. "The kid had very little online presence to begin with, and he's apparently hacked in and wiped what was there."

Brit's face wrinkled up in surprise. "You can do that?"

"*He* can do it, apparently. It's really hard, according to Carlin. But the kid is good. We can hack the sites, find the screenshot caches, and recover them, but it will take time."

"In the meantime, we need to find some human beings, some actual people who know him. Kenny has to have somebody. He probably has a girlfriend. Have you seen that picture of him? He might have more than one."

"What if Z has him?"

Silence. They didn't even want to think about that.

"The kid is secretive," Ian observed.

"You'd be, too, if you were working for Z. That's why Carlin hasn't found diddley." Carlin, the team's computer geek, had been searching relentlessly online for any sign of Kenny. He had hacked into the high school's system and found no leads. He had set tripwires in numerous places online. But Kenny remained at large, off the grid. They'd find him eventually—it was only a matter of time. But, according to their employer, they didn't have much time. And so the visit to Alec Sellars.

Brit watched the house with the patience of the predator she was. "How did the subject in Tampa make us?" She spoke in an Appalachian hillbilly twang, which sounded flat and menacing.

"You should have worn a wig," Ian deadpanned.

"Screw you, Ian." He gave her a look, and she said, "It was an insult, not a suggestion."

Ian smiled and said nothing, but Brit knew he must sometimes imagine what it might be like with her.

Brit admitted to herself that she had misjudged the Tampa situation. And Ian, damn him, was right. People sometimes did notice Brit, if they saw her in action and not as a bystander. A whippy five-foot-ten with spiky blonde hair, she could stand out in a crowd, and she sometimes did wear masks or disguises. But she hadn't done so in Tampa.

Most of the time, she was her own best disguise, hiding in plain sight. In their world, few people expected a woman, much less a distinctive blonde. Ian was a colorless, easygoing Everyman who, like herself, was a stone-cold killer. But nobody noticed him coming, and few people would remember him afterward. Oliver was the most physically adept of the team, but he was a follower, not a decision-maker. And Carlin was capable enough but was usually too valuable for field work. They needed him working the databases.

Ian checked his automatic and chambered a round. Four minutes. "It doesn't matter now. He obviously tipped Kenny, and now the kid's gotten away." Kenny's friend in Tampa had been unequivocal about Kenny's involvement with Z. Brit had a talent for stripping away equivocation.

"Kenny still has to be around," she said. "He's by far the best lead we've got on Z and what Z is up to—maybe the only real one . . . oh, shit."

Ian looked up sharply and grabbed the walkie-talkie. "You see it?" he asked.

"Yes," came Oliver's reply. A white van was turning into the driveway at the Sellars house.

"Stand by." He looked over at Brit. "Who the hell is that?"

"I don't know." She reached for her cell phone. "But we'll find out."

Chapter 4

Alec Sellars's home was unexpectedly nice, a beautiful two-story timber-and-stucco structure on a wooded corner lot in southwest Minneapolis. Apparently the move to Minnesota, which Alec and his current wife had made a year ago, had worked out well financially. Alec's wife, Shannon, was originally from the Twin Cities, and Alec had found a job here as finance manager for a Chrysler dealership, a position similar to the one he'd held in Tampa.

I had called from the airport and found him at home. I imagined he'd taken off work to deal with Kenny's disappearance. As I descended the ramp from my rented van to the driveway, Alec sauntered out of the house. He looked down at me, taken aback. He'd never seen me in a wheelchair. Finally, when I'd completed my descent, he shook my hand. "Pen. Great to see you. You're looking good."

"Thanks." I hadn't seen my former brother-in-law in six years, but he had aged well, still erect and handsome at forty-one, with plentiful dark hair, a smooth face, and a ready smile. "Are you playing hooky today?" I asked.

"I work Saturdays," he said. "I get Mondays off."

"Have you heard from Kenny?"

"Uh, no."

"Have you been out looking for him?"

Alec looked a little surprised at my abrupt questioning but refused to be put out of his friendly mood. "We've done everything we can think of. Maybe you can help us take it from here."

I pushed a switch on my key ring, retracting the ramp and closing the van's side door. "I'll do what I can to help. But I don't have a lot of time."

He nodded. "That's what Marsha said. Come on in." I followed him to the steps leading to a side door, then turned around, facing away from the house.

Alec stood in the doorway, clueless. "Uh—how do you want to work this?"

"Maybe you could pull me up the steps."

"Sure—okay." Alec pulled me up the three steps into the house, through a mud room and into the kitchen, a spacious room with large appliances, granite countertops, and a center island. He pulled a chair away from the kitchen table, and I rolled up to it. "Coffee?" he said.

"Fine." He began fiddling with the coffee pot.

"Here—let me do that," a female voice said. I glanced over at the door, where a woman had joined us.

"Oh, hi," Alec said. "Pen, meet my wife."

Alec's second spouse was in her mid-thirties, short, with dark, curly hair, carrying a bit of extra weight but very pretty. She shook my hand. "I'm Shannon Fine. Pleased to meet you, Pen. I heard you were coming, so I took the afternoon off and came home." She took over making the coffee, and Alec sat down across the table from me.

"I haven't seen Kenny in several years," I said. "Do you have a picture?"

Shannon, who appeared sharp and efficient, answered. "I'll get one in a minute." Alec, I noted, apparently didn't have one in his wallet or on his phone.

"When did you realize that Kenny was missing?" I asked.

"He wasn't here when we got home around noon on Sunday," Alec said. "We were spending a long weekend up north at Grand Casino."

"You believe he left on Friday night?"

"Sounds about right. Marsha called me on Saturday night, looking for him."

"Has he ever taken off before?"

"Not without telling us."

"Why do you think he left?"

He shrugged. "Hard to say. He sort of does his own thing."

"What is his thing, exactly? Is he in school?"

"Well, no—the school year's over."

"Did he graduate?"

"Not yet," Alec said. "He's got a couple of classes left to finish up."

"Does he have a job?"

"Not exactly. He worked at Subway for a while."

Shannon cut in. "That was last summer."

"Yeah, right," Alec said. "Anyway, he does some computer work for a guy. Works here at home."

"What kind of computer work?"

"Hell, I don't know." He smiled. "I know jack about computers. But he spends a lot of time online. He's always been good at the techie stuff."

"Who's the guy he works for?"

"I'm not sure. Do you know, Shan?"

Shannon shook her head as she set two steaming mugs in front of us. "I don't. He's been secretive about it."

"Does he have a car?"

"No," Alec said. "He doesn't seem to need one very often."

"What are his plans?"

"I don't know. He's mentioned college, but of course he'd have to finish high school first. He doesn't talk a lot about it."

I paused and sipped from my coffee mug. I wondered if we were all talking about the same young man, who actually lived in this household.

"What do his friends say?" I asked.

"Well, it's only been a couple of days, and we haven't actually heard from any of them, have we, Shan?"

Shannon shook her head, not meeting my eyes. Alec was making her cringe.

I pulled out my phone and opened the notepad. "Why don't you give me the names and numbers of his two or three closest friends?"

There was an embarrassed silence. Alec said, "There's that girl he's been dating. Pretty girl." He looked at Shannon. "Sierra, right?"

"Yes."

I wrote it down and asked, "Last name?"

Alec didn't respond.

"Bjorklund," Shannon said.

"Do you know how to reach her?"

"Let me see what I can find," Shannon said. She disappeared, seizing on the chance to leave the room.

"Any other friends?" I asked Alec.

"He has a buddy he hangs around with—a tall kid with glasses. I don't remember his name. Haven't seen him in a while."

Shannon returned and sat down at the table. She held a slip of paper, but made no effort to show it to me.

"Why do you think he left?" I asked, addressing the question to both of them.

Alec shrugged. "Hard to say. He didn't seem mad or anything. He left pretty much with the clothes on his back, plus his laptop."

"You didn't have an argument or a fight?"

Both shook their heads.

"Could he have had a fight with Sierra?"

More head shakes, the kind that meant "don't know" rather than "No."

"Was there anything unusual at all that happened during the past week?"

"Well, there was the break-in," Alec ventured.

I almost dropped my phone into my coffee cup. "Come again?"

"Somebody broke in while we were gone—jimmied open the back door. But they didn't take anything."

I forced myself to remain in control. Shannon looked like she wanted to dig a hole in the expensive hardwood floor and disappear inside it. "Do you think that just might have had something to do with Kenny's disappearance?" I asked.

"I don't know. We weren't here."

"Did you report it to the police?"

"Sure. They wrote up a report for our insurance, but the company won't pay to fix the door—it's within our deductible. We told the officer Kenny had taken off, too, but they didn't seem interested. In fact, they said it was probably him or one of his friends who broke in."

"The door was forced from the outside?"

"Right. The window, though—that was from the inside."

"Window?"

"In the upstairs bathroom," Alec said. "We got home, and damned if the window wasn't open. We were air-conditioning the great outdoors."

Suddenly, I felt ashamed for questioning Marsha's concern. "Let me get this straight. Someone breaks into your house but doesn't take anything. Then, probably on the same night, Kenny disappears, possibly leaving through a bathroom window, and hasn't been heard from since. Doesn't that concern you a little?"

"Sure, I guess so. But the police won't help. What are we supposed to do?"

"How about checking with the neighbors? Did they see him leave that night? Anyone chasing him?"

Alec remained silent. "I asked the Hansons next door," Shannon said. "Also the Colemans on the other side. They didn't see anything."

"You don't know of any trouble he's been in? Any disputes or arguments?"

"No," they answered in unison.

"You have to give me something to go on."

Shannon slid a sheet of paper across the table to me. On it were two names, Sierra Bjorklund and Sam Fenton, along with two phone numbers. Alec looked at Shannon. "How did you get those?"

"I asked him."

Alec nodded slowly, clearly impressed by this innovative approach.

Shannon next handed me a photograph of Kenny. I was stunned. The unformed middle-schooler I knew had grown into a remarkably handsome young man, with an angular face, aquiline nose, and dark, curly hair. The kid was hot. He'd inherited Alec's looks along with Marsha's smarts—a formidable combination.

Shannon handed me another item. "His cell phone. He left it here."

"But took his laptop?"

"Yes."

I turned on the phone and let it boot up. It wasn't protected by PIN or pattern, and I looked through it quickly, finding exactly what I expected to find: nothing. "He's wiped it." I flipped off the back cover. "He's taken the SIM card."

"Why would he do that?" Alec asked.

"He doesn't want to be found. He left this phone behind so it can't be used to track him. He probably has another one."

Alec's mouth opened slightly before closing, and his face assumed a troubled look. The gravity of Kenny's disappearance seemed to register with him for the first time. Meanwhile, I was running out of questions and still had very little to go on. I would have asked to see his room, but it was upstairs. I looked again at the picture. "What is he like? What does he do? Who is he?"

After the now-predictable blank look and shrug, Alec said, "He's basically a good kid. Hasn't given us any trouble. I always thought Marsha was too hard on him."

"Is that why he moved up here? To get away from Marsha?"

"Maybe. We never really talked about it."

Now there's a shocker, I thought.

*   *   *

Down the street, Ian and Brit watched as the visitor, a young blonde woman, was lowered down the steps to the driveway and rolled over to the handicapped van. Brit's cell phone buzzed.

"Yes?" She listened for a couple of minutes, scribbling notes on a pad, then said, "Stay on her. And on the kid." She hung up.

"What does Carlin say?" Ian asked.

"The van is a rental and was picked up this morning at the airport by a Doris Penny Wilkinson of Long Beach, California. It looks like she's a sister of the birth mother."

Ian shook his head. "How does he find out shit like that so fast?" Ian was far from a technophobe but was frequently amazed at what geeks like Carlin could find online. For that reason, he was surprised they had found so little on Kenny.

"An aunt," Brit said. "She had to have come because of the kid."

"A reasonable assumption."

"We need the house covered electronically, Ian."

"Tonight. I promise." Brit had touched on a sore spot. He hadn't yet had the opportunity to place a bug in Alec's house. "So what do we know about this aunt in the wheelchair?"

"She's a federal prosecutor in Los Angeles."

"Does that mean the Feds will be on this?"

"I doubt it," Brit said. "She may be able to draw on some resources. But there's no investigation. Where's the crime?"

"So maybe we should hold off on questioning the parents."

21

"I guess." She sounded disappointed.

"Any chance Kenny has been in touch with the aunt?"

"According to Carlin, there's no record of phone or email contact."

"Even so, she's a lead. I'm betting we can follow her to the friends—maybe a girlfriend."

Brit considered it. "You take the aunt. I'll stay here and watch the house."

"Sure." He paused. "Of course, Kenny isn't our only problem."

"Not at all. Z knows we're on the case. And Z is not just a geek in a basement. He's got some real muscle behind him. Russian muscle. The question is: Is Z harboring Kenny or hunting him?"

"Kenny was living in plain sight at his father's house, so he had to be on good terms with Z, at least until the last few days."

"All that has changed, now that Z knows we're after the kid. You can bet Z is hunting him now, too. He can't afford to let us find Kenny. Either way, we find Kenny and we find Z. And we need to find him soon. Let me know the minute you see anything, Ian. And I mean anything."

"Aye, aye, Captain."

Chapter 5

The boutique wasn't very accessible. I rolled past a series of storefronts on France Avenue, a trendy shopping destination in the Linden Hills neighborhood, and found the address. There was a little hump at the threshold, which I had to wheelie over, and the aisles were narrow. The merchandise, hung up high on the racks, would have been hard to reach. The style wasn't to my taste, anyway—slinky items for young women who had a lot of money and didn't eat much. I made my way over to the counter and asked for Sierra. An older woman gestured to someone behind me, and after a moment a young woman with long black hair appeared, stylishly dressed and very pretty except for an unfortunate case of acne. She looked at the older clerk, then at me.

"Hi, I'm Pen," I said.

Sierra looked down at me, then did a little double-take, the kind I often get from someone who didn't expect a person in a wheelchair. "Oh," she said. "Hi." She shook my hand, then looked at the older woman. "Grace, could I . . ." Her boss nodded, and Sierra looked back at me. "Want some coffee?" I'd just had coffee at Alec's, but I'd been up since three in the morning and could use more.

We went a couple of doors down to a coffee shop. France Avenue was crowded with shoppers enjoying the beautiful June day. I bought a small coffee for myself and a Frappuccino for Sierra, and we found a small table on the sidewalk outside.

Sierra worked her hands around her coffee cup but didn't drink from it. "So you're Kenny's aunt?"

"Right. His mother's sister."

"And you're here because you think he's missing?"

"You don't?"

"I haven't heard from him. But it's only been a few days. I just talked to him last week."

"Are you still officially dating?"

"Sure. Not real hot and heavy or anything. We see each other."

"But you don't communicate every day?"

"No. Every few days. We're busy."

"Really? According to Kenny's dad, he doesn't seem to do much of anything at all."

"Well—I've got a job. And Kenny does some programming."

"For whom?"

"I don't know. A guy he met in Florida, I think."

"How can I find this guy?"

"I don't know."

A troubling thought occurred to me. "Is what he does programming or hacking?"

Each additional question seemed to make her more uncomfortable. She took an unsteady sip from her Frappuccino. "I'm sure it's legit. I mean, he fools around online, I know that. But it's nothing serious. He doesn't break into the Defense Department or anything like that."

It wasn't quite the reassurance I'd hoped for. "So the idea that some nasty folks might be after him is pretty much ridiculous?"

She hesitated an instant too long. "I'm sure it's nothing like that."

"What if I told you that his house was broken into the other night, and that he escaped out a bathroom window?"

"Please," she scoffed.

"Let's take a step back. Does Kenny have any plans, other than to continue to do some programming for a guy out of his bedroom?"

"You make him sound lazy."

"Is he?"

She sipped from her Frappuccino. "No. He's just not sure what he wants to do."

"What about you?"

"I'm starting at the University of Minnesota this fall."

"Congratulations. Do you know . . ." I consulted the sheet Shannon had given me. "Sam Fenton?"

"Sure. He's a friend of Kenny's."

"His best friend?"

"I guess. Kenny was new at the school, and he's kind of quiet, anyway, so he doesn't have a lot of friends."

"The address I have here for Sam is in north Minneapolis. But he apparently went to your school?"

"Yes. It's a good school. Kids come from all over the city."

"Why didn't Kenny graduate?"

"He's really smart," Sierra said. "He's just a little . . . unfocused, I guess."

"Could you call him?"

"Not at the moment. He's between phones and his number hasn't been transferred yet."

I was reaching the end of the line. "When he calls, would you have him get in touch with me? And tell him that his mother is really worried about him?"

"Sure. I guess so."

As an afterthought I asked, "Has anyone else been around looking for him?"

She rotated her cup in both hands, apparently struggling to decide what to tell me. "Yeah, there was actually a cop looking for him."

The whole situation just got a lot curiouser, I thought. The police had supposedly refused to look for Kenny. "When was this?" I asked.

"Yesterday."

"On a Sunday?"

She shrugged.

"Did the cop leave a card?"

She sighed, dug through her purse, and produced a card, sliding it across the table to me. I looked at the card, and curious became disturbing. The "cop" was Special Agent Ben Hewitt of the Federal Bureau of Investigation.

*　　　　*　　　　*

Down the block, in the surveillance van, the Aussie named Ian put down his binoculars and picked up his buzzing phone.

"We ran the name," Brit said without preamble. "Sierra Bjorklund. She was a classmate of Kenny's and works at that boutique. Carlin should have the address and other information momentarily."

"How do you want to play it?"

"Stay on the aunt for now. Meanwhile, we'll put this girl under the microscope, check for social media, phone calls and emails."

"Got it."

"But be prepared to move. We'll have to visit her soon."

Chapter 6

I set out in the rental van for Sam Fenton's house at the other end of the city, on the north side. Sam was at home when I'd called, and despite some wariness, had agreed to meet with me. The search for Kenny had spawned two further mysteries: First, why was the FBI looking for him? I put in a call to Special Agent Hewitt, got voicemail, and left a message.

Second, why was Kenny's girlfriend lying through her teeth? I didn't have a lot of experience in sensing deception, but I was getting better at it, and even an amateur would have noticed Sierra's unnatural pauses, evasiveness, and lack of eye contact. It was tempting to conclude that Kenny was in touch with her, or that she knew where he was, or both. But that was speculation. All I could say for sure was that she probably hadn't been straight with me. She apparently hadn't even planned to tell me about the FBI agent, a man who, she said, had asked a few routine questions and hadn't said why he was looking for Kenny. I had to hope that my next contact, Kenny's buddy Sam, would be more forthcoming.

Sam Fenton lived in a diverse, working-class north Minneapolis neighborhood, not far from where I'd spent some time a few months ago looking for a missing witness for one of my cases. I skirted downtown and exited the I-94 freeway at Dowling Avenue, then made my way west. Sam's block was busy with young kids riding bikes, playing ball, and hanging out. I found the house, a well-kept two-story frame structure with a big front porch, and parked on the street.

I hauled myself from the van's front seat over to my wheelchair, which was secured to a rack behind the seat. With my own van, I simply rolled up to the steering wheel and clamped my chair into place. I pressed the button on my keychain that lowered the vehicle's profile, opened the side door, and extended the ramp. Before getting out, I pulled out my cell phone and called Sam, reminding him of our appointment and telling him I had arrived. I made my way up the crumbling asphalt driveway, and when I was halfway up, a tall kid with glasses and unruly hair came out a side door.

I extended my hand. "Hi, I'm Pen."

He looked at my hand, then realized he was supposed to shake it. After we shook, he looked at me, and the steps to the house, with the same kind of confusion Alec had shown. "I'm not sure how to handle this."

I glanced around the corner of the house, spotting a small patio between the house and the detached garage. "We could just sit outside," I said, gesturing toward the patio.

"Okay, I guess."

He went through a gate and let it close behind him, pretty much in my face. I rolled up close to the gate, pushed it open, and made my way through it to the patio. Sam took a lawn chair, and I moved up across from him. "Thanks for making time for me," I said.

"Kenny never mentioned that he had an aunt."

"I haven't seen him in a long time."

"Why not?"

I almost smiled. Sam wasn't big on social graces. "His parents are divorced. I'm his mother's sister, and I live in a different city." It was more complicated than that, but I saw no point in explaining it all to Sam.

"Why do you need a wheelchair?" he asked.

I didn't know whether the kid was direct, awkward, or maybe had a touch of autism spectrum disorder—what they sometimes call Asperger's. Or maybe he was just an insensitive jerk. "I was in a car accident four years ago."

Something seemed to click with him. "Oh, was that the one where his little sister was killed?"

My amusement at Sam's gracelessness was fading quickly. "Yes, that's the one. When did you meet Kenny?"

"Last fall. He was new in school, and we like to, you know, play the same video games and watch the same movies."

"Why do you go to high school all the way at the other end of the city?"

He shrugged. "My parents think it's a better school."

"When did you last see or hear from Kenny?"

"Last week. He was over here on Wednesday or Thursday, I think."

"Do you know Sierra?"

"Yeah, a little. But it's not like the three of us do stuff. Why are you looking for Kenny?"

"He fled from his house on Friday night, and no one has seen or heard from him since."

"Maybe he's just chilling somewhere."

"Where?"

Sam shifted in his lawn chair. "I don't know. I mean, is this really a big deal?"

"The FBI is involved. Doesn't that sound like a big deal to you?" He didn't answer.

"Has the FBI contacted you, Sam? An agent named Hewitt?"

"Yeah."

"What did you tell him?"

He shifted again. "I'm not sure I should be talking to you."

"Why not?"

"Well, why should I? I don't know anything, anyway."

I studied him but couldn't figure out where the resistance was coming from. "So you haven't had any contact with Kenny since Wednesday or Thursday?"

"That's right."

"And you have no idea where he is?"

"No, I don't."

"And no idea who might be after him?"

"How do you know somebody's after him?"

"Why don't you pull out your phone and text him right now?"

"I don't know . . ." He stammered, hemmed and hawed, didn't answer.

"Are you refusing to do it because you know he won't respond? Because you know his phone is sitting at home? Or because you have a different number and you don't want me to know that?" He didn't answer.

"You're his friend, Sam."

He nodded.

"His best friend?"

He considered it. "Well, there's Sierra. His closest friend is probably a guy in Tampa. Liam."

"He's remained in contact with Liam?"

"Yeah."

"What's Liam's last name?"

"I don't know."

"Why doesn't Kenny finish school and go to college?"

"Maybe he doesn't see much reason to do it. He makes some money."

"Programming?"

Sam shrugged. "He does jobs for some people."

"How about you? Do you program, too?"

He scratched the back of his head. "Some. But nothing like the stuff Kenny does. He's really advanced. Way beyond me."

"What did you tell the FBI?"

"I don't really want to talk about that."

"Sam, I don't have much time. Kenny is missing, and the FBI is looking for him. His life may be in danger. Either you tell me what the hell is going on right now, or I'll have some serious police presence on you in a very short time."

He let out a nervous, ragged sigh. "Look, I haven't heard from him. I swear. And I don't know how to get hold of him. He doesn't answer his texts or messages, and he hasn't posted anything online. If he's got a new phone, I don't know about it. That's what I told the FBI, and it's the truth."

"Did the FBI ask why he might have disappeared?"

"No, not really."

Which meant, I thought, that they probably already knew. "If they asked, what would you have told them?"

"That I don't know."

"If he contacts you, will you let me know?"

"I guess so. If he says it's okay."

"At this point I'm not interested in questioning him or getting mad at him. I just want his mother to know he's okay."

Sam nodded. I saw myself out of the back yard, returned to the van, and pulled out my phone to call Marsha.

*　　　　　*　　　　　*

Upstairs, in Sam's bedroom, Kenny Sellars looked with apprehension out the window. Down on the patio, his friend sat with Aunt Pen, whom Kenny hadn't seen in years. Another complication. He should have anticipated that his mother would call in help. Sam was a bright guy, but not too socially adept, and Kenny wasn't sure how good a liar he would be. And Aunt Pen, from what little he remembered of her, and everything he'd heard about her, was very sharp. Kenny gathered his few belongings and shoved them into his backpack in case he might have to flee.

Crashing with Sam was strictly a short-term measure. Sam's parents would be home from their trip tomorrow. The people who searched for him would find him here, sooner rather than later. So would Z. He felt guilty for involving his friend, but other than Sierra, he didn't know who else to turn to. For a fleeting moment, he was tempted to go down and see Aunt Pen, to tell her everything and ask for her help. But he knew she wouldn't be able to help. She was a prosecutor and would be obligated to help law enforcement. He couldn't let that happen. And when it came right down to it, she would be powerless against Z.

He looked carefully out the window again. Pen was leaving. He walked across the hall to the bathroom and looked out the window to the street. He watched his aunt roll up into the van, get herself situated, and drive away. He started to turn away, but something in his peripheral vision caught his attention. Down the street, another vehicle approached the house. A silver SUV. And in a flash, he remembered seeing the same vehicle, under a street light, trying to corral him on Friday night as he'd fled from the blonde woman. He darted across the hallway, grabbed his backpack, and bolted down the stairs and through the kitchen to the back door.

*   *   *

A block and a half away from the house, Ian watched through his field glasses. Sometimes he chafed at the triviality of this assignment, finding and neutralizing a geeky computer hacker—tracking a kid, for God's sake. There wasn't much here for an adrenaline junkie, and nothing for professionals like him. It wasn't like extracting an oil company executive from his captivity in a Colombian jungle, or eliminating a Saudi prince who'd been caught with his hand in the royal cookie jar and fled to the United States, or persuading a rogue Korean executive to give up the codes to his secret bank accounts in Luxembourg. No, it wasn't a typical project for Brit's team, but the involvement of their wealthy, connected employer meant that somehow, there had to be money at stake. Lots of it.

The cyber people at their company had gotten them started. "We've been working on it for months," one of the geeks had told Brit. "We're getting a lot of IP addresses coming from Florida—Tampa specifically. We can even narrow it down to a neighborhood. But you'll have to take it from there." And they had.

Ian lowered the binoculars and reached for his cell phone, punching a speed dial number. "Has Carlin checked out the address?"

"Yes," Brit responded. "Belongs to John and Colleen Fenton. They have an eighteen-year-old son named Samuel."

"Must be a friend of the kid's."

"We'll try to confirm it with school records and social media. Is the aunt still there?"

"She's just leaving now. I'm following. And—shit! The kid is here—going out the back door. I'll call you back." He watched as the figure ran through the Fentons' back yard and over a short chain-link fence toward a neighboring house.

Ian concluded that pursuit on foot was a long shot; the kid had too big a head start. He turned the wheel and gunned the SUV into a U-turn, swerving around the block to intercept his target on the next street. When he reached the next street, Kenny was nowhere to be seen. Ian rolled slowly down the street, peering between the houses, and caught a glimpse of his prey doubling back toward the Fentons' house.

Ian stepped on the gas, shot down to the end of the block, and squealed around the corner. When he got back in front of the Fentons', he saw Kenny vanish between two houses across the street. Two doors down, a bewildered homeowner looked up from his lawn mower but made no move to call the police. Ian decided to stay with the SUV rather than pursuing on foot. Once again, he looped around the block, this time in the opposite direction. But the other side of the street on this block was not fronted by houses, but by a park . . . No, not a park. A cemetery. And Kenny Sellars was scaling the fence to enter it.

It was a large cemetery, at least several blocks in width and in depth. There was no way to predict where the kid would leave it and return to the street grid, and Ian didn't know where to enter with a vehicle. Cursing, he pulled to the curb, jumped out of the SUV, and sprinted to the fence. Though nearing forty, Ian was more athletic than Kenny and got over the fence easily. But by now Kenny had a substantial lead. The youth ran, backpack slapping against his body, to the east, across large expanses of grass and between rows of graves. Ian was gaining on him.

Kenny reached the eastern edge of the cemetery and once again scaled the fence. Ian followed thirty seconds later, by which time Kenny had disappeared between two houses. Ian pursued his quarry through a back yard, across an alley, and into another back yard, dodging a swing set and a sandbox. He lost sight of Kenny after crossing Girard Avenue but plunged ahead anyway, cutting between two of the small houses lining the street, fighting hedges, fences, picnic tables, and toys. By the time he reached the next street over, Fremont Avenue, the kid was nowhere to be seen. Ian glanced up and down the street, spotting several pedestrians, none of whom was Kenny. Then, down to the right, he spotted a transit bus pulling to a stop at the curb and someone getting on. The kid.

"Wait!" he yelled, sprinting furiously toward the bus. But it pulled away, taking his prey with it. Ian continued running. If the bus stopped in the next block or two he might have a chance to catch it. But the bus continued on, block after block, until it was hopelessly out of range. Finally Ian stopped and bent over, catching his breath. Talk about lousy timing. Shit.

Chapter 7

It was four o'clock when I approached downtown. I felt as though Sam hadn't been truthful with me, any more than Sierra had, but it was hard to tell. His conversational pauses, abrupt changes of subject, and lack of eye contact may have resulted from social awkwardness rather than lying. I tried calling Marsha and got a text in return: "Working. Can't talk."

I texted back: "Last name of Kenny's friend Liam in Tampa?"

The response: "Blankenship."

"Thx. Talk tonight."

I turned off the freeway at the downtown exit and headed east, past Target Field, then south to my destination, a high-rise condo building at the south end of Nicollet Mall. I took a handicapped spot in the garage underneath the building, transferred to my wheelchair, and fastened my overnight bag to the back of the chair. Then I rolled over to the elevator. On the twenty-third floor I found the proper unit, pulled out my keys, and let myself in.

The condo, which belonged to James Carter, was nondescript, with a slight musty smell, furnished in plain modern style, with few personal touches. Although James now lived in Laguna Beach, California, he was once a top executive here in Minneapolis at North Central Bank, the same company that had employed me as an attorney. Both of us had become entangled in a sophisticated corporate sabotage scheme targeting North Central. We ultimately found the saboteurs, but more importantly, we found each other. James kept this place for use on his frequent trips to Minnesota, some on business, but more often to see his thirteen-year-old daughter, Alicia, who lived with her mother and stepfather in the suburbs. Ironically, Alicia was now in California, spending part of the summer with her father.

I took a few minutes to unpack and eat a drive-through sandwich I'd purchased on the way here. Then I pulled out my phone and called Kenny's school. The call was short and unproductive. The school secretary told me no administrators or teachers were around and that none of them, due to student privacy regulations, would talk to me about Kenny anyway. She would not even confirm that Kenny had been enrolled at the school.

"I understand," I said. "But I would expect further questioning from the FBI, probably pursuant to subpoena."

"I told them the same thing I'm telling you. We just can't discuss any individual student."

I thanked her and hung up. At least I was able to confirm that the FBI had contacted the school.

I rolled over to the living room window, opened it, and looked down onto Nicollet Mall, where large rush-hour crowds waited at the bus stops. I wished James was here, and so did he, but he didn't feel he could get away as long as Alicia was staying with him.

"I know better than to try to talk you out of going," he'd said when I had called him from the airport. "Just be careful, okay?"

"Sure. But I don't sense anything dangerous going on. Just a troubled kid who needed some space for a while." I knew now, of course, that Kenny might have gotten himself into a boatload of trouble.

My phone buzzed. I looked at the caller ID, expecting it to announce a call from Marsha. But the number was unfamiliar. I answered.

"Ms. Wilkinson?" said a polite male voice.

"Yes?"

"This is Special Agent Gary Sink from the FBI. I'm returning your call to Special Agent Hewitt."

"Thanks for calling back."

"I know you're looking for Kenneth Sellars, and you're probably wondering what our involvement is."

"Yes, I am."

"I'd like to take a few minutes to discuss this matter in person. Are you downtown?"

"Yes."

"Would you be free for a quick cup of coffee?"

"Sure." He gave me the location of a Caribou coffee shop several blocks away, and we agreed to meet in half an hour. I hung up and unsuccessfully tried Marsha again, leaving a message. Then I made my way downstairs and through the skyway system to my meeting, hopeful of getting some answers about the FBI's involvement. It would be nice to have something to tell Marsha, and just as nice to ease my own growing concerns about Kenny.

Gary Sink was a distinguished-looking man in his late forties, immaculately groomed, with a full head of silver hair, wearing a standard FBI uniform of dark suit, white shirt, and muted tie. He leaned down, not reacting to the wheelchair, as if he already knew I was a paraplegic. I returned his firm handshake, and he produced his FBI creds. "I understand you're an AUSA," he said.

I showed him my own ID and handed him a business card. "I am an assistant US attorney, but I'm not here in any official capacity. Kenny is my nephew."

"That means you have to be exceedingly careful about not abusing your official position."

"I do?"

"It also means you have the same duty as any other citizen to cooperate with our investigation."

"I'll keep that in mind." This was not beginning well.

He went to the counter, ordered a cup of coffee, and brought it over to my table. I'd already gotten myself a glass of water, having had enough coffee today. He sat down across from me. "What can you tell me about your nephew's whereabouts?"

"Agent Sink, I appreciate that your time is valuable and that you'd like to cut to the chase. But it would be very helpful if you could tell me why you're trying to find Kenny."

"I can't tell you that."

"Then I'm afraid there's nothing I can do to help you."

He stiffened. "I don't need to tell you the penalties for withholding—"

"No, you don't. But here's what you do need to do, Agent Sink. You need to treat me with respect. Otherwise this conversation is over."

He swallowed a reply, paused, and said, "We're trying to question Kenneth Sellars as part of an ongoing investigation."

"Investigation of what?"

"I can't comment on that."

"Is he a suspect?"

He sipped from his coffee. "I wouldn't say a suspect."

"A person of interest?"

"More like a potentially important witness."

"Is he in trouble?"

"If he's intentionally trying to avoid questioning, he will be in some trouble, yes. As far as the underlying investigation goes, as I said, I really can't discuss that. I will say that we're more interested in some people he's associating with than in Kenny himself." He pulled out a notebook. "So you're Kenneth's aunt?"

"Right. His mother's sister."

"His birth mother? Who lives in Tampa?"

"Right. Do you plan to contact her?"

"Agent Hewitt already has."

I was puzzled. Marsha hadn't mentioned anything about that.

"Are you and Kenneth close?" he asked.

"I'm afraid not. I'm not sure he would recognize me if he saw me. I live in California."

He made a note. "What have you learned so far about his whereabouts?"

"So far, you're ahead of me. I've only been here since this morning, and you've already talked to the same people I have."

"And who are those people?"

I wasn't terribly happy about being interrogated, but I didn't see any harm in answering. "Sierra Bjorklund and Sam Fenton."

He made a check in his notebook. "And what did they tell you?"

I gave him a brief account of my interviews with Sierra and Sam. He didn't look surprised at anything I'd learned. I decided not to mention Kenny's friend Liam in Tampa.

"What do you plan to do next?" he asked.

"I honestly don't know."

His expression told me he didn't believe it. "If you come across any relevant information, please let me know at once."

"In judging relevance, it might help if I knew what this was about."

"I know you think so, but you must deal with the FBI regularly, right? You know we can't release information about ongoing investigations."

Sink may have been a jerk, but he was right. John Gibson, the FBI agent I worked with most closely, was so closed-mouthed that you could waterboard him a few times and not find out what he had for lunch. Still, nobody could blame me for trying.

Sink stood up to leave. "By the way," he said, "if you have anything to tell us, please contact me. Agent Hewitt is a young fellow I used for some legwork over the weekend on this matter, but he's not familiar with the big picture. He's not fully cleared for everything we're doing, and he won't be involved any further."

"Sure," I said. I started to roll away from the table, then stopped. "Agent Sink?"

He turned back.

"In my experience," I said, "if the FBI really wants to find somebody, they usually succeed. Do you really want to find Kenny?"

His look changed in an instant from surprised, to offended, to calm. "We do want to find him. And it's true that when we really pull out all the stops, we usually locate our subject. But we don't have the resources to do that in every case. Even when we do, we can't do it instantly. And in this case we're dealing with somebody who is maybe more skilled than average at staying off the grid. That's why we need your help."

His response made perfect sense, but I still felt something else must be going on. "Well, good luck," I said, although I wasn't at all sure I wanted this guy to find Kenny.

I left the coffee shop and started back the way I had come. Glancing at the busy skyway, I decided to go down to street level to enjoy the nice day and take in some fresh air. I followed a sign back behind an escalator to a darkened elevator alcove. I waited alone in the alcove until the elevator arrived, but when I began to move forward, my path was blocked.

Agent Gary Sink stepped in front of me, his face a mask of quiet menace. I looked around; we were alone.

Sink leaned toward me. "Prosecutors have a lot of power," he said. "You can threaten defendants with eighty years on a rinky-dink drug charge, and so they plead guilty. That's why you hardly ever have to try cases."

He leaned closer, and I could smell his hot coffee breath as he spoke even more quietly.

"You've got no authority here. You are a private citizen. Worse than that, you're a smart-ass private citizen with a ton of attitude." He looked at me in disgust. "Especially for a god-damned cripple. If I were you, I would be a lot more cooperative and respectful. I would be falling all over myself to help the FBI. And when you deal with me, it would be 'Yes, sir' and 'No, sir.' What do you think about that? Does that sound like a good plan to you?"

I watched him, stunned. "Yes," I whispered.

"I'm afraid I didn't hear you."

"Yes, sir," I said, louder.

"Very good. Maybe you're not quite as dim and full of yourself as you appear to be. Now, I'll expect to hear from you, very soon, with a lot of good information. Don't even think about trying to withhold anything from me."

And then he was gone.

I sat in front of the now-closed elevator door, my chest heaving, gripping the wheels of my chair with slick, shaking hands. My face burned with shame. Why hadn't I stood up to this bully? He'd caught me off-guard, confronting me so suddenly and outrageously that I hadn't known how to respond. Who was this man? I'd never met any FBI agent like him. He wasn't just a garden-variety asshole. And I didn't have a clue what his agenda was.

I was on the elevator on my way up to the condo when my phone buzzed. I dug it out just as the elevator door opened, and I rolled out into the hall to answer the call. "Yes?"

"This is Special Agent Ben Hewitt returning your call," a youngish-sounding male voice announced.

Interesting, I thought. He and Sink were not coordinating. And I was not about to heed Sink's warning to refrain from talking to the younger agent. "I'm Kenny Sellars's aunt from California. I understand you're looking for him. So am I."

"And you have some information for me?"

"Not specifically at this time. It might help if you could tell me why you're looking for him."

Hewitt's response was prompt and automatic. "I'm not at liberty to discuss that."

"What's the big secret? Why couldn't we work together and share information?"

"That's just not how we operate. You have a legal duty to disclose to me any facts relevant to Kenneth Sellars's whereabouts."

"Really? Agent Sink didn't seem to think so. I just talked to him. He says you're young and green—implied that you're pretty much out of your depth. He discouraged me from telling you anything."

"This conversation is over," Hewitt snapped and hung up.

I was disappointed. I'd hoped that by pushing a couple of buttons I might get Hewitt to let some information slip, but he was even more tight-lipped than Sink. I rolled down the hall to the condo and let myself in. Then I dug my phone out again and pushed a speed dial button. After a couple of rings, an efficient male voice answered.

"Gibson."

"Hey, John. How's life?"

"Pretty boring, at least compared to your shop," said Special Agent John Gibson. "I hear you're in Minnesota."

"Oh, no," I groaned.

"Yep. It's all over southern California."

"What are you hearing?"

"I talked to somebody who talked to your boss Wade and said he'd never seen him this mad. You really got to him somehow."

"I seem to have a talent for doing that."

"What's the emergency?"

I explained about Kenny.

"Sounds like he's in trouble," Gibson said.

"Maybe. I suppose it's possible that he's just a witness."

"Let's hope that's all it is."

"I was hoping maybe you could tell me something about these two FBI agents I've talked to. Ben Hewitt and Gary Sink."

"I happen to know Hewitt. He's a good guy. Ambitious. Straight shooter. Sink, I haven't heard of."

"Could you check him out for me?"

"Let me make a couple of calls and get back to you."

"Thanks, John."

I hung up and rolled out to the kitchen, where I found a bottle of water in the refrigerator. As I drank the water, I tried to collect myself and prepare for the rest of the evening. I'd been going since 3:00 AM, but the day was far from over. I found my bag and pulled out my laptop. After booting it up and finding the Wi-Fi network, I spread everything out on the kitchen table and called Cassandra back at the office. For the next hour we ran down a number of items that needed to be done. After that, I hung up and spent an hour writing up a series of pretrial motions. Then I took a break, looked through the refrigerator, and found a frozen pizza. After putting it into the oven, I returned to my computer and Googled Kenny's friend Liam Blankenship, along with the word "Tampa." Within seconds, I realized that I would never connect with Liam.

He'd been murdered.

*   *   *

My phone woke me up. I glanced at the time: 9:30 PM. I'd been asleep, my head down on the kitchen table. "Hello?"

"Pen, it's me." Marsha.

"Yeah, Marsh." I tried to clear my head while I rolled my shoulders, trying to get rid of the kink in my neck.

"I'm sorry I couldn't get back to you earlier. I had to work an extra half-shift."

"Okay. Here's what I learned today." I filled her in. "Did you know this Liam?"

"I met him a couple of times. I know they were good friends. And you're telling me he's been murdered?"

"Yes. Shot to death, a couple of days ago."

"My God. And you think it has something to do with Kenny?"

"I think we need to find out."

"It sounds like Kenny is definitely in trouble."

"We can connect the dots. Common sense tells us he's into something bad. Look, we have several things to discuss, but I'd rather do it tomorrow."

"Why?"

"Because I'm coming to Tampa."

Chapter 8

Tuesday

For the second morning in a row, I was on an airplane. My decision to go to Tampa to look into Liam Blankenship's death was impulsive, but I was still convinced it was the right one. Liam had been Kenny's closest friend, and according to Sam, they had stayed in touch. Now Liam was dead, killed a day before Kenny disappeared. I couldn't accept that as a coincidence, and Liam's murder now seemed my strongest lead into what had happened to Kenny. My visit had a secondary purpose: to have an in-person, heart-to-heart talk with Marsha. I had a lot of questions about Kenny, his friendships, and his activities.

As I waited for my plane, I made a series of phone calls. The first was to a car rental agency, which didn't have any handicapped vans available in Tampa, but fortunately did have a hand-controlled sedan. Then I called Lucy Schell, an old friend of mine who was a prosecutor for the state attorney's office in Tampa, and asked if she would find out what she could about the Liam Blankenship murder. She said she would check into it and that I should call her when I got into town.

I used the flight to work on the Vargas case, writing several messages to Cassandra and promising to call tonight.

At the Tampa airport, I endured my usual slow deplaning procedure, then found my way down to the car rental counter. As promised, the company rented me a Chevy sedan with hand controls. I completed the paperwork, rolled out to the parking garage, and found the car. Then I began the laborious process of transferring to the driver's seat and stowing my chair. Because the car was a four-door model, I couldn't reach around to the back seat. In lieu of that, I had to disassemble the chair, taking off the cushion and wheels, and hoisting the pieces, one by one, over myself to the front passenger seat. Twice, I had to lift my legs back out of the car to get enough leverage. All this was made doubly hard by my being dressed up in a business outfit, and my fear of scraping or scratching the rental car as I lifted everything in. I had once thought I would like to drive a regular car instead of a handicapped van, but the hassle of these transfers had convinced me otherwise.

Once inside, with everything stowed, I took a few minutes to catch my breath. The sedan's hand controls were similar to those found in nearly all handicapped vehicles. The gas and brake pedals were attached by rods to a lever on the left side of the steering wheel, which the driver pulled down toward the floor to accelerate and pushed to brake. As often happened, my long legs tended to bump up against the rods leading to the pedals.

Then I called Lucy Schell. "You're in luck," my old friend said. "I got hold of the detective who's handling the case, and he gave me a bit of information."

"Great." I pulled out a notebook.

"Liam was killed in his apartment." She gave me the address, which I wrote down.

"How was he killed?" I asked.

"Gunshot to the head. A close-range .22 shot. There were ligature marks around his wrists."

"Any suspects?"

"Not yet."

"How about a motive?"

"They found a small bag of weed in his apartment. They've labeled it a drug-related homicide."

"Based on the bag of marijuana alone?"

"I'm not sure," Lucy said. "You sound surprised."

"At least a little. My sister was very emphatic about Kenny not being involved in drugs. If that's true, it's hard to imagine that a close friend would be mixed up in drugs enough to get himself killed."

"I see. Anyway, that's all I was able to get out of the detective."

"I appreciate it, Lucy."

"So what are you going to do while you're in town?" she asked.

"I'm going to see my sister."

"Right." A pause. "This is an active, open investigation, Pen."

"I know."

There was another moment of silence, and I could tell she wanted to ask if I was going to poke around on my own. But she apparently decided she was better off not knowing. "Good luck," she said.

I thanked her again, clicked off the phone, and headed off to do what she didn't want to know about.

Chapter 9

Following the directions on my phone's navigation app, I drove north out of downtown on I-275 toward the University of South Florida campus area, then turned east on Fowler Avenue. I hadn't attended USF but was familiar with the neighborhood. I found Liam's address a few minutes later, in a complex of half a dozen three-story apartment buildings south of the campus.

I parked, went through the now-tiresome process of extracting and reassembling my wheelchair and bumping my legs on the control rods, and rolled up to the vestibule of Liam's building. I pressed the buzzer for the office.

"May I help you?" a female voice asked over the intercom.

"Hi. I've got a couple of questions about Liam Blankenship."

"Are you from the police?"

"No. I'm an attorney." I rolled back a little so the camera could get a better picture of me, reasoning that the wheelchair would make me look harmless.

"Come in, please." The door buzzed, and I awkwardly pulled it open and got myself through.

A short way past the elevator, a young woman stepped out into the hallway. "I'm Emma," she said. "I manage the complex. Come in."

"Thanks. I'm Pen." We shook, and I handed her my business card.

The office was cramped, and we had to move a plastic chair aside so I could get completely in. Emma, who looked to be in her late twenties, appeared intelligent and energetic. She studied my business card. "US attorney? California?"

"I'm not here on official business." As succinctly as possible, I explained about Kenny—his disappearance, and his friendship with Liam.

"Have you talked to the police?" she asked.

"Not directly, but I got some information from a prosecutor friend."

"Are they making any progress in solving the case?"

"They seem to think so. They've concluded it's some kind of drug-related killing."

Emma rolled her eyes. "My bosses have been calling three times a day wondering if the case has been solved yet. They're worried about bad publicity. They especially don't want the complex to get a reputation for drugs."

"They found a small bag of weed in the apartment. I saw no indication that they found anything else drug-related."

"So what do you think the murder was about?"

"I don't know." I wondered if I was getting further and further from anything related to Kenny, and time was short. "Do you know if anything was stolen from the apartment?"

"Not for sure," Emma said. "I know the police didn't find a computer. One of the cops who did the search told me so. Liam always carried around a laptop in his backpack."

"You knew Liam?"

"We said hello once in a while. That's about it. He was a polite guy. Quiet. A little disheveled. He always came in and paid his rent in cash."

"That doesn't sound good. It's consistent with running an illegal business."

Emma shrugged. "Some people—that includes a lot of students—don't have bank accounts."

"Is there anything you can tell me about what happened?"

"I helped the police go through our surveillance footage. Eventually they found what they were looking for."

"What's that?"

"Here—I'll show you." She rotated a large monitor toward me and began typing on a keyboard. Eventually the image of the vestibule where I'd just entered the building appeared on the screen. After a few seconds, a heavyset woman came through the front door, holding a tote bag and a shopping bag. The video didn't have any sound.

The woman slid her key into the slot and pulled it out. Then, after she struggled to open the door, a second figure—a large man with a shaved head and a couple of big, offensive tattoos—suddenly appeared in the picture. His arm shot out, holding the door open. The woman turned to protest, but quickly backed down. Both went through the door. The screen went blank.

"Shortly after this incident," Emma said, "the police responded to reports of a gunshot. As it turns out, the call was made by the woman who was intimidated into admitting the big scary guy. She saw him go into Liam's apartment."

"Did Liam let him in?"

"No, he didn't."

"So he kicked the door in?"

"No. He just walked in. The door was open. The gunshot came a couple of minutes later, and Barb, the lady you saw, made the call to 911. The video feed from the front door shows him leaving the way he came."

"Looks like he must be the guy."

"The police seem to think so. But let me show you something else." Emma gave me a smile, and I could tell she was enjoying the presentation. She pulled up another video feed, this one looking out across a parking lot toward one of the buildings.

"This footage was taken from a neighboring building," she said. "Do you see beyond the parking lot—that building on the left?"

"Yes."

"That's the back of the building we're in right now, where you saw the tattooed guy go in the front."

"Okay."

"Notice the time?"

"About four hours earlier."

"Right. Now, notice the man walking into the picture from the right?"

"I see him." A well-built black man, casually dressed, wearing a ball cap and sunglasses, sauntered toward the building from across the parking lot.

Emma pointed to the right side of the screen. "You can't see his vehicle, but it has to be parked off the screen this way. Now watch."

The man, carrying a backpack, glanced around casually, but didn't seem to be showing unusual vigilance. He walked up to the back door and put both hands up to the doorknob. He appeared to be doing something to the door, but I couldn't see it; his body shielded the action.

"He's picking the lock," I said.

"Has to be. Watch."

In less than a minute, he had the door open and walked through it. Within seconds, another figure appeared, this time from the left side of the screen, walking with the same efficient but unhurried gait. Like the lock-picking guy, this figure wore a cap and sunglasses, but her figure clearly showed she was a woman. And, although you couldn't see her face well, a small tuft of blonde hair stuck out from under the back of the cap. When she reached the door, it opened a crack from the inside, after which she opened it and walked through. Someone — probably her lock-picking predecessor — had let her in.

The screen went blank, and Emma was typing again. Then another image appeared, from the same camera. I looked at the time counter; forty-one minutes had elapsed. The blonde woman came out the back door, looking down at the ground, the bill of her cap pulled low. She walked off in the direction she'd come from. The black guy did the same about a minute later.

Emma gestured toward the screen. "What do you think of that?"

"They parked out of range of the camera. They used the back door, where they couldn't be seen close up. They hid their faces. They picked the lock pretty easily. They looked professional."

"That's what I thought, too."

"But why were they there? What would it have had to do with Liam?"

"Good questions."

"What do the police think? They had to have seen this."

"They did. I helped them access the footage. They seemed perplexed, maybe a little troubled. But I heard one of them tell the other that the break-in doesn't match the time of death. The tattooed guy's visit does."

"They might have gone in there to—I don't know—talk to Liam? Do a transaction with him? Interrogate him?"

"It could be any of those things. They don't look like people buying or selling drugs."

"Their visit could account for Liam's door being unlocked when the tattooed guy showed up," I said.

"I hadn't thought of that. Anyway, the cops said they'd ask around the complex to see if anybody had spotted the man and woman. What they really wanted was a vehicle they could trace. Otherwise all you've got is a man and a woman. Nothing to go on."

"And if they found something, it might complicate or undermine their drug theory. Especially since the shooter was apparently somebody else: the shaved-headed galoot."

We were silent for a moment. Finally I asked, "Why did you show me all this?"

"I'm looking for help. Something is going on here, something more than a drug sale. This team broke into one of my buildings in a very professional manner. I want to know why, and I don't think the police are going to find out."

I shifted uneasily in my chair. "I'm not an investigator. And I'm not sure if any of this is related to my nephew's disappearance. But I'd like to know more. Is there anything else you can tell me about Liam? What kind of work he did, or where he spent his days?"

"I think he must have done some kind of computer work, although I can't give you any specifics. His hours seemed to be irregular. He spent a lot of time down at the Mosey coffee shop—he was always carrying one of their cups when he walked through. Apart from that, I don't know. He was just another tenant. Lived quietly."

"I'll have to think about it. Do you have a card?"

She gave me one. I thanked her and began rolling out, but then something occurred to me. I turned around. "Emma, could we look at the footage again?"

"Sure."

"Let's look at where the first guy goes in."

She pulled up the footage, and the image of the lock-picker walking toward the back door came into view. "Stop," I said. "See that? He's carrying a backpack."

"So?"

"Just take a good look at the backpack. Now, move forward to where the same man comes out of the building." She found the spot. "Now, here he comes," I said. "Wait until he turns, so you can see the backpack . . . there. Stop. See the backpack?"

"Heavier. There's something in it."

"And what do you think that might be?"

"A laptop."

"It certainly could be."

I turned back toward the door. "I don't know what the police are thinking, but if they think this whole thing was about drugs, they have to figure out why both the tattooed guy and the team of two other people forced their way in, but neither took the bag of weed. But they probably did take the computer."

53

*   *   *

I'd just finished my rental car contortion act when my phone rang. It was Lucy Schell.

"Lucy?"

"Hi. I decided to do a little more asking around about your case. I ran a check on Liam."

"Don't keep me in suspense."

"The guy barely existed."

"Meaning?"

"Meaning he basically lived off the books. No tax return that anybody could find. No employment record. No criminal record. No cell phone account. He wasn't a student and was well into his twenties—he should have had at least some of those things."

"He probably used burners."

"And what does that tell you? Drugs, right?"

"Some kind of illegal operation, probably. If it was drugs, though, why didn't the killers take the bag of pot from the apartment?"

"That would have been small potatoes. What they really would have been after was a bigger stash—or money. And who knows? They might have gotten a lot of it."

I thought about the weighted-down backpack. Somehow it still didn't sound right. "Did you find out anything else?"

"I did. But the next part is sort of weird. I got hold of a copy of the ME's preliminary report. It's especially interesting to read about the cause of death."

"Gunshot, right?"

"Yes, but that's not all. According to the ME, there are a lot of signs of asphyxia."

I waited.

"The ME isn't sure what happened," Lucy continued. "She found . . ." I could hear the rustling of papers over the line. ". . .

congestion and cyanosis with petechial hemorrhages in the skin of the face and beneath the conjunctivae."

"And in English that would be?"

"I can't explain all of it, but it appears the victim suffered from severe oxygen deprivation—maybe some kind of smothering or suffocation—before he was finished off with the gunshot."

"That might account for those marks on his face. How do you explain this finding?"

"I can't—not without more information."

I couldn't, either. But a couple of possibilities arose in my mind. The tattooed guy hadn't been in the apartment very long —probably not long enough to tie Liam's wrists and try to smother him. But what about the man and woman who'd been there earlier? They'd been with Liam for forty minutes, long enough to do plenty of things to him. I decided not to tell Lucy about the duo, or about my suspicions. What I did voice was an even worse scenario.

"I think it's possible that Liam may have been tortured. You've got him being killed up here, and then a day or two later somebody shows up in Minnesota looking for Kenny."

"So you think these people—whoever they are—were actually looking for Kenny? That they tortured Liam, who gave up his location?"

"Not exactly. I don't think they were looking for Kenny when they approached Liam. Kenny was living openly in Minnesota—he wouldn't have been hard to find. No, I don't think they were looking for Kenny until they talked to Liam. From that questioning they concluded that they needed to find Kenny, and so they tracked him down."

"But Kenny got away," Lucy pointed out. "You think Liam warned him somehow?"

"That's possible. Maybe he anticipated the visit from his killers."

"You keep saying 'they,' as if there were more than one. Do you know something I don't?"

I did, but I decided to keep it to myself. "Figure of speech."

"What were the killers trying to find out?" she asked. "You think Kenny was at the northern end of a drug pipeline?"

"I'd be shocked if he was. But I do think his disappearance and Liam's murder are connected."

"I'm sorry to have to tell you these things."

"No, no. I appreciate it. Thanks for everything, Lucy."

"This is an interesting one—a real whodunit. We don't get those too often."

Maybe so, I thought, but I ended the call a lot more worried about Kenny than when I'd begun the conversation. The word that came to mind was not interesting, but horrifying.

With the killers/torturers still on the loose, I needed to tell somebody, to warn someone. I pulled out my phone and made four calls, getting voicemail all four times, and leaving similar messages. I told Sierra Bjorklund, Sam Fenton, and Agents Gary Sink and Ben Hewitt that Kenny was linked to a murder victim in Tampa, and that Sierra and Sam might be in danger from the people who were hunting for Kenny. I hung up, looked at the phone, and exhaled. It was all I could do at the moment. Then I started the car and set out for my next stop.

Chapter 10

Sam Fenton sat in the family room in late afternoon, shooting his way through a ridiculously high level of Grand Theft Auto, but making way too many mistakes. He couldn't focus, not while Kenny was still on the run and in trouble. He tried calling Sierra, but she didn't answer her phone or respond to messages. And there was no way to call Kenny himself—his cell was disconnected. He told himself Kenny was still out there, still okay. By fleeing, he was probably protecting Sam as well as himself. Sam wouldn't be able to give away anything about Kenny's whereabouts because he didn't know—his friend had simply taken off. Sam also wouldn't be able to say anything about Kenny's relationship with the friend he referred to simply as Z.

Sam found the subject of Z exciting, but a little scary. Kenny, by contrast, didn't seem to be concerned at all. He had acted as though Z was a close friend. But then something had changed early in the year. Kenny talked less and less about Z and seemed wary of the entire subject. Then a couple of days ago he had called, saying he needed a place to crash. And yesterday, after his aunt's visit, he had vanished.

He sat up with a start. Someone stood next to him. "What the—"

"Hi, Sam," said a blonde woman with some kind of hillbilly accent.

Sam dropped the controls and sat up straighter. He couldn't stand up, because the woman stood directly in front of him. "Who are you? You can't just walk in here."

She gave him a puzzled expression and looked around. "Seems to me I just did."

Sam glanced around and noticed a second person, a man, who stood by the front hallway. "Who are you?" he asked the woman.

"Nobody special. Just somebody who is going to learn every single thing you know about Kenny Sellars."

Sam shrank into the couch, and for a terrifying moment he feared he might lose control of his bowels. "You can't just walk in here," he managed to say. "My parents will be coming home."

"I doubt that. Their plane isn't due for another hour. And I really hope they don't arrive early, because then one of my assistants will have to kill them."

"Jesus," Sam gasped. And then his cell phone rang.

He looked at the phone, which sat on the couch beside him. The woman picked it up, glancing at the screen. "Who is D.P. Wilkinson, Sam?"

"I . . . don't know." The name didn't ring a bell.

"It looks like a Los Angeles area code," the woman said. "I'm guessing that would be Kenny's aunt, the nice lady in the wheelchair you talked to yesterday."

Sam just shook his head.

The woman smiled again, producing a set of handcuffs along with a heavy plastic bag. "Well, we have all the time we need to learn that, and so many other things. Let's get started."

Chapter 11

The Mosey coffee shop was a funky, independent, student-type place about a mile from Liam's apartment. It wasn't crowded when I rolled in, but there were a few people, hunched over laptops, who looked like regulars. I made my way between two large burlap sacks of coffee beans that flanked the front door and rolled up to the counter. It took me a minute to get the barista's attention over the noisy hiss of the espresso machine, but finally the young woman came over.

"Can I help you?" She looked to be in her mid-twenties, an oval face framed by magnificent thick, flowing, wavy dark hair. I ordered coffee, paid, and made a point of putting a couple of dollars into the tip jar.

"Thanks," she said. "Enjoy."

"Actually, maybe there's something more you can help me with. Have you ever see this guy?" I showed her the picture of Kenny.

"I don't think so."

"Are you sure?"

She smiled. "I'd remember him."

"How long have you worked here?"

"About ten months."

That might explain it, I thought. Kenny had moved away from here about a year ago. I showed her a picture of Liam, an apparent yearbook photo of some kind, which I'd cut out from the newspaper article reporting his murder. "How about him?"

She looked stricken. "That's Liam. Sure, I remember him. But he was murdered, just a couple of days ago."

"What can you tell me about him?"

She stood up straighter, assuming a wary expression. "Wait. Are you a cop or a PI or a bill collector or something?"

I held up the picture of Kenny. "He's my nephew. He was a good friend of Liam's. And now he's missing."

"Wow. And you think there's a connection?"

"Maybe."

"You should talk to Sid. He knew Liam pretty well." She pointed to a young guy at a corner table.

"Thanks." I took my coffee and rolled over to the table where Sid, who sported a buzz cut and a three-day stubble, worked furiously at a laptop. He wore cutoffs, a tank top, and, strangely, because it was ninety degrees outside, a scarf.

"Sid?"

No response.

"Sid?" I repeated, louder.

He looked up with an annoyed expression. "What?"

"Hi. My name is Pen. I'd like to talk about Liam."

"Why?"

I had his full attention now. "Because of him." I held up the picture of Kenny.

"That's Kenny."

"He's my nephew. And he's missing."

"And you think that's connected to Liam's murder." It came out as a statement, not a question.

I sipped from my coffee. "Is it?"

"I don't know. Nobody knows who killed Liam."

I rolled a little closer. "Tell me about Liam."

"What do you mean?"

"How well did you know him?"

"A little. We didn't hang out or anything. He usually worked at that table over there." He gestured to a corner table, currently unoccupied. I almost expected to see a bouquet of flowers there in honor of its deceased occupant.

"Did he work here a lot?"

"Quite a bit. Of course, nobody would do serious work here. Just routine stuff and odds and ends."

"Because the public Wi-Fi isn't secure?"

"Well, duh."

"Was Liam into drugs?"

"No. I mean, he might have smoked a little pot once in a while, but who doesn't?"

"What did he do for a living?"

Sid shrugged. "A little of this and that."

"Did he take classes?"

"No."

"Did he have a job?"

"Like I said, nothing steady. Just some programming work here and there."

"He lived in a decent place. He wasn't poor, apparently. Did he get support from his family?"

"I doubt it."

"Was he a hacker?"

Sid's expression gave him away. I'd tried to set up the question so that he wouldn't see it coming and have time to prepare himself. "No," he said without conviction, his voice trailing off.

"What kind of hacking did he do?"

"I didn't say he did."

"How about you?"

His features hardened. "Look—I don't know who you are, or why you think you have the right to ask these questions. But I think we're done here."

I touched his arm. "I'm sorry if I came on a little strong, Sid. I'm asking for your voluntary cooperation, because of my nephew and for no other reason. I don't care what you do for a living. I only care what Liam did because he might have done it with Kenny."

He appeared only slightly mollified.

"If I can just get a few answers, I wouldn't see any reason at all to have the police come down here and question everybody about hacking and how it might relate to an unsolved murder."

I saw a flash of fear in his eyes, which pretty much confirmed for me that what he did on that laptop might be a little sketchy. "What do you want to know?" he asked quietly.

"Was Liam a hacker?"

He nodded.

"How about Kenny?"

"I didn't know Kenny as well. He started hanging with Liam maybe a couple of years ago. They worked together on some stuff."

"What kind of stuff?"

After considerable sighing and internal deliberation, he said, "Look, none of this is coming from me."

"All right. None of what?"

He almost whispered. "Anything about Z."

"What's Z?"

"Not what—who. You're telling me you don't know who Z is?"

I shook my head.

"He's like, famous. You really haven't heard of him?"

"Tell me about him."

"Well, he's sort of a legend. He can get in anyplace. And he's made some big money."

"Doing what?"

"Ransomware. Sticking up evil corporations. He did it back before everybody was doing it."

This was not sounding good. "I've heard that term 'ransomware' a lot. How does it actually work?"

"Pretty much the same way it's always worked. Hell, everybody does it now. But Z was one of the first to do it. He gets into their systems and encrypts or corrupts or deletes their data. Then he makes them pay to leave them alone, or to get their data back."

"That sounds like a dangerous business. Is that what Kenny was doing?"

"I'm not sure. He might have helped Liam some."

"But Kenny knows this Z?"

He shrugged. "They've been in touch."

Suddenly, the interest shown in Kenny by the FBI was beginning to make sense. "And if the FBI is investigating Z, they might be investigating Kenny, too."

He recoiled at the mention of the FBI. "I suppose."

"What does 'Z' stand for?"

"Nothing, as far as I know. It's just a name he uses."

"So where is this Z located?"

He gave me a baffled look. "You mean where do you find him online?"

"No. Where does he live? Here in Tampa?"

His look changed from pitying to disgusted. "Nobody knows *that*, for heaven's sake. He could be in Russia or Germany or wherever."

"Or Tampa. Or Minneapolis."

He looked dubious. "I suppose."

"What else can you tell me about Z?"

"Nothing, really. I know Liam worked for him, and Kenny might have helped him and Liam with some things. I think Kenny was becoming distracted during the last few weeks he was here."

"Distracted by what?"

"A girl—what else?"

"Who was the girl?"

"I never found out her name. He didn't talk about her. Hell, none of us here really talks about ourselves much. The girl was fairly pretty. Kind of tall. They just started talking here one day, and I saw them a few more times. But then he moved."

"Did Kenny talk about why he was moving?"

"Just for a change, mostly. He said his dad was moving to Minnesota, and he just thought he'd give it a try."

I tried to collect my thoughts. "What is going on here, Sid? Was Liam killed because of his hacking?"

"No, no. I mean, how would anybody even find him? And Z is the one they'd want if they were ticked off about a hack."

"Liam ticked somebody off."

Sid looked scared and bewildered. "Yeah."

Back in the car, I pulled out my phone and checked my messages. There was one, from Special Agent John Gibson in LA: "Pen, it's Gibson. Listen, I made some calls to check out Agent Gary Sink, and I'm afraid I struck out. I talked to a couple of people who had heard of him or met him, but nobody who actually knew him. Sorry, but the FBI's a big organization—thousands of agents. It was just lucky that I knew Hewitt. I'm thinking maybe somebody in your shop might have a connection. If you try that and still can't find anything, let me know."

I exited voicemail and hit #1 on my speed dial list. James Carter answered on the second ring. "Hey, Pen. How's Minnesota?"

"I'm actually in Tampa."

"Why? What's going on?"

I explained about Liam.

He didn't respond right away, and I knew what he was thinking. "Look," I said, "I don't see any danger—"

"Pen," he said, calmly but with an edge of exasperation. "How long has it been since the last time?" He was referring to our involvement in a scheme called Windfall, which involved high-level corruption and the murder of James's ex-girlfriend.

"I know it's only been a few months, but this is different."

"I hope it's different. But it sort of sounds the same to me. Corporate crime, bad dudes with guns, people disappearing."

"No, no. It's just—"

"Are you starting to like this?" he said, getting angry. "Is it a lot of fun, getting beaten up and having people stick guns in your face?"

"Come on, James. That's not fair—none of that has happened."

"Not yet, you mean."

"I'm just trying to help Marsha."

He sighed. "I know you mean well. Of course you're not doing this for fun. And I know you feel as though you owe Marsha. But where does it stop, honey? There has to be some limit. You can't keep putting yourself in harm's way."

"But it's—"

"All just an unlikely string of coincidences, right. Just remarkable, that it keeps happening to you."

I didn't respond.

"Just promise me you'll be careful."

"I will," I promised. And I meant it. Really.

"So what's your next move?" he asked.

"I need you to make a call."

"To whom?"

"Somebody in Minneapolis who can lend me a geek. I need a cyber-security expert to answer some questions about hacking."

"I'll give Dustin a call. He's got access to all sorts of people like that."

Dustin Blount, a friend and ally of James for many years, was chairman and CEO of Columbia Central Bank. Columbia was the successor to North Central Bank, the company that once employed James and me. Last year, North Central had merged with another huge bank, Texas Columbia Bankshares, to form Columbia Central. The resulting corporate behemoth was a huge player in the financial services industry, including not only banking but products such as mortgages, insurance, investments, and credit cards. "Dustin is in trouble," James commented.

"He's facing a proxy challenge, right?"

"Yep, from our old buddy Ozzie Hayes." Osborne Hayes was the former chairman of North Central Bank. James had been named by the board of directors to be Hayes's successor but never got the chance, thanks to a corporate sabotage scheme. "The challenge is serious," James continued. "The stockholders will be voting on whether to throw Dustin out and put Hayes back in."

"Why would the stockholders want Hayes back?"

"I don't know if they're wild about Hayes. But they want a change. The stockholders who will be voting are institutions, who usually think short-term. Pension funds, hedge funds, mutual funds. The bank's earnings and stock price have been in the tank. In some ways, they've never really recovered from Downfall." A year and a half earlier, corporate saboteurs had manufactured a series of incidents that had nearly taken the entire company down.

"I hope Dustin can find somebody to help me," I said. "When it comes to computer hacking, I'm out of my depth."

"I'm sure Dustin will help. Listen, just promise me you'll be careful, okay?"

"I will. 'Bye, James."

"Good luck, hon. Love you."

I looked down at the phone. Was James right? Was I getting some kind of adrenaline rush from being involved in dangerous things? I guessed it was true that I didn't scare as easily as I used to. But I'd never planned to put myself, or anyone, in harm's way. And it wasn't fun.

Chapter 12

I waited for Marsha in the lounge of a hotel near the airport, my feelings a mishmash of apprehension, annoyance, and awkwardness. Apprehension, because the stakes in Kenny's disappearance had increased dramatically in the past day, a fact I now had to tell Marsha. Annoyance, because I was fairly certain Marsha knew some things she should have told me. And awkwardness, because, well, things had always been awkward between us, even before I had killed her daughter.

I barely recognized her when she walked into the lounge. The sister I had last seen was about twenty pounds overweight and a little on the frumpy side, her reddish-brown hair worn in an unflattering helmet. The new Marsha had clearly lost weight and gotten a dramatic makeover, with hairstyle, makeup, and clothing all upgraded. She leaned down and embraced me.

"Good heavens, Marsh. What happened to you?"

She gave me her trademark shy smile as she sat down. "Why do women usually do these things?"

I gave a little shriek. "You haven't told me anything. What's his name?"

Shy changed to embarrassed. "I'll tell you about it in a minute. First you've got to update me on Kenny. Did you meet with those people in Liam's neighborhood?"

"Yes."

"If you could have just waited until four, I could have gone with you."

"I told you, I didn't have time. I have to be on a plane in an hour."

"Of course. You have important things to do, people to see."

"Come on, let's not start on that stuff."

We ordered drinks, a Cosmo for her and white wine for me. I filled her in on what I'd learned from Sierra and Sam. "I also met with the FBI," I said. "You didn't tell me you'd talked to them."

"Who did you meet with?"

"An agent named Sink. But he said another agent named Hewitt called you."

"Hewitt. Right. That was the guy."

I let out an exasperated sigh. "Why didn't you tell me the FBI was looking for Kenny?"

"Was he FBI? I thought he was from the Minneapolis police, calling me back. The bottom line was that he didn't make any commitment to help."

I reined in my frustration. Marsha knew the difference between the FBI and a local police department. Maybe she just wasn't thinking clearly in her stress over Kenny's disappearance. "This is serious, Marsha. The FBI is looking for Kenny, which means he's mixed up in something pretty bad."

She nodded slowly, letting it sink in.

"And that something is hacking," I continued. "Did he ever mention anything to you about a hacker named Z?"

"No, he didn't."

"Did he ever talk about using ransomware to shake money out of corporations?"

"Never."

"Did he talk about hacking at all?"

"No."

Maybe not, I thought, but Marsha didn't look totally shocked by the prospect. "Did he ever say what Liam did for a living, or what he and Liam did together?"

She shook her head.

"He must have told you something."

She looked away, fingering her glass in both hands. "I know I must sound like a terrible mother, like we never talked and I didn't know or care what he was doing. It wasn't like that. I actually thought we were doing pretty well, that we were close."

"Why did he move to Minnesota?"

"He said it was his idea, but I would bet Alec talked him into it, as a way of getting at me."

"Are you sure it wasn't Kenny's idea?"

She waved her hands in vague futility. "Who knows? He's a teenager. Why do they do anything? It was something different. An adventure." She started to say something, stopped herself, and set her drink down. "Look, Kenny is an awkward kid. Like me."

"You're not—"

"I am. You know it, I know it. And Dad knew it." We were moving into painful territory. As hard as our father, Ken, had tried to love us equally, it hadn't worked. His favoritism may have been unacknowledged—even unconscious—but it had been there. Marsha recognized it a lot sooner than I did, of course. The discrepancy was doubly painful because Marsha was the dutiful daughter, working hard and trying to please. She had even named her son after him, a gesture that everyone appreciated. But it didn't eliminate the perceived favoritism, and both of us knew that Marsha's insecurity and shy personality contributed to the problem. Our father's parenting struggles were doubly painful because for most of our lives, he was the only parent we had. Our mother had died when I was seven and Marsha ten. I barely remembered our mother, but everyone said she had been the one with the outgoing personality, and that I took after her.

"Have you seen a picture of Kenny?" Marsha asked.

"I have. He's handsome. Gorgeous, in fact."

"And believe me, the girls noticed."

"There might have been one girl in particular, shortly before he left for Minnesota." I told her about the girl Sid had seen Kenny with.

"There was no actual girlfriend down here—not that I knew of. He'd occasionally talk to girls, of course. School friends, mostly. But he didn't know how to deal with the attention. He felt shy around them. He found it hard to relate to other kids in general."

"He's a lot smarter than most kids."

"That made it harder. He didn't fit in."

"He spent a lot of time online."

She took a sip from her glass. "I tried hard to encourage him to get out and see friends, and get involved in some school activities. But it was a losing battle. He lived online. When he said he was thinking of moving up to Minnesota, I didn't fight him very hard. I thought maybe a change would be good, that he'd meet some new people. And I thought the schools might be better up there. But now you're telling me he was working for this hacker guy—what's his name?"

"Just 'Z.' That's all we know."

She shook her head. "Obviously I'm not objective about this, Pen. But he's a good kid. He's decent. He's got a good heart. He wouldn't do anything illegal. He wants to stay out of trouble."

"How closely have you kept in touch with him since he moved to Minneapolis?"

"Pretty closely, I think. We texted just about every day or two and talked at least a couple of times every week. I know he didn't graduate, but he assured me he didn't have much to finish up, and he said he might still be able to start college this fall. He said he was dating a nice girl named Sierra—I was very encouraged by that, of course."

"What else has he been doing up there?"

"He said he was doing some programming for a guy—I didn't get any details on that. Obviously I should have. He might have been talking about this Z."

"Tell me about Liam."

"I met him a couple of times. Never a substantive conversation. He was older than Kenny."

"How did they meet?"

"I'm not sure. Mutual friends, I think. They were good buddies. They hung out together. But mostly, they did computer stuff."

"Liam lived off the books. No tax returns—not even a cell phone account."

Marsha looked surprised. "Didn't he have a job of some kind?"

"Apparently not the kind where you get a W-2 or pay taxes."

"Oh, jeez." She sighed. "What on earth were they up to?"

"The police think Liam might have been involved in drug dealing."

"I can't believe that. Kenny wouldn't have hung around with a dealer." She looked into her drink for a long moment, then up at me. "What did they do to Liam?"

I sucked in a breath. "They shot him."

She studied me. "What else?"

I hesitated.

"Tell me," she said sharply.

"They might have tortured him."

She stared at me for a moment, then let out a series of long, ragged sobs. Eventually she pulled out a tissue, drying her eyes and blowing her nose.

"I'll be in Minneapolis day after tomorrow if he hasn't been found," she said at last. "I don't know what I'll do there, but I have to go and do something. I can't just stay here."

"Fine. You can stay with me."

More silence.

"Tell me about the lucky guy," I said.

She managed a fleeting smile. "His name is Nathan. He's an anesthesiologist."

"What's he like?"

"A few years older. On the quiet side, like me. Not real tall. Losing his hair. But hey, I've gone the tall-and-handsome-and-outgoing route, and how did that work out?"

"He's divorced?"

She nodded. "Two kids, in high school."

"How long have you been dating?"

"Ten months. It's going well."

"That's great. Look, Marsh, do you think you could stay somewhere other than your house tonight?"

Her happy features crumpled suddenly. "You think I'm in danger?"

"Probably not, but it's better to be safe. There were two sets of violent assailants after Liam. We don't know if they're after Kenny, too, but they could be, which means they could be tempted to pay you a visit, too."

"I could stay at Nathan's place tonight."

"Good."

She looked away, blinking back the tears, before slowly turning toward me. "Is Kenny still alive?"

I didn't know what to say. "Let's not get ahead of ourselves, Marsh. It's way too early—"

"He's still out there. It can't be too late."

"We have to believe it."

Chapter 13

Special Agent Ben Hewitt drove toward southwest Minneapolis, trying to make sense of the whole Kenny Sellars mess. Sink had put him onto the case without telling him why it was important to find the kid. What did it mean, that Sink wouldn't trust him with the big picture? The powers that be in Minneapolis hadn't given Hewitt much choice when they assigned him to work temporarily for Sink and his mysterious cyber task force. Hewitt knew Kenny was involved somehow with a hacker named Z, and that was about it. So he'd done his job, interviewing witnesses, checking cell phone and bank records, and checking at the school, only to find that this highly intelligent kid had taken a highly serious powder.

He had dutifully reported on his efforts to Sink, who promptly blew him off, canceling the assignment. Then came the weird call from Kenny's aunt, purportedly a federal prosecutor, who pointedly alleged that Sink was disparaging Hewitt and his efforts. And then, a second call from the aunt, claiming that a friend of Kenny's in Tampa had been murdered and that two other friends, Sierra and Sam, whom Hewitt had previously interviewed for Sink, might be in danger. Hewitt couldn't imagine why; his interviews of both had been uneventful.

What was he to make of this woman? Was she a crank? Or was she on to something? To top it off, she said she had called Sink with the same warnings, yet he, Hewitt, hadn't heard anything from his boss. Did Sink not take the warning seriously? Or was he cutting Hewitt out of the loop? Too many questions, and Hewitt figured he deserved some answers.

His first query, a call to an FBI agent he knew in LA, yielded an important insight. Special Agent John Gibson, who happened to work closely with Pen Wilkinson, vouched for her without reservation. "She's the real deal, Ben," he'd said. "If she says her nephew is involved with some dangerous people, you need to take that seriously." And so here he was, approaching Sierra Bjorklund's house, which he had visited only a few days ago for an unproductive interview. He had received no answer when he'd tried calling. He thought about asking the Minneapolis police to swing by the house but decided he could do it himself on his way home from the office. After that, he'd give Sam Fenton another call.

He spotted the first lookout a block and a half from Sierra's house. The figure sat in a pickup truck on the street, wearing a baseball cap, and looked away when Hewitt passed the vehicle. Hewitt didn't slow down as he cruised past. Of course, the man didn't have to be a lookout, but if he was, he was in the right spot. Hewitt passed Sierra's house, which had lights on in the main level. Nothing looked amiss from the outside. As he drove through the intersection at the next block, he glanced to his right. A sedan was parked half a block down. By looking across the lawn of the house on the corner, the sedan's occupant, if any, would be able to see Sierra's house and both intersecting streets. He couldn't see if anyone was in the vehicle.

Hewitt proceeded through the intersection, went down a block, and made three right turns, coming up slowly behind the sedan. His headlights silhouetted a figure in the driver's seat. Hewitt had seen enough. He pulled over behind the car and got out. The figure behind the wheel leaned slightly to one side, as if talking on a radio.

"FBI, sir! Please step out of the car!" The figure didn't move, and Hewitt moved his hand toward the Glock in its shoulder holster.

The figure remained motionless.

"Sir, step out of the car and keep your hands in sight! Do it now!"

"All right!" the figure yelled. It was a man's voice and sounded British or Australian. His right hand went into the air. His left hand pushed open the door. His legs swung out and onto the ground.

"Keep your hands in sight!" Hewitt yelled again.

"All right, all right!"

Hewitt couldn't say, then or later, what was unnatural about the man's motion. But it was wrong. Hewitt reached for the Glock, but when the gun appeared in the man's hand, he knew he was too late. As the first shot was fired, Hewitt dived behind the car, rolled, and came up with the Glock to return fire. He peered underneath the car, looking for the man's legs, but didn't see any.

The car door slammed. Still no feet. The man had gotten back into the car. Hewitt stood up as the engine started. The car squealed away. Hewitt got down onto one knee, aimed, and fired. The car kept going, and he couldn't tell if he hit anything. The sedan tore around the corner to the left and came to a stop in front of Sierra's house. Hewitt ran after the car on foot, cutting across the lawn of the corner house. He saw a figure run out of the house toward the car. It was a woman.

"Stop or I'll shoot!" Hewitt yelled. But he was too far away. The woman jumped into the car, which squealed off down the street. Hewitt kept running toward the house, gun drawn. He stopped at the curb and pulled out his cell phone to call for back-up. After relaying the address and situation he said, "We need a welfare check on another witness. His name is Sam Fenton. The address is in my system." Hewitt hung up and resumed his sprint to the house. He knew it was foolish to clear the house himself, but he sensed that something very wrong had happened inside.

He pushed the front door open, ducked in, and faced a hall-way and dining room. Both were empty. He crept down a dark hallway, hearing a faint noise behind an open door on his left. He first cleared a kitchen on his right, then headed for the open door. He peeked around the corner and scanned the room, Glock extended. He lowered his gun. A young woman sat in a chair, sobbing.

"It's all right. You're safe," he said, striding across the room. "I'm Agent Hewitt, from the FBI, remember?"

Sierra didn't react.

"Are you hurt?"

She shook her head.

"How many were there?"

She didn't respond.

"Was there anyone other than the woman?"

Head shake.

"Come with me. Let's get to my vehicle until we can clear the rest of the house."

Back in the car, as they waited for the police and paramedics, his cell phone rang. "Hewitt."

"Agent Hewitt? We had the police check out your witness, Samuel Fenton."

"And?"

"We were too late."

"What do you mean? Is he alive?"

"Yes. But he's really messed up."

*   *   *

My flight back to Minneapolis was an hour behind schedule. I sat at the gate, staring at the materials I'd brought to work on for the Vargas case but unable to focus on them. Kenny Sellars was a mystery, to his parents and maybe, to some extent, to his friends. After being so sure Marsha would have some insight into his hacking activities, I had learned nothing. I wasn't sure about my next move back in Minnesota, but I couldn't see anything more to be done here.

I checked in with Cassandra at the office and made some notes. Then I called Wade Hirsch, got his voicemail, and left my boss a calm, detailed message setting forth the status of the Vargas case. That done, I forced myself to work on an exhibit list for the trial.

My cell phone buzzed. I glanced at the caller ID: Columbia Central Bank, with a Minneapolis area code.

"Hello, this is Pen."

"Hi, Pen. It's Dustin Blount."

"Oh, hi. I didn't expect you to call personally."

"No trouble at all," said the confident CEO with a Texas drawl. "It was nice talking to James. I understand you could use some help?"

"Yes. My teenage nephew has gone missing, and there's some indication he might be into hacking. I'm hoping to consult a tech person who might be able to give me some insight."

"I know just the person for you. Her name is Emily Radatz, and she's done some consulting for us. I'll have her give you a call in the morning."

"I really appreciate it, Dustin. I know you're busy these days."

He chuckled. "That's one way of putting it. Say, any chance you might be available for a drink late tomorrow afternoon?"

"Sure," I said, puzzled and pleased.

"I'll have my assistant give you a call. See you tomorrow. And good luck finding your nephew."

"Thanks. See you then."

I hung up, wondering why Blount wanted to see me. He was a friend of James, and I'd met him briefly and shaken his hand once, but didn't know him otherwise. I'd find out soon enough . . . if I could ever get back to Minneapolis. I glanced at the monitor; the flight was delayed again.

*　　　　　*　　　　　*

Sierra waited until the master bedroom light went off upstairs. Her mother had been "out shopping" with her friends when the intruder arrived. In practice, "out shopping" usually meant "out drinking," but she was, after all, only fulfilling the minimum purchases mandated by the social membership at her country club. At any rate, the blonde woman had seemed confident enough that her mother would not be home any time soon. But after the blonde woman fled, the police had insisted on calling her mother, who'd seemed more put out than concerned when she'd arrived. In fact, she'd declined the police officers' offer to watch their house overnight and had been annoyed by the trip to the police station to file a complaint and make a statement. She'd been openly skeptical of Sierra's version of events, inclined to believe that a prank or misdeed by Sierra's slacker boyfriend, or other friends, had accounted for the intrusion.

Sierra made sure her mother was in her room, sleeping it off. Then she switched on a light, found her backpack, and emptied it of the high school folders and notes she had never unloaded after graduation. Next, she quietly packed a change of clothes and toiletries, along with her laptop, cell phone, and the remaining money from the jar on her dresser. Downstairs, she hurried through the kitchen and out into the garage. She opened the garage door and got into the Toyota Corolla her mother had bought her for graduation. Out on the street, she closed the garage door and left slowly, heading toward the freeway.

Angry as she was, Sierra couldn't really blame her mother for being skeptical. Why would unknown intruders, not interested in robbery, want to question her daughter? Her mother was wrong in believing that Kenny was a slacker, when in fact he was brilliant. But she was correct in believing that he was trouble. She felt bad about not being able to tell the FBI agent anything. He'd come to her rescue, but he was looking for Kenny. She couldn't help him with that.

Sierra glanced in her rearview mirror, spotting a pair of headlights. She made a sudden right turn and glanced back again. No lights. When it came down to it, she was basically on her own. Her mother was hopeless. The police, taking their cue from her mother, dutifully took her statement, but seemed dubious. The FBI agent was helpful, but it wasn't his case, and his primary concern was finding Kenny. She briefly considered contacting Kenny's aunt, who seemed competent and concerned. But her agenda wasn't necessarily the same as Kenny's. And Kenny? She wasn't sure exactly where he was, or what his plan was. But one thing was certain: she couldn't stay home. The blonde woman and her accomplices knew where she lived, and although they'd been thwarted by Agent Hewitt's arrival, she knew they wouldn't stop trying.

Another glance into the mirror. The headlights had returned. Probably not the same lights, she told herself. But, to be on the safe side, she made a right turn onto a side street.

This time, the lights followed.

The street was quiet. It was now past midnight.

Another right. The car stayed with her. The headlights got closer, gaining on her. Now, as she tried belatedly to gain speed on the quiet residential street, the trailing car swerved to the left, threatening to overtake her.

She braked to a halt at the curb, hoping she hadn't failed Kenny.

*   *   *

Sam Fenton couldn't escape. He lay on his side, curled up. The mental loop repeated endlessly despite every effort to break free, to re-enter the world he had inhabited only a few hours ago. On some level, he knew he was in a hospital—he remembered his parents bringing him to the emergency room. He even understood that he was physically intact, with no permanent injuries.

He willed the memories to stop, but they took control of his brain, replaying the mental tape of the blonde woman endlessly. He felt spasms seize his body, in sympathy with the jolts of agony that had shot through him again and again as he had gasped for breath, his chest tightening. Blacking out, being revived. And then repeating the process. He had quickly told her everything he knew, but the woman's smiling reply, delivered in some kind of southern or mountain accent, had chilled him.

"But we need to make sure, hon."

Chapter 14

Kenny stood on the light rail platform just after midnight, watching and waiting. He saw nothing threatening in the small groups of passengers waiting for the train to take them home from the downtown bars. The people chatted easily on the warm night, most of them at least a little drunk. And why not? They didn't have to worry about killers coming after them. A train glided to a stop on the platform, but Kenny didn't get on. He kept watching, fingering the disposable cell phone in his pocket.

He hadn't taken Liam seriously at first. His friend's voice call—a rarity in itself—had come last week, late at night.

"Hey, man. What's up?"

"We've got trouble, Kenny. I think they're onto us."

"Whoa, take it easy. Who are 'they'?"

"Does it matter? It could be anybody."

Maybe not anybody, Kenny thought. But it could be a lot of people. People who didn't appreciate being held up for a lot of money. He asked the next question with considerable unease. "Have you talked to Z?"

"Hell, no. You know we're on our own if there's trouble. Z told us that from the beginning. What could he do to help, anyway?"

Kenny wasn't sure. But he didn't want Z's help. It was Liam who'd made the online introduction to Z, and at first it had been fun, an interesting game. He'd learned a lot, first from Liam and then from Z, and he'd gotten a chance to make a little money and work some interesting plays on some all-too-deserving targets. But then it had all gone south.

"Just calm down," Kenny said. "Why do you think they're onto us?"

"Somebody is looking hard, online. Somebody good. I've set a few tripwires, and they're going off."

"So just shut it down for a while. Wipe everything—they'll hit a dead end."

"Dude, it's more than that. I think they're here."

"What do you mean, 'here'? Like, physically present?"

"That's exactly what I mean."

"Come on, man. You're paranoid." But the prospect, however unlikely, was chilling. Being online meant anonymity, safety. When danger intruded into the physical world . . . who knew what to do then?

"Paranoid," Liam snorted. "Easy for you to say."

"Depends on how serious they are. If they go backward in time, they could find me, too."

"They wouldn't have to go back very far."

"I know. But I'm out of it now."

"Sure," Liam replied with heavy sarcasm. "You just want to be a normal teenager, going to a normal school, with a normal girlfriend. A nine-to-five schmuck. You've decided the boring life is for you."

"Maybe boring is better than crooked."

"'Crooked'? What a joke. The targets we go after are the real crooks."

"You know that even if they're looking, it's not about us."

"Of course not. It's about Z. But that doesn't mean they're not coming after us in order to find him. They are. And I've worked more closely with Z than anybody else has."

"So what have you actually seen there?" Kenny asked.

"A woman. A blonde woman. I've seen her a couple of times. She doesn't look like a Fed or a corporate security type, but I know she's trouble. She's after us."

Kenny's immediate reaction had been to dismiss his friend's fears as more paranoia. But what if he was right?

Liam's second call had come two nights later. "It's for real," he announced, breathless and without preamble.

"What's for real?"

"The blonde woman. I saw her again today, outside my building, and up at the market when I went out for some groceries. And Sid saw her down at Mosey. There was a guy with her, a tough-looking black guy."

"So there's a blonde woman hanging around your neighborhood. Lots of people live in your neighborhood. How do you know it has anything to do with you?"

Liam's voice was desperate, pleading. "I just know it does, man. I can feel it. And I'm telling you, you need to bail."

"Where would I go?"

"I don't know. But you'd better figure out something, and fast." Liam hung up.

Kenny had looked at the phone. It had seemed premature to run. But he'd figured he should be ready. And now, standing on the platform, waiting to make a call, his best friend dead, he knew it had been the right decision. But had he made it in time?

Chapter 15

Special Agent Ben Hewitt was walking down the hall toward Gary Sink's office when a fellow agent spotted him. "Sink wants to see you," the guy said.

Hewitt nodded. He and his boss needed to have it out. He had never wanted this temporary assignment, but after he'd completed his work on a credit card fraud task force, they weren't sure what to do with him while he'd waited for a promised posting in Washington, DC, where he had grown up. He knocked on Sink's door.

"Come," said the smooth voice. Sink sat behind his desk in shirtsleeves, wearing reading glasses. He gestured toward a chair.

Hewitt sat down. Sink continued to read something on his desk. Finally, he signed his name, put the paper into his outbox, and looked up at Hewitt. "Thanks a ton for the big shit sandwich, Ben."

"Thanks for all the trust and communication," Hewitt retorted.

"I had to go in and see the special agent in charge this morning and explain to him why we're involved in a local incident in southwest Minneapolis."

"Why did you have to explain anything? You don't report to the Minneapolis special agent in charge."

"But you do. And I, God help me, am responsible for you."

"What did you tell him?" Hewitt asked, genuinely curious.

"The truth. That a young agent, disregarding orders, took it upon himself to conduct a personal stakeout and blundered into an alleged home invasion. After another half-dozen questions on the reasons for your involvement, and the nature of the alleged crime, the special agent in charge gave up, because I had no answers."

"You know what I know. More, actually."

Sink ripped his glasses off. "You're missing the point. It shouldn't have been necessary to 'know' anything. The incident shouldn't have happened."

"Oh, it would have happened. We just wouldn't have been involved. The girl would have been attacked—probably hurt like Sam Fenton. You keep saying 'alleged.' Why don't you ask Sam how alleged the whole damned thing is?"

"It's a mess that has nothing to do with us."

"Really? And how would you know that?"

Sink's features tightened. "I told you to stay away from this case. Your role is finished."

"I was informed of impending danger to a civilian. I checked it out. I would have done that, case or no case. And I'd do it again in a heartbeat."

"You did it without checking with me." Sink's face was getting red.

"I can't prevent a crime without running it past you first? But now you're the one missing the point. You weren't communicating with me. You didn't tell me you were notified of the same threat and decided to do nothing. And you know what? I'll bet you didn't tell the SAC that, either."

Sink didn't respond.

"You also told the kid's aunt that I was an incompetent fool and not to talk to me. We're lucky she's a good judge of character, because we might have a girl hurt or dead if the aunt didn't decide to warn me anyway."

Sink shot to his feet. "Goddamnit, who the hell do you think you are, talking to me like that? You think you're a hot shot, a young man in a hurry. But to me, you're nothing but a punk. A flunky. You're all I could get for help when I was assigned here."

"You think I wanted this assignment? You come in here, all mysterious and secretive and superior, getting me to do your donkey work without telling me jackshit. Agents weren't exactly lining up for it."

Sink glared at the younger agent for a long moment, then sat down. "I looked at your file when I first got here. You came highly recommended. They didn't tell me you were some kind of half-assed rebel."

"I insist upon being treated right. If that makes me a rebel, so be it."

Sink sighed heavily, then stared off into space. He didn't look back at Hewitt when he said, "I'm placing a letter of reprimand in your file for insubordination. And I'll see about getting you out of Minneapolis to a new assignment." He looked back at the younger agent. "It won't be Washington."

Hewitt, face flushed, stood up. "We're not finished. I will fight this."

Sink, looking bored and tired, waved him away.

Chapter 16

Stefan Fedorenko sauntered into the office next to the shop area. His men had gone out on an errand, and the place was quiet. Four vehicles sat in the shop in various stages of disassembly. He pulled out his cell phone, wondering what to tell Z and hating himself for wondering. Stefan was a cunning, violent, elaborately tattooed veteran of the Russian mafia. Why, honestly, was he worried about the reaction of a nerdy kid twenty years his junior?

There were several reasons, he supposed. Z paid Stefan's considerable salary, and if the current project succeeded, Stefan would be a rich man. He went way back with Z's family, back to the old country. His bond with Z was complex. He was Z's confidante, right-hand-man, link to the non-virtual world, and, he supposed, father figure and protector. But behind Z's frightening intelligence, behind the controlled countenance, behind the unimpressive physical presence, Stefan sensed . . . he wasn't sure what. It could be a hardness, or actual malevolence. And that uncertainty, along with the intelligence, was what unsettled him.

Z picked up on the first ring. "Well?"

"I looked into it," Stefan said.

"Go on."

"When the kid disappeared—"

"He was scared."

"Of course he was. With good reason." They spoke Russian. It was Stefan's first language, Z's second. "The parents finally reported him missing."

"And the police responded? Usually they don't."

"Technically it wasn't a missing person's call. It was a break-in."

A pause. "Oh, shit."

"That's right," Stefan said. "They went after him. The back door was forced. The bathroom window was open. He probably got out that way."

"So the opposition is definitely here."

"Yes."

"What happened next?"

"No way to know if he escaped or if they got him."

"If they had him, we'd know it by now. They wouldn't take long to break him. Which would lead them to me. And they'd be taking steps to stop the project."

"We don't know how much he knows about the project."

"I might have told him too much. And what he doesn't know, he can probably put together. Are the police going to do anything more?"

"They're not investigating the disappearance. They took a report on the break-in. But nothing was reported taken from the house, so I don't expect any follow-up."

"We're a step behind," Z said. "We're late to the game. But if Beast had gotten there on time . . ."

"He went two days after he said he would."

"Damnit, Stefan, I depended on you to get somebody reliable."

"Beast has worked for us before. He'd always done okay."

"Well, he didn't this time. So where does that leave us?"

"The opposition showed its hand in Tampa. Liam must have seen them coming. I'm sure he tipped Kenny off before they got him, and by the time they got up here, Kenny was gone. We've been a step behind ever since."

A long pause. "Time to take it to the next level, Stefan. Lean on everybody harder. Find him."

"Okay."

Z hesitated. "I'm genuinely fond of the kid. But . . ."

"I understand."

"We can't let him fall into their hands. We just can't. When we find him, he'll have to go."

The conversation seemed to be at an end, but Stefan didn't hang up. In a tentative voice, Z asked, "Do you think they have him?"

Stefan didn't answer.

Chapter 17

I waited at a table in the restaurant of a hotel in downtown Minneapolis, gulping down a cup of coffee, trying to wake up enough to talk coherently with Dustin Blount's tech consultant. The stress and lack of sleep were starting to catch up with me, as was the realization, driven home by James, that I might have gotten myself into something bigger than I could handle.

"Pen?"

I looked up. A very large man with prematurely gray hair in a crewcut stood next to a very pregnant young woman.

"I'm Doug Lamm," said the man. "Columbia Central's CTO." We shook, and as we did so, he studied me carefully, eyes narrowed.

"And this is Emily Radatz," he said, introducing the woman. I nodded to her across the table. They sat down. "Emily does some consulting for us on security issues," he said. "Hopefully she can help you out. I understand you're meeting with Dustin later today."

"Right." I wondered yet again what Dustin Blount might want from me, and Lamm looked as though he wasn't sure either. Blount was pulling out all the stops, sending not only a consultant but his chief technology officer.

"Maybe you could fill us in on what you're looking for," Lamm said. He listened closely, asking incisive questions, as I spent five minutes explaining why I needed to learn the basics of hacking, as well as the particulars of a hacker named Z.

After I'd completed my explanation, Lamm stared at me for a long minute, considering what he'd heard. At last, he stood up.

"Well, I'll leave you two to figure things out. Nice to have met you, Pen." He left, and I turned to Emily Radatz, who'd settled herself awkwardly into a chair across from me. She was tall—about five nine, I guessed—with dark hair and smart-looking glasses, wearing a perfume with a nice jasmine scent. She ordered coffee but didn't appear to need it.

"Thanks for making time for me," I said, chewing an English muffin.

"No problem. I'm always looking for an opportunity to suck up to Blount and Doogie."

"Doogie?"

She nodded back toward the direction Lamm had gone. "He calls himself Doug, but to the rest of the world he's Doogie."

"He seems a little cautious."

"'Cautious' doesn't begin to describe it. I'm not even sure 'paranoid' is adequate. He trusts no one."

"You're consulting for him. He must trust you."

"No more than he has to. I guarantee he ran a check on me—a very detailed one. I'd bet he ran one on you, too."

"Have you done a lot of consulting for Columbia Central?"

"A fair amount. They're not my biggest client, but I nearly always have some kind of project going with them. I'd like to do more, though." She glanced down at her large belly. "Kids aren't cheap."

"How long have you been in the consulting business?"

She frowned slightly. "I guess I've been doing programming and systems work . . . well, for as long as I can remember."

Probably like Kenny, I thought.

"Anyway," she continued, "I began my consulting career working with law enforcement agencies in the Boston area, where I grew up."

"Interesting. How did you get started with that?"

She looked embarrassed. "I was . . . encouraged to do it by a judge. If I declined to help the authorities, I was probably looking at some jail time. I'd done some hacking. Stupid hacking."

"Stupid in what way?"

"I broke the law. Not only that, but I didn't make any money from it. The judge got creative with the sentence, and . . . well, community service helping the police was better than the alternative, so I took the deal."

"And you've been on the straight and narrow ever since?"

"Absolutely. But I do keep track of the bad guys. In fact, that's what I do now. So you're a friend of Dustin?"

"More like a friend of a friend." I explained about James and his connection with Dustin Blount.

"I see. I understand you'd like to know more about Z."

"Right."

Emily asked several more questions about Kenny, Liam, and the mysterious hacker they may have been working for. Then she asked about the attacks on Sam and Sierra. She thought about my story for a long moment and sighed. "If Kenny was working for Z, he probably should have kept it to himself."

"What do we know about Z?"

"I know a few basics, I guess. Most people in my business do. The FBI thinks his real name is Yevgeny Mishkin, that he was born in New Jersey, and that he's in his early thirties."

"How sure is the FBI about all that?"

"Not totally. They can't confirm any of it. And they've had no success actually tracking him down. They don't have a picture of him, and they don't know where he lives."

"So he could be a teenager."

"He might have started at a young age. But he's been at it a while."

"Or a woman?"

"That's an intriguing thought. But all my sources say he's a man. Nearly all hackers are." She shrugged. "But who really knows?"

"How about his real name?"

"They aren't a hundred percent sure."

I took a long gulp from my coffee cup. "How did he become legendary?"

"He was a pioneer in the use of ransomware. Are you familiar with that?"

"I've heard the term a lot. I know it's nasty malware."

"Right. It can infect an individual's computer, and often does, but of course there's much more money in holding up bigger entities. A hacker infiltrates an organization's system—sometimes using an innocent-looking email to an employee, or sometimes breaking a password. The victim could be a business or a nonprofit, and usually a smaller to medium-sized outfit. The hacker plants a virus or malware of some kind. A lot of times, the malware encrypts all of a company's data. The company can't get its data back unless the hacker sends it the encryption code, which he won't do unless the business pays a ransom. The money is usually paid to a numbered offshore account or with Bitcoins."

"Do the businesses pay?"

"Sometimes not, but oftentimes yes. They can usually detect what's in their system, but they can't get it out, at least not within a short time frame. The company's data could be deleted or rendered totally inaccessible, and its systems could be damaged or compromised."

"That sounds serious."

"The effects are devastating and could even put the company out of business, especially if they're not adequately backed up. The victims hate it, of course, but sometimes paying the ransom seems their only option."

"And Z does this?"

"Yes, and he's made tons of money from it. He has a genius for finding vulnerable systems and companies."

"Why can't the authorities track him down?"

"Hackers are good at covering their tracks. They use proxy servers, rerouted messages, and temporary IP addresses. It's really tough to physically locate them. Now, the FBI did make some progress in locating Z. Nobody will talk on the record, but my sources tell me they identified him as Mishkin and traced him to New Jersey three years ago. Then they lost the trail. And within a few months, Z resurfaced online, selling some of the data he lifted from companies that didn't pay."

"How do you sell illegal data online?"

Emily smiled. "There's a robust online market for stolen credit card numbers, bank account numbers, Social Security numbers—all kinds of things. It's not too different from Amazon or Ebay. It's not just information, either—the feds busted a large online drug operation a few years ago. It all takes place on the Dark Web, which can't be accessed through normal web addresses and search engines. You sort of have to know where to find it. But it definitely exists, and it's a constant cat-and-mouse game between the FBI and the players on these markets."

"Could Kenny have helped Z do some of these things?"

Emily shrugged. "It's possible. Z definitely has a crew—his operation has to be bigger than just him sitting at a computer. But it's like so much else about him—nobody knows how many accomplices he has."

I thought some more while I sipped at my now-cold coffee. I looked at Emily's cup, which she had refilled twice. "Isn't that—"

"Bad for the kid?" She shrugged. "It's not like drinking or smoking. I'll just have a wired kid, that's all."

"So," I said, "the FBI traced Z to New Jersey three years ago. Weren't they able to work backwards, to find his family and known associates and trace him from there?"

"Apparently not. He made a clean getaway. Also, he'd gone back and erased a lot of his online history."

"Mishkin is a Russian name. Is the guy even an American?"

"The Bureau thinks so, although his family may have moved here from Russia before he was born. He could be anywhere now, Pen. Chances are good that he isn't even in this country."

"Where would Kenny have met him?"

"Online. The chances that they ever physically met are close to zero."

I paused a moment to take it all in. "So what is Z doing now?"

"No one knows. His name still pops up in hacker chat rooms and discussions relating to the online markets for illegal information and hacking. He may still be doing ransomware, but as far as I know, no one has been able to trace anything recent to him. And of course, everybody is doing ransomware now—he could have moved on to the next big thing, whatever that might be. He's got a lot of money—maybe he's retired." Her smile told me she didn't believe that for a moment.

"Or he could be planning the next big heist," I said.

"Sure."

"Could he go after a big company?"

"How big?"

"Say, one the size of Columbia Central?"

She smiled and shook her head. "I doubt it. He's got the skills —no question. But why beat your head against a wall? Big companies can throw a lot of resources at security. They can hire a lot of people like Doogie and me. Oh, hackers still try—banks are more or less constantly under attack. But with ransomware, it's much easier to establish a credible threat to bring a company down when you're dealing with a smaller outfit. And that's been Z's pattern."

"What is the FBI doing about all this?"

"Hard to say. They cooperate with businesses to a certain extent but are pretty secretive about their own efforts. They've established an interagency task force directed at Z and other ransomware players."

"Is Gary Sink part of that?"

"He is. He's a rather obscure agent, and I really know nothing about him. They sent him here from Pittsburgh a few months ago."

"Why Minnesota?"

She smiled and shrugged. "Maybe he likes the winters."

Chapter 18

After working for a couple of hours back at the condo on my trial preparation, it was time for lunch. I left the building and rolled several blocks down Nicollet Mall. It was a beautiful summer day, but the streets weren't as busy as might be expected. A lot of the pedestrians still used the skyway system one level up.

But there were plenty of people on the streets, and I found myself scrutinizing them. You couldn't tell a killer by sight. And, since this was Minnesota, blonde women, including me, weren't going to stand out much. I didn't. But someone, blonde or not, female or otherwise, had murdered Liam Blankenship. Someone had chased Kenny from his home, forcing him into hiding. Someone—a killer—was still out there.

Over the past year and a half, I'd had some close encounters with violent criminals, and the experiences had spooked me to the point where I'd considered buying a gun. My FBI agent friend, John Gibson, had even taken me to a range and taught me a few basics about how guns operate, and I'd done a little shooting. But in the end, I'd decided against owning a firearm. I wouldn't have been able to bring one on a plane, anyway. Still, on this beautiful day, I felt a familiar chill of fear beginning to descend over me, and I didn't like it.

Special Agent Ben Hewitt waved to me as I rolled up to the outdoor seating area of an Irish pub. He had emailed me and asked to meet for lunch, and I'd readily agreed. And then he'd asked a question that was always easy for me to answer: "How will I recognize you?"

I entered the seating area by the restaurant's front door, then threaded my way down the rows of tables. Hewitt, a tall, good-looking guy with short, sandy-colored hair, looked to be about my age—mid-thirties. He stood up to shake my hand, and I noticed that he had considerately removed the chair across the table from him.

I rolled up to the table, and he sat down. "What's the occasion, Agent Hewitt? I thought you were no longer involved in the Kenny Sellars case."

"Technically, that's true. But I've—well, taken an interest. I'm sorry I hung up on you."

"And I'm sorry I jerked your chain a bit."

"Great—we've got that little awkwardness out of the way. You established your cred by warning me about Sierra and Sam."

"You established yours by following up on the warning."

"And John Gibson says I should listen to what you have to say."

So he had checked me out, as I had him, both of us consulting the same person. "High praise, coming from John."

Hewitt smiled, his grin showing friendliness, polish, and confidence. "Absolutely. I take it you two worked together pretty closely on that big corruption case out in LA."

"Very closely. He saved my life from a psycho killer."

"Funny. He says you did the same for him."

"So that makes us responsible for each other now, I guess. What do you mean, you've 'taken an interest' in my nephew's case?"

"I'll get to that—I have some things to tell you first. But before any of that, would you mind telling me what you know about Kenny's dad?"

"I don't know that much about Alec—he's been divorced from my sister for six years."

"Look, I don't mean to offend you—maybe you really like the guy. But is he as . . . oblivious as he appears?"

I waved off his concern. "You do wonder how he could be Kenny's father, but yes."

Hewitt considered that as we stopped to order lunch, a sandwich for him, a salad for me, and mineral water for both of us. "I think there's something Alec isn't telling me," he said when the waiter left.

"It's certainly possible."

"Could he be responsible for Kenny's disappearance somehow? Or complicit?"

"I doubt it. He's an airhead, but he doesn't strike me as evil."

The waiter delivered our glasses of water, and we each took a sip. "I understand you talked to Marsha," I said.

He nodded. "I did a quick check with her and confirmed she didn't know Kenny's whereabouts. I wish I'd talked to her at greater length."

"Why didn't you?"

"Alec told me she was basically out of the picture—that she lived in Florida and hadn't seen Kenny in ages."

"What a bastard."

Our food arrived, and we ate silently for a few minutes, enjoying the day with our own thoughts. Eventually Hewitt put his sandwich down. "Let me tell you about Sam and Sierra."

I felt the fear return and intensify as he told me about rescuing Sierra from a team led by a blonde woman.

"A blonde woman—that sounds like part of the team that visited Liam."

"Who's Liam?"

"Oh, boy. We need to bring each other up to date." I told him about Liam and my trip to Tampa.

"All right, now it makes sense," he said when I'd finished. "That's how you figured Sam and Sierra might be in danger and warned me. It's a good thing you did. Now let me pick up the story." He looked down at the rest of his sandwich and decided against it. "Sam Fenton was attacked late yesterday afternoon, before the incident with Sierra. He was tortured by someone who fastened a plastic bag over his head, bringing him to the point of suffocation repeatedly."

"The blonde woman?" I realized I had whispered the words.

"Or possibly other members of her team. Or maybe somebody else altogether—we don't know. Sam is still alive and physically unhurt. But he is severely traumatized and hasn't been able to tell the police much that's useful."

"At least they didn't kill him, like they did Liam," I said, terrified by the knowledge that the same people were looking for Kenny.

"They may not have killed Liam, either, based on what you've told me."

I gave him a puzzled look.

"He was tortured like Sam was, and he was shot. Maybe the big tattooed guy came along and finished him off."

"That makes sense; the time of death matches up with his visit, not the blonde woman's. So who is he? And why would he do it?"

"I don't know. But it looks to me like Liam must have spotted the blonde and her team while they were watching him, and warned Kenny. That's why Kenny took off, and that's why the blonde and her accomplices are up here looking for him, going after his friends."

"They haven't gone after Alec, Shannon, or Marsha."

"Curious, isn't it?" He picked up his water glass and studied it as though longing for something stronger. Then he took a sip. The sunny day and the street and the crowds had receded as we pondered the evil that had invaded this wholesome place. "It could be that the parents simply don't know anything."

"But how does the blonde know that?"

"Good question. Maybe Sam told them that Kenny kept his folks out of the loop. Another explanation is that they're simply prioritizing and figure the friends are likelier to know."

I felt clammy. "That means they could still go after the parents." *Or me,* I didn't add.

He nodded. "There's a good chance they're watching the parents." Neither of us spoke for a couple of minutes.

"I guess I might as well finish the story," Hewitt said.

I waited.

"Sierra Bjorklund went missing last night."

My stomach gave a lurch as I sat back, stunned.

"Her car was found abandoned about a mile and a half from home," he continued. "The police believe she voluntarily left home in the car. This had to have been several hours after the police and I left."

"So what do we do now?" I asked, feeling small and helpless, but hopeful now that an experienced, capable law enforcement professional was interested in the case.

"I'm meeting with the Minneapolis police later this afternoon. We'd like you to be there."

"Absolutely. Now, how about telling me why you're interested in Kenny's disappearance?"

He gave me a troubled but amused look. "It's personal."

"In what way?"

"It's selfish."

I studied him. "Okay, then, so confess. Good for the soul."

He met my gaze. "I have an axe to grind. Agent Sink rather forcefully took me off the case this morning."

I waited.

"He also put a career-crippling letter of reprimand in my file and is trying to get me transferred out of here like yesterday. All of which has made me more than a little curious about this case."

"I'm really sorry to hear that, and I appreciate your willingness to help. Tell me, where is Sink coming from? He threatened me—tried to browbeat me into giving him information. Is he a bully, or a control freak, or what?"

"I'm not sure what the hell he is. When he first arrived in Minneapolis, he seemed like a decent enough guy. He showed up at some office functions, brought his girlfriend along. She was a nice lady. A redhead—I think her name is Lindsay."

"He probably likes puppies, too. But he's an asshole."

He shrugged. "It's probably nothing sinister. It's just bureaucracy. He wants to be in control. But sometimes we forget that what we do at the FBI affects real people in the real world. Sink's bureaucracy, my future—none of that is of much concern to Sam, or Sierra, or Kenny. Somebody ought to care, at least a little."

"And Sink doesn't, so . . ."

"Time to put my super-hero cape on, I guess."

"I knew it wasn't all selfish for you."

His smile was weary and a little sad, I thought.

"So how do you read this case?" I asked. "You've got a hacker named Z out there, whom Kenny probably worked for. Is it Z who hired the blonde woman?"

"It's possible. If so, Sink should be really interested. He's been spinning his wheels, looking for Z, ever since he came to Minnesota. Sink is definitely interested, but not in the way he should be."

"Maybe your police contact will have some insight."

"Let's hope so."

He leaned back in his chair. "So tell me about yourself, Pen. How'd you end up in that thing?" He gestured toward the wheelchair.

"Car accident."

He nodded. He could see I didn't want to talk about it. "You seeing anyone these days?"

The question didn't surprise me; I'd been getting the vibe almost the entire time we'd been together, and I imagined the thought processes that went with it. *Interesting . . . I wonder if she can . . . What would it be like . . .* And maybe he'd been getting a vibe from me, too, although he'd probably picked up a little guilt along with the attraction.

"I see Gibson didn't tell you everything," I said.

"He mentioned that you'd been dating a guy for more than a year. I thought I'd ask you."

"It's true."

He smiled, showing big, perfect teeth. He really was handsome. "That's a shame."

"So, did you always want to be an FBI agent when you grew up?"

"Not quite. I wanted to be a cop. But my dad wanted me to be a lawyer—he was a partner at a big firm in Washington, DC. We lived in Potomac, Maryland. Dad kept pushing me to go to law school, and finally I did, at Georgetown. But after graduating, I branched off. I joined the FBI instead of practicing law."

"How do you like it?"

"It's been good. I put in about a year in Raleigh. Then I went back to DC and worked in counter-terrorism. Now, that was interesting."

"How did you end up here in Minnesota?"

"They sent me here to help with the Somali pipeline."

"The—what?"

"There's a large Somali population here—the largest in the US. There has been some money flowing from here to al-Shabab in Somalia. That's a terrorist group—an offshoot of al-Qaeda. It can be hard to separate those money transfers from the ones going to families. But more troubling than that is the human pipeline. Young men are being recruited to go to the Middle East and fight for al-Shabab, or even to Syria to fight for ISIS. I spent a lot of time working with community leaders and organizations, and with families, to try to reach those young men before the bad guys do. And, of course, I caught and prosecuted the ones who tried to go."

"Why would they go to the Middle East? What's there for them, except danger and death?"

"A lot of them don't see much for themselves here, either. They're from poor immigrant families who live in crappy neighborhoods. They're racial minorities. They're religious minorities. And there's the stigma. Politicians label them—sometimes all Muslims—as disloyal and violent. They call for all Muslims to be rounded up, deported, put into camps, whatever. If these guys go off to fight, they see that as their chance to be somebody and do something worthwhile, even if it means martyrdom." He shrugged. "Somalis are making progress here. They're gradually getting educated, moving into careers—even running for public office. But it's a tough battle."

"Why were you being reassigned?"

"I asked for it. I want to move back to the DC area. My dad died two years ago, and now my mother has to move into a nursing home. She has early-onset Alzheimer's."

"I'm really sorry to hear that."

Hewitt signed for the check, then pushed his chair back. "We're in the same business, I guess. I catch the assholes. You put them away."

"And we've got some seriously bad guys here."

"Amen." He stood up. "It was great meeting you, Pen. See you in a couple of hours."

After lunch, I called Alec and told him about Liam's murder and the attacks on Sam and Sierra. "This is getting nasty," I said. "These people appear ready to do just about anything to find Kenny. Can you and Shannon go away somewhere?"

"Do you really think that's necessary, Pen?"

"It would be a good idea. They've gone after Kenny's two closest friends. You and Shannon are logical targets."

"I don't know . . . I'll talk to Shannon. We'll think about it."

"Yes, do that. And be careful."

I hung up, thinking that all the reassurances I'd given James about my own safety were sounding increasingly hollow. I needed to watch my back, and Marsha's. Alec, on the other hand, didn't seem to feel that he had much to worry about. And I wondered about that.

Chapter 19

Stefan Fedorenko kept the Beast waiting for nearly an hour. When Stefan walked into the shop area from the outer office, he sauntered into an alcove with a couple of chairs. His men left through a side door, taking a discreet cigarette break. Byron "Beast" Waddle, an enormous man with a stubbly haircut and big, menacing tattoos, sat in one of the chairs, playing a game on his phone. *No clue*, Stefan thought.

Waddle looked up. "Hey."

Stefan nodded.

"You got some more work for me?" Waddle asked.

Stefan sat down across from the big man. "Maybe. But let's talk about the last job."

"Aw, man—I told you . . ."

"Let's talk about it," Stefan said—slowly, softly, and with menace.

Waddle, who outweighed Stefan by a hundred pounds, straightened up in his chair. "All right, what about it?"

"You were two days late in getting down to Tampa."

"Man, I told you, something came up. Shit happens. I'm sorry about that. But I took care of the guy."

"Yes, you did. But somebody else got there first and questioned him. He told these people where to find Kenny."

"But they haven't found the kid, right?"

"If you had done your job, there would have been no need to find the kid. But now he's disappeared, and the opposition is up here looking for him. They're ahead of us. Your delay put us behind them at every step. I relied on you."

Waddle was unrepentant. "Look, if they haven't found the kid, then it's not over yet, right? No harm, no foul."

Stefan didn't reply.

"Hey," Waddle said. "If you want, I'll go out and find the kid now. No charge."

"I don't think so, Byron."

The huge man shrugged. Still not a clue, Stefan thought, as he idly studied the tats on either side of the Beast's neck. On one side, a big middle finger extended from a fist, flipping off the observer. Someone looking at the other side stared down the barrel of a revolver. He was a man who was used to fearing no one. "Have it your way," Waddle smirked. "I got paid."

"Yes, you did. And to show you I'm not a bad guy, I won't ask for our money back."

Waddle's expression changed suddenly. Now he got it. But it was too late.

Stefan drew an automatic and shot him.

The Beast's forehead erupted, blood oozing into his eyes and down his face. He slumped in his chair, his phone clattering to the cement floor. He finally slid down and died, his eyes open, his face a mask of utter shock.

An hour later, after Stefan had cleaned things up and, with the help of both of his men, loaded the massive body into a vehicle for disposal later that night, he called Z. "It's done," he reported.

"Good. It still pisses me off. If he'd gotten there on time, they wouldn't have been able to question Liam and trace Kenny to Minnesota."

"Yes, I know."

"And then Waddle had to go overboard and kill him. That got the aunt and the FBI involved."

"You know, it wasn't as though we needed the Beast anymore, or that he was going to talk. It wasn't strictly necessary to do this."

Z's voice sounded weary. They'd had this kind of discussion before. "Yes, it was. I just don't need to have people messing with me. Years ago, maybe. But now, at this stage in my life, there's just no need to put up with it. Anything on Sierra?"

"Still gone. My police source tells me they didn't get anything out of her last night. The FBI got there first."

"But they might be questioning her now, if they have her. And now they have whatever Sam knows. Any chance we can talk to him?"

"It won't do any good. Sam is too messed up even to talk to the cops. And what would he say, anyway? That a blonde woman and one or two other guys asked about the kid. We already know that."

"But maybe he knew where Kenny was."

"I doubt it. They wouldn't have gone after Sierra."

"So," Z said, "now the police will be looking for Sierra. We need to find her first. Try hacking into her voicemail. I'll do what I can online."

"All right."

"And make sure Kenny's parents know we want him alive."

Stefan wondered if the parents cared that much, or why they would have any reason to believe the lie.

"We're just about ready with the project," Z said. "We find Kenny and we can move."

Stefan didn't respond.

"Damnit, just find him," Z said.

Chapter 20

After working a couple more hours back at the condo on the trial, I set out in my rental van and drove across downtown to City Hall, a big nineteenth-century building with a clock tower. I found a handicapped parking spot in the underground garage across the street at the Hennepin County Government Center and took a tunnel over to the striking, castle-like edifice. On the main floor, I found Agent Ben Hewitt waiting for me in the hallway.

"Hi," I said. "Who are we meeting with?"

"Her name is Candiotti. She's a detective—a lieutenant, actually."

"Working what kind of cases?"

"I understand she's an unassigned floater."

After we'd stopped at reception, a trim woman in her mid-forties came out from her cubicle in the detectives' bureau and gave us businesslike handshakes. She was of medium height, with dark, shoulder-length curly hair and intense green eyes. She nodded to Hewitt, then said, "Ms. Wilkinson? Lexi Candiotti. Thanks for coming in." We followed her down the corridor to a conference room and got ourselves situated inside. "Can I get you anything?" Candiotti asked.

We declined.

"Agent Hewitt has told me a little about his involvement in your nephew's disappearance. Our main focus is the attacks on Sam Fenton and Sierra Bjorklund, and Sierra's disappearance. We haven't actually opened a file on Kenneth Sellars, but he's a strong person of interest, and so we're trying to find him, too."

I nodded.

"So let's see if we can piece this story together. Agent Hewitt, why don't you start?"

Hewitt described his assignment working for Gary Sink and his questioning of Kenny's friends and family. Then he nodded to me. I began with the call from Marsha and my meetings with Alec, Sierra, and Sam. Candiotti listened with particular interest when I described my trip to Tampa and my discussions with the witnesses in Liam's neighborhood. Then Hewitt, after describing his rescue of Sierra, told her about the hacker named Z and his possible relationship to Kenny and Liam.

Candiotti nodded. "Then let's talk about Sierra's disappearance. I did a song-and-dance for the county attorney and got a warrant to check her cell phone records. She received a call last night—this morning, actually—at 12:08 AM. It was from a burner that was bought for cash at a Target store several weeks ago."

"Where was Sierra when she got the call?" I asked.

"That's hard to pin down. They tell me it was received in the vicinity of her home, but it's likelier that she was away from the house a short distance."

"What about the burner?" Hewitt asked.

"We checked the disposable and learned that the call was made to her from the western side of downtown. So then I tried to narrow it down further."

"How do you do that?"

"You first consider what's open in the area at that hour. Bars, basically. But there are dozens of bars in that area. If the call came from one of them, we're pretty much out of luck. But what if the caller is too young to get into a bar?" I gripped the wheels of my chair.

"Of course," Candiotti continued, "the caller could have been parked in a car, or standing on a street corner. If that's true, we're pretty much out of luck there, too. But then I wondered, What if he or she doesn't have a car, and doesn't want to be loitering on a street corner at midnight?"

We waited.

"So then I thought, 'What else is open at that hour?' Let me show you something." She motioned us around the conference table to a desk against the wall, which held a computer and screen. We crowded around the desk while she logged in and entered a series of commands.

I held my breath as a video feed flickered to life on the screen. It was a view of a rail platform at night. The time counter in the bottom corner showed 12:06 AM this morning at Target Field station. Perhaps two dozen people sat or stood at different points on the platform.

"I had this sent over from the transit police," Candiotti said. "See the guy down at the end? With the white T-shirt?"

I squinted at the image. There was a restless-looking man off to one side of the screen. "He's trying to stay away from any cameras at the ends of the platform," Candiotti said. "But those aren't the only cameras." She entered more commands, and another image came up, this one from a different angle.

I gasped. "That's Kenny." There was no mistaking the angular face and curly dark hair. The counter now showed 12:07 AM.

"Here's the call," the detective said. Kenny pulled a phone out of his pocket, punched in a number, and held it up to his ear. The conversation lasted less than half a minute. Then he clicked off and replaced the phone. Candiotti switched back to the full-platform view, then fast-forwarded through additional footage, which showed Kenny to be vigilant, peering out at the streets and sidewalk at different locations, checking his phone. At 12:30, Candiotti slowed the video down to normal speed. And then, at 12:32 . . .

"There he goes," Hewitt said, pointing at the screen, where Kenny glanced impatiently at his phone and walked off the platform.

"I decided to keep watching for a while," Candiotti said. She speeded up the video again, and at 12:35, a figure appeared from the right side of the screen, walking briskly down the platform, surveying the scene. Candiotti froze the video at a particularly revealing spot, with the pursuer's hair flying back, directly under a light. The figure was athletic and female, the hair blonde. She exited the platform, and camera range, less than a minute later.

Candiotti turned to look at us. "She didn't miss him by much. I've got a guy who's spent the last two hours checking other cameras across downtown, trying to pick up the trail. We caught a couple of images of Kenny just to the west, about a minute and a half later. We didn't see the blonde woman, but the station is pretty close to the edge of downtown, and the camera coverage gives out quickly."

"So we don't know whether she found him or not," Hewitt said.

"Not for sure," the lieutenant replied. "But there was another call made from Kenny's phone in northeast Minneapolis, near the river, at 1:04 AM."

"To Sierra?" I asked.

"Yes. Her phone was in the middle of downtown. After that, both phones went silent."

"So there's hope."

"I'd say yes."

"How did the blonde and her team find him?"

Hewitt responded. "I can think of three possibilities. One, they knew to look for him at the station—they'd followed him partway there, for example. Two, they got Sierra, who gave up his location. Three, they have the ability to do their own cell phone checks."

Candiotti nodded. "I'd say the odds of each of those scenarios are about the same. We also don't know whether it was Sierra who took the calls, or whether the bad guys took the phone, or made her answer under duress."

Hewitt and I returned to our spots at the conference table. None of us spoke for a long moment. Finally I asked, "Where does this leave us?"

"I've put the word out," Candiotti said. "We're looking for them. Sierra's disappearance will probably be on the news tonight, although I don't know whether that helps us or not. We'll continue to monitor the cell phones. We have only two real leads on the disappearances: the blonde woman and Z, the hacker. On the blonde, we've got nothing—no vehicle, no physical evidence. That leaves us with the hacker."

I told her what I'd learned about Z from Emily Radatz.

Candiotti shook her head. "We've got cyber-crimes people here at the department and at the state, but let's face it: if the FBI has been trying for years to catch this guy and hasn't been able to do it, we don't stand much of a chance. We'll have to concentrate on old-fashioned detective work—witnesses, phone records, and so on. You guys are free to do whatever you can on the hacking angle. Just stay in touch."

We thanked her and left.

Hewitt walked with me as I found the elevator and descended to the tunnel under the street.

"I hadn't expected the police to be so helpful," I said, "or to assign such a capable officer. In fact, I sort of wonder what's going on with this case."

"I asked around, and Candiotti is a high-powered cop. She's actually the top homicide investigator in Minnesota."

"Homicide?" I said, alarmed.

"But she's not in Homicide anymore."

"Why not?"

"I'm not sure. I gather it's a long story and had something to do with department politics. It happened before I got here. I do know she was once in line to be chief."

"Now I really wonder why she's helping us. I'm just glad she is. But when it comes to finding Z, we don't have a plan. The police can't do anything, and Sink—who knows what his agenda is? Candiotti is right—the Bureau has been after Z for years."

We reached the elevator leading down to the Government Center garage. "We don't understand how any of this fits together," Hewitt said. "Is Z trying to find Kenny? If so, why is he so desperate to do it? Is he the one who hired the blonde woman?"

I pressed the elevator button. "Or are we on the wrong track altogether? If Kenny was working for Z, why would Z be looking for him—even trying to kill him—now? What if somebody else hired the blonde woman?"

"Like who?"

"Z has ticked a lot of people off. He's shaken down a lot of businesses. Maybe one of them took it personally. Maybe they're using Kenny to find Z."

The FBI agent lifted an eyebrow. "You might be right."

"So what's your plan?"

"As of now I'm still employed by the FBI, but I'm officially awaiting reassignment. Unofficially, I'm on thin ice. I suppose I should be careful."

"According to Gibson, that's not your style."

He gave me an enigmatic smile. "We'll see. What are you going to do?"

"Go back to the beginning. I'm going to talk to Alec again."

Chapter 21

On the way to Alec's, I called Marsha, got her voicemail, and left her a message saying that Kenny had been sighted alive last night. I didn't add that he was being pursued by the people who had tortured and maybe killed Liam. Then I called Alec's cell and found him at home. He was taking some time off until Kenny was found, he said. I told him I'd be there in ten minutes.

Alec came out to pull me up the steps, looking cheerful as always, but with a touch of wariness. In the kitchen, I was on him before he could sit down. "Why didn't you tell me about the FBI?"

He paused briefly, then sank into a kitchen chair. "They said it was a confidential investigation."

"Alec, that is a steaming pile of horseshit. The mere existence of the interview wouldn't be confidential. And you were ready to let me run around the country asking questions without knowing the FBI was looking for Kenny. I'll bet they also said to call them if anybody came around wanting to talk about Kenny."

"Yes, they did."

"And when I came around asking about Kenny, did you call them?"

"Well, no."

"So much for obeying the FBI. Your son is in grave danger, Alec. His best friend has been murdered. Another friend was tortured. A third was rescued from a home invasion and then disappeared. Killers are chasing him. Do I have your attention here?"

He looked chastened but not surprised.

"I hope you're listening," I continued, "because if you're going to save Kenny's life, you have to get your head out of your ass, pronto. And you and Marsha have to put aside your differences and cooperate. Last but not least, you have to tell me the truth. Your failure to be forthcoming may have placed Kenny, Sam, and Sierra at risk. Are we communicating here?"

He nodded.

I told him about the sighting of Kenny last night at the light rail station downtown and the pursuit by the blonde woman. He listened intently, but he didn't display the type of relief I would have expected.

"Now, tell me about the FBI," I said.

"A young agent came around asking about Kenny."

"Ben Hewitt?"

"Yes. I told him what I told you, that I didn't know where Kenny might have gone."

"Did he ask about hacking?"

"Yes, he asked me if Kenny was good with computers and if he'd associated with any hackers. I told him I didn't know, but that Kenny was a good kid."

"Did he mention the names 'Z' or 'Mishkin'?"

"Not that I can remember."

"What do you know about Liam?"

"Kenny mentioned the name a couple of times. I knew he was a friend from Tampa. That's it."

"What's going on, Alec? Why are these people after Kenny?"

"I don't know, and that's the truth."

I continued to stare at him, feeling in my bones that he was holding back on me. "I swear to God, Alec, if you're lying to me, and anything happens to Kenny, I won't rest until the prosecutors come down on you with everything. Obstruction of justice, lying to investigators, accessory—you name it."

He gave me a long look, then turned away. "I'm sorry, Pen. I can't help you."

Alec helped me down the steps from the kitchen, then returned to the house. I rolled toward my van in the driveway, but before I could get in, a Volvo sedan appeared in the driveway beside my vehicle. Shannon, wearing a smart, businesslike outfit, got out.

"Hi," she said. "Any news?"

"That's a good question. I told Alec a number of things. I'm not sure if any of it was news to him."

She glanced at the house, then back at me. "Can you spare a few minutes?"

Ten minutes later we were at a Caribou Coffee shop a couple of miles away, looking at each other awkwardly across the table. Finally she said, "I'm sorry about Alec."

I nodded.

She sighed heavily. "I really like Kenny. I'd like to help if I can."

"So you get along well with him?"

"Not exactly. He's really a sweet kid, but he keeps me at arm's length—hardly acknowledges my existence. We've barely exchanged two words since he started living with us. I understand, I guess. I can't replace Marsha."

"I appreciate your giving me the names of his friends. But I'm afraid it hasn't gone well for them." I told her about the attacks on Sam and Sierra, along with Sierra's disappearance.

Shannon's hand shot up to her mouth. "What is Kenny mixed up in?"

I told her about Z and my suspicions about hacking. She took a long sip from her coffee cup, and I followed suit. "So he's probably still alive," she said.

"He was as of late last night."

"What can I do to help?"

"The most useful thing you could do is get the whole truth out of Alec. I think he's still holding out on me."

"Why would he do that?"

"You tell me."

She looked away, and then down at her hands. "He loves Kenny. I'm sure of that."

Alec loves Alec, I wanted to respond. But I kept my opinion to myself. "Is he still angry at Marsha?"

"No, he's let go of Marsha. I don't think he ever felt much animosity toward her."

"Did he talk Kenny into leaving Marsha and moving up here?"

She shook her head firmly. "It was Kenny's idea. I'm not sure Alec was actually that wild about it. He . . . well, let's just say he didn't welcome additional responsibility."

It made sense, I thought. "Responsible" was not exactly Alec's middle name. But then why had Kenny moved up here?

"Why did you and Alec move up here?" I asked.

"I grew up in this area, and I was a little homesick, I guess. Alec wasn't that happy with his job in Tampa, and he was open to making a change."

I waited.

Her face reddened. "Alec and I were having problems with our marriage. I thought a change of scenery might help."

"What do you do?"

She shrugged. "The same thing I did when I was up here before. Executive assistant. It's an okay job."

"I keep wondering if Alec knows something I don't. He doesn't seem that concerned about Kenny."

Her look was grim and embarrassed. "He's not a bad man, Pen. He tries hard."

"If we're going to find his son, he has to try harder."

Shannon left. I sat at the table with my now-cold coffee. Unlike her husband, Shannon seemed intelligent and concerned. But could I trust her? Maybe she was just a better liar than Alec. On impulse, I pulled out my phone and did a Google search for Chrysler dealerships in the area. There were two of them within ten miles of Shannon and Alec's home. I called the first one and asked for Alec Sellars. Nobody by that name worked there, they said. I called the next closest dealership.

"Good afternoon. Southdale Chrysler."

"Alec Sellars, please."

"I'm afraid Alec isn't employed by us any longer."

I thanked the receptionist and clicked off. Alec wasn't taking vacation or playing hooky or looking for Kenny. He was unemployed. What else had he lied about?

Chapter 22

Brit Herbst's mother had smoked in bed. That's what had made the whole thing possible, really. And that, indirectly, had helped make Brit what she was. She wished she had grown up to be like her father—gentle, affable. But it was not to be. For better and worse, Brit had been born with her mother's angry intensity, and in hating her mother, she knew on some level that she was probably hating herself.

Brit sat on a bench in a skyway above the street, with a clear view of the bar where Pen Wilkinson met with a distinguished-looking man in an expensive suit. She had sent Carlin a photograph, which the geek had used, along with face recognition software, to identify the man as Dustin Blount, chairman and CEO of Columbia Central Bank. As she chewed on the significance of the meeting, Brit felt confident that sooner rather than later, the lady in the wheelchair would lead her to her prey. And Brit always caught her prey. That was one thing she had taken from her father: the patience and focus of the hunter. That, and the love of the hunt.

She and her father had spent untold hours together in the hills, mountains, ravines and woods of southern West Virginia, stalking their targets—mostly deer, waterfowl, and grouse, but squirrels, turkeys, and raccoons would do in a pinch. Though naturally talkative, Bob Herbst said little on these excursions. They walked silently with their guns and sometimes the dogs. Brit knew he savored the peace of the hills, away from the incessant grinding, grating background noise generated by Brit's mother, Sally. He also may have appreciated the quick explosion of violence, the sudden ending of a life, in which hunting culminated. It was a small zone of control which Bob, an inventory manager for a heavy-equipment dealer, had blocked out in his small, limited life. It was a small moment of triumph, an instant of mastery.

Brit's mother had murdered her father. That's not the way the law had seen it, but Brit knew it, and most of their neighbors undoubtedly agreed. They sensed the meanness and aggression behind the facade of sweetness that Sally Herbst presented to the world; there were no real secrets in a small town. Day in and day out, her nagging, abuse, and belittling had assaulted Bob Herbst, eaten away at him, destroying the soul of a good man.

Increasingly, Brit had found herself the target of similar treatment. Sally had seemed to possess an unlimited supply of vitriol, plenty for both father and daughter. But unlike her father, Brit had fought back, resisting her mother's controlling ploys and incessant criticism. As she grew into adulthood, she had wondered how it would end, for both herself and her father. In either case, she'd known it wouldn't end well.

Bob had been in a reflective mood on that day in early November, a couple of months before Brit's eighteenth birthday. As they'd climbed the mountain to their favorite ruffs area, a former clear-cut forest, he'd told stories about his boyhood and his time in Vietnam. Stories about the mountains and the woods. He'd even talked about Brit's younger brother, who had died in infancy, leaving Brit as an only child. They had walked for hours without a hint of a flush, separating now and again to explore different trails. It was during one of these periods of separation that she had heard the blast.

Brit knew what had happened. She had followed the sound and within a couple of minutes found his body. Now she understood his nostalgic mood. The authorities may have ruled the fatal shotgun blast self-inflicted, but that was a technicality. Sally had murdered him. She had killed his spirit—berating him, degrading him, telling him how worthless he was, how big a failure he was, how he wasn't much of a man. And her treatment of Brit had been similar, with particular emphasis on her daughter's alleged laziness, stupidity, and ugliness. Day after day, year after year, father and daughter had absorbed the nonstop abuse.

Brit had swallowed her rage for four days until Bob was buried, during which time Sally put on a grieving-widow routine. Brit didn't think it was a very good act. In fact, Sally seemed to assume that life would not change very much with her husband dead. She still had a daughter, who could now absorb the incessant criticism.

But Sally smoked in bed.

Brit's phone buzzed. She looked around; the skyway was deserted. She took the call, speaking quietly. "Yes?"

"Anything?" Ian asked.

"She's still meeting with Blount."

"Covering Blount would be difficult."

"I know. And we're spread thin as it is. But I don't like it. She's getting close to things she shouldn't be getting close to. Anything on Sierra?"

"No, she still hasn't resurfaced. Do you suppose Z has her?"

"I doubt it, but there's no way to know for sure. Anything happening on Kenny's cell?"

"Reston reports no further activity." The organization that employed Ian, Brit, Oliver, and Carlin as covert operatives for hire was headquartered in Reston, Virginia, a Washington, DC suburb.

"I think Kenny's call to Sierra was a setup, to see if we had monitoring capability."

"I don't know, Brit . . ."

"He's a smart little bastard. I wouldn't put it past him."

"What else has the crippled aunt been up to?"

"Nothing since the meeting with the parents, and we had those covered. She's starting to suspect the father, I think."

"But according to Sam, the father doesn't know," Ian said.

"I know. Otherwise we would have gone back to question him."

"We're spinning our wheels. Do we need to pull in the aunt and question her?"

"I'm about ready to do it. Let's plan it for tonight."

"There's some risk involved."

"Sure there is. She's a federal prosecutor—anything happens to her and we might have the Feds coming down on us. But we need to shake something loose here. We need to make a move."

"Understood," Ian said.

"Anything more on that computer consultant? Emily something-or-other?"

"Carlin says she appears to be on the up-and-up. She's an established consultant."

"The aunt was probably just looking for general background information on hacking."

"Hell, it sounds like she's way behind the curve."

"Maybe for now. She seems pretty sharp, though. Hold on a minute." Brit smiled at a young businessman who walked past her on the skyway, then resumed the conversation. "I wonder where the FBI is on all this?"

"I wouldn't be too concerned about them."

"If they're in Z's pocket, we need to be incredibly concerned. The Bureau knows how to find people."

"But they're a bureaucracy. They need a legitimate reason for the search."

Brit didn't answer, but she didn't see that it would be all that hard for a bent FBI agent to invent a pretext for finding a missing kid.

"I almost forgot," Ian said. "Carlin found an interesting lead. Sierra has an uncle who owns rental properties."

"How many properties?"

"Thirteen that we know of. None of them has a vacancy advertised. But we don't know if the uncle owns other properties using other entities. Maybe we should question him tonight, instead of the aunt."

Brit thought about it. "The aunt is a pretty good lead, too."

"We'll be ready either way."

She felt a mental tingle as she thought about the plastic bag. "Good."

"So, landlord or aunt?"

She sighed. "Let me think about it."

"We'll need to know soon so we can start the prep."

"I know." Brit sighed. "It's a tough call. All these players, trying to find this kid. And all the time pressure . . ."

"It might already be too late."

"We'd know if Z's plan had gone down already. No, we're down to the wire, but there's still time."

Chapter 23

Dustin Blount was shorter than I remembered—probably about five foot nine. But at fifty years old, tanned and distinguished, with a little graying at the temples, he still looked the part of a banker and CEO. He shook my hand before sitting down across from me at the secluded table in the lounge of the Discovery Hotel in downtown Minneapolis. "A pleasure to see you, Pen. You're looking great."

"Nice of you to say, thanks."

"How is the search for your nephew going?"

"We have some intriguing leads, but he's still missing, and it looks like he was mixed up with some sketchy people."

"Was Emily helpful?"

"Very. She gave us some good background on hacking." I changed subjects. "How are you holding up, with the proxy fight and all?"

He smiled. "It's a little awkward, showing up for these meetings with institutional shareholders wearing a flak jacket. It's been a tough fight, and we're going right down to the wire. So, is James getting bored yet?"

"I know a part of him would like to be back in the game, in the trenches with you. But he's immersed in the venture capital business and enjoying it a lot."

Blount turned serious. "I don't know if he's ever told you this, Pen, but I begged him to come back and work with me. The merger just hasn't gone well. There was a lot of fear and confusion after Downfall."

I opened my mouth to respond, but Blount held up his hand. "I knew he had baggage, from being implicated in a phony scandal and then forced out. I didn't care. I needed him. Nobody could kick ass and get things done the way he could. We would have made a great team. But I understood that he needed to move on, for his daughter and for you."

He paused, then lowered his voice. "Ozzie Hayes left a lot bigger mess than either James or I realized. A bad mortgage portfolio. Big losses on derivatives. But I think the most frustrating thing was not knowing whom I could trust. We weren't sure we'd found everybody who was involved in Downfall. There could have been saboteurs still on our payroll. We'd have people underperforming or screwing up, and we didn't know if they were incompetent or deliberately undermining us."

"What is Hayes pledging to do differently?"

"Nothing specific. He's running on a platform of not being me. Ozzie never accepted being put out to pasture. He never sold his house in Minneapolis. He's been waiting and scheming for the past year and a half. Of course, if they win, he wouldn't be CEO himself. His group has nominated Hayes's son, Skip—Osborne Hayes III. The old man would be chairman."

"What is Skip's background?"

"He's held senior positions at several banks. He seems to be reasonably competent. But personally . . . well, his father affects this southern gentleman persona, right?"

I nodded.

"Not Skip. He's just a straightforward, abrasive jerk. People hate working for him."

"Do the shareholders know that?"

He smiled and sipped his bourbon. "You've got to understand, Pen. They don't care. The typical 'shareholder' is a pension fund or mutual fund or exchange-traded fund. All they see is numbers. They have no interest in employee satisfaction. The bottom line is all that concerns them, and the Hayeses are promising better results."

"Do you think they have a chance?"

He blew out a long breath. "This is not for public consumption, but yes, they do. The election is a lot closer than is generally known. Right now, we're slightly ahead, but there are a significant percentage of proxies that aren't in yet. A decisive percentage. And the votes can be changed right up until the annual meeting, which is a week from Friday. It could still go either way." He shrugged. "If I get thrown out, it's not the end of the world—for me. I'll just go back to Dallas and manage my family investments. But this bank and its employees deserve better, and that's why I've stayed to make the fight."

"Well, good luck."

He hesitated. "There might be a way you could help."

"Sure—what can I do?"

"You apparently had some dealings with Hayes."

I stiffened. "I'm not sure I would put it that way."

"You talked to him after Downfall was busted."

"Yes," I admitted, wondering if he was guessing or actually knew somehow. I was sure James hadn't told him.

"Hayes emerged from Downfall with apparently clean hands. He seemed to be a victim as much as any other shareholder. But I'm not at all sure that's an accurate characterization."

I said nothing.

"I think," he continued, "it's very likely that you discovered some damaging information about Hayes in the course of your ordeal. And I'm thinking you might have reached some kind of understanding with him, which is why it hasn't come out."

Again, I didn't reply. I looked at my empty wineglass but couldn't remember drinking from it.

He leaned forward. "Pen, if there's anything you know that could help us, now is the time. We're in a fight for our lives here. Hayes can't be allowed to win."

I looked away, avoiding his gaze. Blount had guessed correctly. I had in fact made a deal with Hayes to keep quiet about things I knew, damaging things. It had galled me to have to make such a pact. But for my future, and James's, I needed to honor it.

"I'm sorry, Dustin. I wish I could help you, but I just can't."

He smiled. "You can't blame a guy for trying."

"I don't. Good luck, Dustin."

Chapter 24

I made the five-block trek down Nicollet Mall back to the condo, thinking hard about what Blount had said. I suspected there was more to his seeking me out than a simple desire to dig up dirt on Osborne Hayes, although that was certainly a logical goal. I thought some more while eating the Subway sandwich I'd bought on the way home. Then I called Ben Hewitt.

The FBI agent answered right away. "Hewitt."

"It's Pen," I said. "I need a favor. Do you still have access to Bureau resources?"

"Maybe, if I'm careful. I'm still awaiting reassignment, which means I'm just finishing up old paperwork. I'm not supposed to be actively working on cases. What do you need?"

"Just some research."

"On what?"

"Ransomware."

"Ah. Do you have a lead on the mysterious Z?"

"Not specifically. It's more like a long-shot hunch."

"Let me take some notes . . . All right, go ahead."

I hoped I wouldn't get him into trouble. "I'd like to research Columbia Central Bank to see if they've ever been a target of a ransomware attack. You'd need to include their predecessor banks, North Central and Texas Columbia."

"Okay. I'm on good terms with a researcher here at the office. I think I can manage that."

"There's more. I'm wondering if you can answer the same question with respect to companies owned by Dustin Blount and his family."

"He's the current CEO of Columbia Central?"

"Right."

"And what basis do you have for researching this?"

"A gut feeling."

"I see." There was a long pause. He didn't see at all. "What if I told you we needed to do better than that?"

"I understand. I'll just do what I can with Google."

Another pause. "Let me see what I can do."

"Thank you. Another question?"

I could hear his chuckle over the line. "Why not?"

"The FBI thinks Z's real name may be Mishkin, and that he's the son of Russian immigrants."

"I've heard that, yes."

"Has Sink investigated any Russian connections here in Minnesota? Like Russian hackers or the Russian mafia?"

"Not as far as I know."

"Do you know why he hasn't?"

"No, and I don't think I'll find out from Sink."

"It would be interesting to know."

"I guess. Is there anything else?"

The question had a sarcastic edge to it, but I pretended not to notice. "Actually, there is," I said. "I've been thinking about these people who keep turning up and creating trouble."

"The blonde woman and her accomplices."

"Exactly. Who do you think they are?"

"I've been thinking about them, too. I think they're professional operatives—mercenaries or contractors."

"Have you run searches for them?"

"I've been trying to keep a low profile. This is not my case, and I'm not supposed to be doing anything substantive while I'm awaiting reassignment."

"But?"

"But now that I've decided to stick my neck out and check for ransomware incidents, I guess it's in for a penny . . ."

"You're a good man, Agent Hewitt."

"Yeah, yeah. I'll talk to you tomorrow."

I hung up and checked my watch. Marsha's flight would be arriving in two hours.

*   *   *

Kenny finished punching the number into his disposable cell. Then, his heartbeat accelerating, he pushed the Send button. One ring. Two. He reached for the button to cancel the call, then pulled his thumb away.

Three rings. Four.

"Yes?"

"It's me," Kenny said.

"Kenny, are you okay?"

"So far, no thanks to you."

"Thank God. They don't have you yet."

"You can drop the act. I know it's you who's trying to get me. You and that Russian goon of yours."

Z's reply was urgent. "It's not me, Kenny. And it's not Stefan. You have my word."

"You warned me against breaking ties with you. You said you wouldn't allow it."

"I was upset. I still am, but we can work it out, Kenny. Talk to me."

"Talk? What is there to talk about? You killed Liam. You sent thugs to my house. You attacked Sam—almost killed him. And you went after Sierra. Call it off."

"Kenny, you have to believe me. It's not me. I would never do any of those things."

"You think I'm an idiot? I know you. Of course you would."

"Look," Z insisted, "whatever else I've done in the past, I didn't do those things."

"Then who the hell is it? Who do the blonde woman and her crew work for?"

"They were hired by someone who's trying to stop what I'm working on."

"What do they want with me?"

"It's a way of getting at me."

Kenny hesitated. He wanted to believe it, badly. But he had gotten to know Z too well. "Just call it off," he said. "Then we can talk."

"I told you, I can't call it off. They don't work for me. Come in, where I can protect you."

Kenny's finger hovered over the Disconnect button. He hesitated, then clicked it firmly.

Chapter 25

I was already exhausted when I returned to the condo, but I needed to work on my case until it was time to pick up Marsha, who was flying in tonight. I'd spent nearly an hour on the phone with Cassandra, my colleague in LA, going over our outlines of testimony for key witnesses, and I had just hung up when someone knocked at the door.

I was puzzled. This was a security building. The doorman wouldn't just send somebody up. I rolled over to the door, cell phone in hand. "Who is it?"

"It's me," a female voice said.

I unlocked the door and opened it. "Marsha. What are you doing here?" I rolled back to let her in.

"I caught an earlier flight and decided to just take a cab."

"Thanks. I'm pretty tired. How did you get up here?"

"The doorman let me in, but before he could ask where I was going, some kind of alarm went off, and he went hurrying toward the back. So I just came up."

Marsha stepped inside, and I did a double-take when I saw her; I still wasn't used to her new slim, fashionable look. She set her purse and overnight bag down and took a long look at me. "You look awful. Have you slept at all?"

"I'm okay."

"Before we do anything, fill me in."

"Why don't you sit down?"

"Just tell me." And so, as she stood in the kitchen, I told her about my conversations with Agent Hewitt, Alec, Shannon, and

Lieutenant Candiotti, as well as the attacks on Sam and Sierra. I didn't spare her any of the frightening details.

When I'd finished, she stood for a long moment, trying to take it all in, composing herself.

"Are you ready to sit down now?" I asked.

She nodded.

"Have you had dinner?"

"Not hungry."

"How about some wine?"

"That's a spectacular idea." I selected a Malbec from the small rack in the dining room and handed it to Marsha for cork removal. I told her where to find the wine glasses, and she brought two of them out to the living room along with the bottle. Marsha wasn't looking too hot herself; she was a worrier in the best of times, and even more so now, with ample cause.

"Cheers," she said, lifting her glass, and we sipped the wine. "So what does all this mean?"

Analyzing all the events proved to be an up-and-down process. There had been no contact from Kenny—but he'd been sighted at the rail platform. Sierra had gone missing—but her phone had been used after her disappearance. Alec hadn't provided any useful information—but an FBI agent and a Minneapolis detective were willing to help. For every scary development, there seemed to be a hopeful one—so far.

Marsha took a drink from her glass and sat for a long time, saying nothing. Tears began to form, and her hand trembled. She set her glass down and stared straight ahead. Finally, she gave voice to the fear that haunted us both. "He's all I have left. I can't lose another one, Pen. I just can't."

"I know. I won't let it happen."

She turned toward me. "For God's sake, who is after him?"

"I don't know. But I'll find out."

She managed a small smile through the tears. "I know you will. You're the smart one, after all."

I returned the smile. It had been our standing joke since childhood. Although tests had shown that Marsha had a higher IQ than I did, she suffered from dyslexia, which made her a mediocre student despite a lot of hard work. But, Alec notwithstanding, it was not a fluke that Marsha had raised a genius.

"What did I do wrong?" Marsha asked, taking a gulp from her glass. "I know I wasn't a perfect mother, but . . ."

"We all make mistakes," I said, "but if there's one thing I learned after Downfall, it's that sometimes you don't do anything wrong, but it all goes bad anyway. Sometimes you just happen to be in the way of a bad person with a bad agenda."

"Wrong place at the wrong time?"

"Exactly."

"Why do I feel like I've been in the wrong place my whole life?"

"Come on, Marsh—"

"I mean it. I'm just out of sync with the world."

I took a hefty drink from my glass. "There are days when I feel like that, too. But for you, at least, it's not true. What about all the thousands of babies you've helped to deliver? The joy you've given to their families? The lives you've saved? Seems to me you've been in exactly the right place at the right time, a lot."

"Damnit, stop patronizing me."

"I'm not—"

"All right, so I won't win any awards for mother of the year. I didn't know what my kid was up to. I don't know his friends. I let him go off to Minnesota to get rid of him . . ."

"For heaven's sake, Marsha. I'm not judging you."

"Of course you are. You always are. I've never been good enough. For you, for Dad, for Alec—for anybody."

"Don't start on this shit," I groaned. It was the same old conversational and emotional rut, the one we never seemed able to escape.

"Just don't tell me how I should feel. You always thought you knew what was best, what everybody should be doing."

"I never tried to boss you around."

"You never had to. All I had to do was look at Dad, just look at him, and I knew what he was thinking: 'Be more like Pen.'"

"Come on, Marsh—"

"'Make some friends. Get good grades. Go to college. Just be happy.'"

"He never said anything like that."

"He never had to."

I opened my mouth to respond, then closed it. It was all true.

"You were oblivious to all of it," she continued. "You never even noticed me, struggling. You just cruised along, having fun, living a charmed life."

We sat in silence. Finally I said, "Are you done? Have you hurt me enough yet?"

"So now you're the victim?"

"I hope not. And I'm damn well not a professional victim like you are."

Now it was her turn to be silent. Why couldn't we get out of this destructive pattern? I wondered. And we hadn't even faced the Elephant in the Room. "So you were dealt a shitty hand," I said. "You play it anyway, as best you can."

"Spare me," she said. "I'll watch Dr. Phil if I need self-help advice."

"I know you blame me. But there's nothing I can do now. Maybe I wasn't always a model sister. I was probably a little insensitive."

"A little?"

"I don't know. I can't change any of that. I'm just doing the best I can right now."

"Well, isn't that big of you? Isn't that sisterly of you? Are you enjoying being a martyr in a wheelchair?"

I didn't respond.

Her hand flew up to her mouth. "My God, I'm sorry. I didn't mean that." She looked down at her hands and took a deep, ragged breath. "I just . . . I just . . . miss Tracy." She put her glass down. "God, I miss her."

"I miss her, too."

"Sure you do, and you feel really bad, because you . . . you . . ."

"Because I killed her." I finished the sentence, my voice rising. "I killed her! I know that. I *know* I shouldn't have given her that soda in the back seat. I should have *known* she'd spill it and unhook her seat belt. I *know* I should have found a place to pull off the freeway instead of unbuckling my own seat belt to try to help her. And I *know* I should have anticipated that the pickup truck would veer into my lane and run me off the damn road. I know! I killed her!" There was a long minute of silence. We avoided each other's eyes. Finally I said, "What do you want me to say, Marsh? What do you want me to do? If there was anything I could—"

"I know!" she shrieked. "I know! It wasn't your fault. It was an accident. A goddamned accident. I can't blame you. I can't blame anybody. I just have to swallow my feelings and move on."

I said nothing.

"One of my children died in a ditch in Florida," she said. "And now the other one's going to be tortured to death, suffocated, and dumped in an alley somewhere with a plastic bag over his head."

"No!" I screamed. "It *will not happen!* Not while I have an ounce of strength left!" And Wade Hirsch and his job and case could just go to hell until Kenny was safe, I vowed to myself.

She looked at me, startled, for a long moment, and then began sobbing. "I've been such a shit."

"No, no."

"You didn't kill her. Don't you think I understand that? I look at you in that horrible wheelchair, and I think about what you were—tall and athletic and vigorous—you were a damned Amazon. And now I think about you living like this for the rest of your life, and it makes me feel sick. You pay such a terrible price, every day, for something that wasn't even your fault. I feel so guilty—so disgusted with myself—for being angry with you. Don't you get that?"

I just shook my head. We were having the honest conversation we'd never had, and I didn't know what to say.

She wept, her face in her hands. I rolled over next to her, put my arms awkwardly around her, and joined in. We cried for what seemed like an hour, having finally faced down the Elephant.

Chapter 26

Brit liked it a little too much. She'd be the first to admit it. She had come to that realization when she'd killed her mother. And she'd be able to experience it again when they got the kid. But first they had to get him. And that task was proving to be a nightmare. Had she ever had an assignment with so much bad luck, so many near-misses?

She and Ian rested back at the team's motel while Carlin and Oliver watched Kenny's parents and aunt, respectively. They were running short on time, but there was no need for desperate measures—at least not yet. Desperate people made mistakes.

She'd made her own share of mistakes. The kid's escape from his house was on her. She should have caught him, period. The escape through the cemetery was on Ian, but of course that ultimately came back to her, the team leader. The fact was that this part of the assignment was simply different from what they'd believed it would be. How hard, they'd reasoned, would it be to simply snatch a teenager? But this was a teenager who'd been warned. He'd known they were coming, and he was extremely smart. And so far, he'd also been lucky. That wouldn't last forever.

The team had located Sierra Bjorklund's uncle, who owned a number of rental properties, but he was out of town until noon tomorrow. They would visit him then and find out if Kenny and Sierra were hiding in any of his units. And she had no doubt the uncle would tell them. Getting people to tell the truth—that was a talent she had. But it was more than a talent—it was a deep-seated need, which she'd discovered after her father's suicide.

She had waited until a week after her father's funeral, late at night, when her mother lay in bed, watching TV and smoking, after two stiff drinks. Brit had gone to the bedroom with the thought of smothering the old bitch with a pillow. It was easy enough for her to straddle Sally, pin her arms with her knees, and press down with the pillow. In fact, it was too easy. She felt her mother struggle underneath her, fighting for her miserable life, while her cigarette burned in an ashtray on the bedside table.

Brit sat up abruptly and tossed the pillow aside, looking at her mother's terrified expression, watching her gasp for breath. What to do now? She had to die. But Brit wanted—no, needed—to watch the process. She glanced around the room and noticed Sally's black funeral dress, back from the dry cleaner, still in its plastic bag, draped over a chair back. Brit walked over and tore the bag off the dress. Then she started back toward the bed.

"N—no!" her mother managed to gasp. "Don't!"

Brit approached the bed, holding the bag. Sally struggled, trying to sit up. "No—my God!"

Brit kept coming.

Then she was on top of her mother again, securing the bag over her head, holding it tightly, furiously. And then Brit watched. She watched the face darken, the head move back and forth, and the arms and legs thrash as her mother fought for her life. She felt Sally's chest heave under her knees.

And then she removed the bag. Her mother gulped in air, her color gradually returning, her face showing relief.

Then Brit put the bag back on. This time, after a similar struggle, her mother lost consciousness. Brit pulled the bag off and revived her, slapping her and pouring water over her face, allowing her to recover again. And then Sally watched her in horror, knowing the bag was coming again.

And again. Brit repeated the process several times, eventually losing count. Finally, the procedure seemed to come to a natural end. Brit simply kept the bag on, and her mother ended her struggle for life. She was gone. Brit pulled the bag off and slowly got off the bed. She tossed the still-smoldering cigarette onto the quilt, waited until the cloth caught fire, and seemingly floated out of the house on a wave of euphoria. Outside, a few minutes later, she looked back at the now-burning house, shaking with joy, enveloped by the feeling.

And knowing she could not live without feeling it again.

Chapter 27

Agent Ben Hewitt sat by himself at a table in the FBI cafeteria, drinking a cup of coffee and wondering about his future. He pondered other subjects, too, like Kenny Sellars, and Pen Wilkinson, and Gary Sink. But more than anything, he wondered if he still had a career path in the FBI. And if he was finished, he wondered if he would ever really know why.

After a few more sips and a little more cogitation, he sensed a figure standing beside him. He looked up to see Special Agent Gary Sink, holding his own cup of coffee. "Mind if I join you?" his former boss asked.

Hewitt suppressed his shock. "Why not?"

Sink sat down, and Hewitt stared at the now-hated figure, the man who had become a secretive bully but who, by all accounts, had once been a pretty good guy.

"You know," Sink said, "in the Hoover days, we could have been fired for this."

Hewitt nodded. J. Edgar Hoover had banned coffee-drinking on Bureau premises. It was an act, he believed, reserved for lazy bureaucrats—never by tireless guardians of public safety. Anyone caught with a cup of Joe, if he kept his job, might be exiled to Butte, Montana or Minot, North Dakota.

"You could get fired for a lot of things in those days," Sink continued. "That's changed a lot, of course. But some things are still no-no's. Disobeying orders, for example. That's pretty basic."

"Got it," Hewitt said. "Important safety tip."

"Which makes me wonder about you, Ben. Do you have some kind of death wish?"

Hewitt didn't answer.

"No, I don't think that's it. You don't seem like the type." Sink blew on his coffee and took a sip. "I find out you've been poking around in our databases, in direct violation of my orders, and I figure it's either your way of flipping me off on your way out the door, or . . ." He set his cup down. "Or there's something about this case."

Hewitt cradled his own cup in both hands. "You seem to enjoy sizing people up, guessing at their motives. Maybe I've done the same. And maybe I figure you don't want to push this any further, that you don't want to do what it takes to get me fired."

"And why would that be?"

"It would take a lot of time and effort, of course. But more than that, it would draw attention to yourself and what you're doing. You might be called upon to answer some tough questions. Maybe tougher than the ones I'd have to answer."

Sink's expression didn't change. "That's quite a risk, betting that you've judged me correctly. So what is it, exactly, that you're putting your future on the line for?"

"Curiosity, that's all. What's going on with this kid? Why did he flee for his life? Who's after him?"

"Only curiosity?"

"He's eighteen. Which means he's probably pretty clueless and pretty scared. It would be nice if somebody cared about him."

"And you've taken it upon yourself?"

Hewitt shrugged. "No, just kidding. I'm flipping you off."

Sink actually laughed. "All right, then, as you extend your middle finger, why don't you tell me what you unearthed in the course of this little electronic treasure hunt?"

"The same as you did, I imagine. At least I assume it was you. Somebody was there ahead of me, doing the same search.

It took me maybe ten minutes to input what we know about whoever is chasing Kenny Sellars. Operatives or mercenaries, 'mercs'. Expensive mercs, operating domestically. They're ruthless; they use rough interrogation tactics. Their team includes a blonde woman. And they're good. You put all that in and the magic box spits out four names, but one of them stands out."

The older agent nodded. "SSI. Security Systems International. Headquartered in Dubai, with their US office in Reston, Virginia. Formed during the Iraq war, like a lot of similar outfits. But they're different."

"They are," Hewitt agreed. "They operate in the good old US of A. That takes balls. It's one thing to throw your weight around in some third-world country, terrorizing civilians, ignoring local law enforcement, conducting break-ins and illegal wiretapping. Maybe even committing a murder or two. But domestically, different story. If they raise too big a stink, they risk losing government contracts and protection. If they get caught, they could be prosecuted under our anti-terrorism statutes. And they're up against us, not some corrupt, underpaid, incompetent third world security service or police."

"That's why they're paid so handsomely."

"So who's paying them to find Kenny Sellars? Who would pay somebody to find any eighteen-year-old kid?"

"Not just any kid," Sink corrected. "A computer whiz, who might work for one of the bigger cyber crooks around."

"A guy named Z. So who's trying to find Z? Is it our side? If it is, we could expect a call from a nameless guy from a shadowy agency in Washington, telling us to leave SSI alone so we don't jeopardize national security. Have you gotten the call, Gary?"

The older agent thought for a long time before answering. "No."

Now it was Hewitt's turn to think. If a US government agency wasn't employing these operatives, who was? He now decided to change the subject, knowing that if any question could actually motivate Sink to fire him, this would be it. "We've talked about my motivation. What's yours?"

Sink's expression hardened. "You mean besides doing my job?"

"Not exactly. It's how you're doing your job. You're secretive. You want to find Kenny and find Z, but without involving anyone or letting anybody else know what you're doing. You're avoiding obvious avenues of investigation, like the Russian mafia."

"How I do my job is my business."

"Again, not quite. It may not be my business, but you're accountable to somebody. Who's your master?"

Sink shook his head. "You really don't want to go there."

"Right now you don't appear to be doing much of anything to find Kenny or Z, even though that's your job. You tried to use me as your front man, but that backfired. What's your strategy now? To let SSI flush them out?"

Sink stood up but made no move to leave. After half a minute, having apparently reached a decision, he said, "This case is very important to me. It's my only real case. If you screw it up, I won't have any problem taking the time and making the effort to get you fired. I could do it now. For the record, I'm repeating my directive to have nothing to do with it."

Hewitt noticed that Sink apparently wasn't aware of the searches he'd run on ransomware attacks against Columbia Central Bank and companies connected to Dustin Blount. "And off the record?"

"If you find anything, I want to know about it, completely and without delay. And I mean you tell only me, not the Minneapolis cops and not the aunt in the wheelchair. Any deviation from that, and you're in the street, looking for work as a deputy sheriff in some one-light shithole of a town." He walked away.

Chapter 28

The phone woke me up. I glanced at the clock radio on the nightstand: 8:08 AM. I gasped. My alarm hadn't woken me up. I'd been sleeping off accumulated exhaustion. The phone rang again. I reached over to the nightstand, pulled the phone off the charger, and answered. "Yes?"

"Good morning, Pen."

"Agent Hewitt."

"Ben will be fine. I may be a civilian soon, anyway. There are some developments I thought you might be interested in." He was crisp and thorough in describing the research he'd done. There were no reports of ransomware attacks on Columbia Central Bank and its predecessor entities, although there'd been plenty of attempted cyber-penetrations of other types. There were likewise no reported ransomware attacks on companies owned or controlled by Dustin Blount or his family. I was relieved that Blount, a man I liked, wasn't involved in hiring thugs.

"So we're back to square one," I said.

"Not entirely. I had an interesting conversation with Agent Gary Sink this morning." For the next ten minutes, he filled me in on their talk, including the conclusion that mercenaries or contractors from an outfit called SSI might be searching for Kenny, along with the frustrating conclusion that the firm's government connections might make them untouchable.

"Untouchable?" I said. "I can't believe that. They've committed crimes—maybe even murder. The police are investigating."

"I'll tell Lieutenant Candiotti what I've told you—maybe she'll be able to run with it. She deserves to know."

"She won't like it."

"None of us likes it."

"There has to be something we can do. We have to find them before they find Kenny."

He chuckled. "I think you have it backwards, Pen. Our best hope is to find Kenny before they do."

I swallowed my frustration. "I guess you're right. So what's the deal with Sink? Where is he coming from?"

"I wish I could answer that, because my future with the FBI may depend on it. But the fact is, I don't have a clue."

I clicked off the phone, sat up in bed, and listened. The apartment was quiet. "Marsha?" I called out. No response. I got up and launched into my morning routine, assuming that she had probably gone out for breakfast.

Marsha returned with a bag of groceries as I was rolling out into the kitchen. "Good timing," I said.

"There was no food here," she scolded. "Have you been eating anything?"

"I'm fine, Mom."

"At least you got some sleep." She pulled bagels and cream cheese from the bag while I started the coffee.

We sat down at the kitchen table and began eating. "It's going to be a busy day," she said.

"Yes," I replied noncommittally. We hadn't talked about our agenda for the day.

"I rented a car at a hotel down the street." She pulled a list from her purse. "My first stop will be at Alec's."

"Are you sure that's a good idea?"

"It will be okay. We don't get along great, but we can talk to each other. That doesn't guarantee he'll tell the truth, of course. But if he's sincere about wanting to find Kenny, maybe we could put our heads together. There's a chance we might think of something we've missed."

It was a good idea, I thought.

"Then," she continued, "I'm going to go over to Kenny's school and see what I can find out."

"Nobody's been able to pry anything out of them. Privacy laws, you know."

"I'm his mother. Maybe they'll have to disclose his records to me."

"He's eighteen. He might have to sign off."

"I have to try."

"What's next on your list?"

"A visit to Sierra's mother."

Again, it seemed a decent idea.

She returned to her list. "And then, if there's time, I'm going to visit Sam Fenton in the hospital—see if he's recovered enough to talk."

"Sounds good."

"So what are you going to do today?" she asked me.

I smiled.

"What?" she asked.

"I just . . . it's just that . . ."

"You expected me to just sit here, waiting for you to tell me what to do?"

"Maybe something like that," I admitted.

"I'm sure you'll let me know if I do something stupid."

"You won't. And I . . . I'm glad you're here."

She studied me. "You mean that, don't you?"

"I do."

She reached across the table and grasped my hand, sealing the bond we'd formed last night.

When Marsha left, I spent an hour on the phone with my office in LA, doing what I could to keep preparation for the Vargas case moving. I explained, however, that I now needed to work on Kenny's situation full-time. "I've got it covered," my colleague Cassandra said. Her claim was mostly bravado, I thought. The trial was a two-lawyer project. More than that, Cassandra was inexperienced and had only recently returned from maternity leave. All the same, I was thankful for her help.

"But you'd better talk to Wade," Cassandra added. "He's been on the warpath, demanding to know when you're coming back."

"Thanks for the warning." I owed her big-time for holding down the fort, fending off Wade, and handling the bulk of the trial preparation.

"Anything else?" she asked.

I hesitated, then decided to plunge ahead. "Cassandra, I need you to be honest with me. Wade has it in for me, and I need to know why. I refuse to believe he just doesn't like handicapped women."

"I don't know, Pen."

"Don't know what his problem is, or don't know whether you should tell me?"

"It doesn't matter."

"Cassandra, this is me you're talking to. Just imagine we're out on a Wednesday night." Most Wednesday nights, I went to a girls' night out with Cassandra and a third friend, Pam La Rue.

I sensed her hesitation over the line. "All right," she said at last. "You should know. He thinks you're a showboat. A publicity hound."

I had more or less expected this, but it enraged me nonetheless. "I've tried to avoid publicity. I've never given a single interview—not a word or comment—to anybody in the media. Ever."

"I know, I know."

"He thinks I went out looking for somebody to take a shot at me, just so I could come off as a hero?"

"I'm not saying it's rational, Pen. But you've been on TV, and I'm just saying that's the problem he has with you."

"The publicity about Windfall didn't even last that long." Several months earlier I'd been in the news after helping to thwart a high-level scandal called Windfall, which had implicated several large defense contractors and a US congressman. Unfortunately, the incident hadn't reflected well on some other federal prosecutors in our office, including the US attorney, Dave O'Shea. I figured that had to be the rub.

"The bosses figure it's our job to make them look good," Cassandra said.

"I know." Although I'd gone way beyond what might be expected of a junior prosecutor, and had produced a good result, those in charge hadn't gotten the credit.

"Don't worry," Cassandra said. "We'll get through this."

"Thanks for being honest with me. I guess when we're done with all this, buying you dinner won't be enough. I'll owe you a new car or something."

"I've always been partial to Beamers. Actually, just babysit David a couple of times."

"Deal." I always enjoyed watching her infant son.

Dutifully, I called Wade Hirsch and was relieved when his voicemail, rather than the pissed-off boss himself, picked up. I left as concise a message as I could, summarizing our trial preparation efforts. And then I smoothed over the question of when I'd return in the most expedient and effective way: I lied, telling him I expected my family emergency to be resolved in the next day or two.

In fact, I had no idea how I was going to find Kenny or how long it might take. Marsha would be touching bases that needed to be touched, but which were unlikely to produce any new information. But my own leads were nearly exhausted, too. I'd talked to just about everybody who knew Kenny, checked out all his movements as best I could, and looked into his hacking activities. All these leads had played themselves out. There were new paths to explore, but they were long shots, tangential to the search. I concluded that I needed to explore them anyway. It was all I could do.

Since John Gibson hadn't been able to help me with information about Gary Sink, I decided to take Gibson's suggestion and tap my own sources. I called Trey Mathews, a lawyer back at the US attorney's office in LA who'd been there forever, and told him I needed to find somebody who'd worked with or knew Special Agent Gary Sink. He said he'd get back to me. Then I called Emily Radatz, the computer consultant, and asked if we could get together for some more questions. We agreed to meet at her office at four this afternoon.

That done, I checked my notes from my first conversation with Alec and Shannon. According to Alec, Kenny had worked at a Subway sandwich shop last summer, when he'd first come up from Florida. As far as I knew, nobody had checked at the restaurant or talked to their employees. Alec hadn't said where the shop was located, so I used Google to pull up locations near their home. I called the closest one first and asked if anybody could remember Kenny working there. The employee who answered put me on the phone with the manager, who said he'd heard the name but hadn't been at the store when Kenny worked there. He added that if I wanted to come in after the lunch rush, I might be able to talk to a couple of employees who had worked with Kenny. I thanked the manager and said I would stop by. I was glad to have found the right store on my first try. But it was a long shot.

Chapter 29

I checked my watch; it was now nearly noon, and I'd have to leave soon. I was wondering what to do next when my phone rang. I checked the caller ID: Minneapolis Police.

"This is Pen."

"Ms. Wilkinson? This is Lexi Candiotti."

"Yes, Lieutenant?"

"I'm in the lobby, and there are a couple of things I'd like to bring you up to speed on. Do you have a minute?"

"Of course. Come on up."

When I let her in, she was eating a protein bar and carrying a bottle of water. "I hope you don't mind," she said. "Eating lunch on the fly today."

"Not at all. Come in."

She walked ahead of me, a lean figure with a wardrobe that fit her personality—a pantsuit that was simple and no-nonsense, moderately priced, with sensible, street-cop shoes.

"Sit down," I said. She took a chair at the kitchen table, and I rolled up across from her. She looked focused and intense, as she had at our first meeting, but also a little sheepish as she related what had happened at the police precinct in northeast Minneapolis that morning. Sierra Bjorklund had walked in, identified herself, and produced a driver's license. Then she had made a statement that she was of legal age, had left home voluntarily, and was not under any duress or in any danger. She said she was sorry to have abandoned her car on the street in south Minneapolis and would reclaim it from the impound lot soon. Then she had left.

I listened with growing excitement, but my hopes for finding Kenny were soon dashed, however. Candiotti explained that due to a bureaucratic mix-up, the officer on duty had allowed Sierra to leave without questioning her about Kenny. The officer recalled that Sierra had looked coached on what to say and do, and I suspected that was Kenny's doing. Candiotti agreed. "He really doesn't want to be found, even by the good guys," she concluded.

I thought about Gary Sink and wondered if any of us could be totally sure who the good guys were.

She stood up to leave.

"Lieutenant? I just wanted to thank you for all of your work on this case. I mean, an in-person update and all . . ."

She gave me a weak smile. "I know it would be a cliché to say that it's my job, but, well, it's my job."

"I doubt that," I said.

She gave me a sharp look.

"It's more than your job," I said. "So much more, in fact, that I wonder a little about it."

"What's your point, Ms. Wilkinson?"

"Why do you feel strongly about this case?"

She shrugged. "Just a feeling."

"Look, I don't want to seem unappreciative. But I would really like to be able to fully trust you, and that means understanding your involvement in the case."

"You should understand. You of all people."

"Understand what? What does any of it have to do with me?"

"Don't you think I checked you out?"

"Checked . . . *me* out?"

"Look, I'm helping you. Let's just leave it at that."

"I want to know why."

She headed for the door. "I need to go now."

I just watched her, mystified.

She opened the door, paused, and looked back at me. Then she let out a long breath and gently closed the door.

She walked slowly back into the kitchen, put her purse on the table, and sat down.

"I was the department homicide commander," she said at last. "I was the mayor's choice to become chief. We've had a female chief since then, but I would have been the first."

"What went wrong?"

She was silent, her gaze far off, for so long I thought she wasn't going to answer. But then I heard her say, "I killed a kid."

The words slammed into me like a two-by-four. She had researched me.

"I was chasing two 'bangers who were suspects in a drive-by," she said. "They abandoned the car and ran. I followed them into an alley. They fired at me from behind a Dumpster. I fired back and hit one of them. The other one ran. I let him go and tried to help the kid I'd shot, but he died before the ambulance got there. He was sixteen."

Her gaze wandered, and I knew she saw the kid in her mind. "We never found the second kid," she said. "And he apparently took the gun with him. We flooded the streets with cops, but they didn't find him. And, for good measure, they couldn't find the slug from the shot they took at me, either. They tested the kid I shot, and he hadn't fired a gun. I hit the wrong one."

"Wasn't there some evidence showing what happened?"

"Not really. There were no witnesses; I was working alone that night, and we were in one of those 'nobody saw nothing' neighborhoods. There was a bit of gunshot residue on the Dumpster, but it might have come from my hands. There were some footprints that suggested a second assailant, but that was inconclusive. No, it was pretty much just my uncorroborated story. So the protests began. Ministers, politicians, community activists—they all claimed there never was a second shooter, that I'd killed an unarmed black kid in cold blood. And I couldn't prove otherwise. Bottom line, I hit the wrong kid. Not the shooter."

I was stunned. It was a perfect storm of bad events, a chain of circumstances which had lined up just as they had on a Tampa freeway four years ago. "It was totally understandable," I said. "The law wouldn't find you at fault for the shooting. In fact, the kid without the gun would have been prosecuted as an accessory for shooting at you, just as if he'd been the actual shooter."

Her smile was weary. Of course she knew all that. "By then, the law didn't have much to do with it. They did submit the case to a grand jury, but I wasn't prosecuted. The city paid out one-point-two million to the kid's family. But the real problems were political and racial, not legal."

I could well imagine the scenario that followed.

"There were marches and protests and editorials," she continued. "Everybody howling for my scalp. Calling me a murderer and a racist and an executioner and a fascist. Meanwhile, I was at home, on administrative leave, not able to do anything about it. There were days when I began to doubt myself. I wondered if I'd imagined the second shooter. I couldn't sleep. In the first few weeks after the shooting, I used to go back to the scene and look for the slug. I'd go at night and run a metal detector over the grass in the vacant lot across the street. I was lucky I never got caught, since I was on leave."

"What happened next?" I asked.

"The mayor had me fired. He said it was nothing personal. He really wanted me as chief, but he was tired of taking the political heat. I had to go to the civil service board to get my job back."

"But you didn't go back to Homicide."

"I asked not to go back. Everybody in the department was nice about it. Everybody was supportive. But Homicide is high-profile, and I wasn't exactly hungering for more publicity. The mayor and the new chief didn't want me there, either, where I'd attract attention and criticism and remind everybody of old wounds. So I agreed to go quietly. I kept my rank and pay grade. But in return for leaving Homicide, they let me sort of do my own thing."

I didn't say anything.

"I still see the kid's face all the time, in every kid I meet."

I nodded. I saw Tracy's face in every little girl I encountered at a playground or a shopping mall. And sometimes I just saw her in my own mind.

"And so," she said, "I've got something useful to do. I try to help kids. I'm glad they let me do it."

She got up, slung her purse over her shoulder, and walked to the door. She opened it and began to leave, then turned back. "Every once in a while, though, when I'm under stress—especially late at night—I feel the urge again."

"The urge to do what?"

"To go back to the alley and look for the slug."

She left.

Chapter 30

The Subway restaurant was located just off West 50th Street, a major east-west route in south Minneapolis. The day was sticky, with hazy clouds breaking up the sunshine. It took forever to find a parking spot; both handicapped spaces in the tiny lot were taken, and I couldn't find anything on the street, so I circled several times and finally found a spot on a residential block around the corner and across 50th. Then I nearly got run down by a turning car as I crossed the street. I really hoped my visit would be worth the trials of pulling it off.

Inside, there were only a few customers left over from the lunch rush. I found the manager, a bespectacled, overweight young man who turned out to be the same guy I'd talked to that morning. He'd found an employee named Teresa, a thirtyish woman with dark Native American features, who had worked with Kenny. She sat down across from me.

"I'm glad you remember Kenny," I said. "Do you remember anything unusual that happened while he worked here?"

She frowned. "Well, there was sort of a tense moment once."

"What happened?"

"He'd started school by then, and I guess word must have gotten around that he was dating this girl—Sierra—who was a classmate of his. One night after closing, Sierra's old boyfriend was waiting for him outside—at least that's what I gathered—and the kid had one of his buddies with him. I was already halfway to my car, but I heard the guy yell at Kenny, so I turned around to see what was going on."

"What did the kid say?"

"He said to stay the hell away from Sierra, or he'd mess up that pretty face. I started back toward them—they were near the entrance to the store—but I didn't want to get too close. Then I saw the kid give Kenny a shove."

"What happened next?"

"I pulled out my phone to call 911. I saw Kenny back away, holding his hands up, saying he didn't want any trouble. Then the kid's friend stepped in. He gave Kenny a shove, too, harder than the first kid had. Kenny stumbled back and hit a car. And then—this was really weird—as I was starting to dial 911, this older guy appeared, like out of nowhere. He was gray-haired, and even under the street light, I could see that he had a lot of tattoos. He punched each of the boys—the boyfriend and the buddy—and they both went down. Pop, pop—just like that. Then he checked on Kenny, who was fine."

"Did Kenny know this guy?"

"He seemed to, yes. I don't know what the gray-haired guy was doing there—if they'd arranged to meet after work, or what. I remember thinking it was weird—I mean, why would he know an older, scary-looking guy? But he got Kenny out of the situation. The two boys picked themselves up and ran off. I was still going to call 911. But Kenny saw me and came over. He said the whole thing was no big deal and there was no need to call the police. Kenny tried to just shrug off the whole incident. We never talked about it again, but I didn't forget."

"Did he leave with the older guy?"

She thought about it. "No, they left separately."

"It wasn't Kenny's dad?"

"Not unless he has gray hair and tattoos."

"Can you tell me any more about this person, or about the incident?"

She shook her head. "Kenny seemed really embarrassed and was very clear that he didn't want to talk about it. I was just glad he didn't get hurt."

I thanked her and was preparing to leave when she said, "Wait." I returned to the table.

"There was somebody else," Teresa said. "Shortly after he started working here, I saw him get into a car with a girl."

"Not Sierra?"

"No, this was during the summer; he hadn't started dating Sierra yet. This girl was maybe a little older—I wasn't sure. Fairly pretty. Tall, with dark hair."

"You seem to remember her in some detail."

Teresa blushed. "Well, I'll admit, maybe I had my eye on Kenny a little bit, even though I'm quite a bit older, of course. I was interested in whether he had a girlfriend."

"Did this woman seem like a girlfriend?"

"Maybe. I suppose she could have just been a friend. They didn't look like brother and sister. Anyway, that was the only time I saw him with her."

"Do you remember anything else about her?"

"She drove a green BMW. A very nice car. I thought maybe she was a friend from Florida. That's about all I can remember."

I wondered if this girl was the same one the guy named Sid had seen Kenny with in Tampa. "One last question: Do you know why Kenny moved up here from Florida?"

Her face wrinkled up in thought. "No, he never talked about it that I can recall."

Once again, I prepared to leave. "Good luck finding Kenny," she said. "I hope he's okay. I really liked him."

"Thanks, Teresa."

I rolled back to my car, thinking about the two new players that had come into the picture: a scary-looking older guy and a dark-haired girl who may have been a girlfriend. It was the first I'd heard about either of them. Even more interesting was the sudden appearance of the man to rescue Kenny, as if he'd been acting as a bodyguard. I wondered if the man had been working for Z. Or maybe it was Z himself.

Chapter 31

Marsha pulled her rental sedan up in front of the two-story colonial house on a wooded lot. She remained in the car for a moment, trying to focus on the task at hand. She was, remarkably, on her way to making peace with Pen, and with herself. But it wouldn't mean much if she couldn't find Kenny.

It had always been hard to separate her anger with Pen over Tracy's death from her resentment at Pen in general. For years, Pen—outgoing and popular—had irritated her. When Pen had been involved in Tracy's death, the uneasy relationship between the two sisters had snapped completely, and Marsha had suspected it could never be repaired. Now, thanks to another crisis, there was hope. But she had to find her son.

Marsha paused at the curb, took a deep breath, and walked up the sidewalk to the front door. Susan Bjorklund had ignored repeated phone calls, but Marsha felt it was important to talk to her. Sierra appeared to be with Kenny, and Sierra's mother was the only known link to Sierra. She rang the doorbell and waited. A minute later, she rang a second time. She was ready to walk away when the outline of a face appeared in the door's frosted-glass window.

"Who is it?" asked a husky female voice.

"I'm Marsha Sellars. I'm—"

"I know who you are. I can't help you."

"I think you can."

The door opened slightly, and a haggard face peered out. "All right, then. I don't want to help you."

"Let's talk, mother to mother. Our children are missing."

Susan Bjorklund opened the door, shrugged, and said, "My daughter wants to be missing."

"So does Kenny. That doesn't mean we shouldn't find them. They're in danger."

Susan surveyed her with a long, disgusted, exhausted look. "Come in if you want."

Marsha opened the door and followed her down a short hallway and into a den, where a large scrapbooking project was laid out on a work table and a well-stocked bar stood against one wall. Several magazines, a television remote, and a glass containing a clear beverage sat on a side table next to an easy chair. Susan sat down in the chair. Marsha sat, uninvited, on a leather love seat across from her.

"Have you heard anything from Sierra?" Marsha asked.

"No. Whatever she does, I'm the last to know it." She took a sip from the glass, which didn't look like it contained anything alcoholic. Susan didn't appear to be drunk, but she did look hung over, carelessly made up with her gray hair in a ponytail, wearing an expensive sweatsuit.

"Why bother?" she said without looking at Marsha. "A cop called—some woman with an Italian name—and said Sierra went into the station and told them to stop looking for her." She now looked directly at Marsha. "And the police, being the accommodating folks they are, were happy to stop looking. They said sure, we don't give a rip where she is or what she does. She can go off with some kid and do whatever."

Marsha said nothing. She understood why the police wouldn't act, but her emotional reaction had been the same as Susan's.

"Did you spoil your kid?" Susan asked.

"I don't think so." In fact, Marsha felt she hadn't given Kenny enough. Not enough time, attention, or supervision.

"I spoiled Sierra. I spoiled myself. 'Why not?' I thought. My life sucked. I divorced well. I don't have to work. Why shouldn't

I give Sierra what she wants? It's not like her father gives a rat's ass, the bastard. Tell me, why didn't you spoil him?"

"I couldn't afford to. I might have otherwise."

Susan's wide mouth twisted into an unpleasant smile. "Well, isn't that empathetic and non-judgmental of you?"

Marsha tried to get the conversation back on track. "They're mixed up in something bad. We need to find out what it is."

"Correction. Your son is mixed up in something bad. Sierra is mixed up with him."

"I guess that's not an unreasonable way to look at it. But that doesn't make it any less dangerous."

"She likes him a lot. When she met him, he was getting over a breakup."

"Say that again?"

"You heard me. He was on the rebound."

"He told her that?"

"I don't know. But that's the impression she had."

Marsha was unable to think of any relationship Kenny might be getting over or, indeed, any prior relationship at all. According to Pen, there had been a fleeting sighting of him with a girl by some guy named Sid in Tampa, but that was it. "Had Sierra left home before?" she asked.

"Nope. She'd never done anything like that until she met your son." She wouldn't use his name. "But I don't care to be bothered with it anymore."

"Is this your way of dealing with the problem? By detaching from it?"

Susan sipped from her glass. "Don't try to psychoanalyze me, dear. The results would be very simple and depressing as hell. They would show you that I just don't care anymore."

"I don't believe that."

"How can I care? How does that help anybody? It doesn't help me—I'm just a lush and a shitty mother whose life has descended into a sinkhole. And it doesn't help her. She's made her choice. She's got a bright future and admission to the University of Minnesota. Instead, she decides to go off with this loser."

"My son is not a—"

"Oh, spare me. He's an unemployed high school dropout, running from the police, or criminals, or somebody. What would you call him?"

"I'd call him a good, normal kid with some problems. Just like Sierra."

Susan lifted the glass absently to her lips and paused. "She is insecure, that's true. But I don't care. I can't."

Marsha tried to think of more questions, but she had just about run out. "You have no idea at all where they might be?"

She shook her head, then got up, walked over to the bar, and refilled her glass from what appeared to be a water bottle. "Look, I've called all her friends. I've called my mother—she lives nearby and Sierra is close to her. I even called my former brother-in-law, Glenn. Sierra likes him, even though he can't be bothered to give us a call. Too busy counting his money and collecting the rent from all his properties."

Marsha sat up straight. "Properties?"

"He's a landlord. He owns a lot of apartment buildings and rental houses. Fixes them up and rents them out."

"What's his name, and how do I find him?"

"Glenn Walsh. He lives by himself in a townhouse in Golden Valley. His wife couldn't get him to return her calls, either."

Marsha felt her heartbeat galloping. "You say Sierra is close to him?"

"They seem to get along fine."

"When did you last speak to him?"

"A few days ago. Before Sierra left."

"Could Sierra have contacted him?"

Susan shrugged again. "How should I know? And why should I care? Sierra is going to do what Sierra wants."

Marsha jumped to her feet, willing herself not to lash back, thinking of all the times she'd wanted to pull back—to disengage, because caring about Kenny and Tracy hurt so much. "Call him," she said.

Susan dutifully picked up the phone on an end table and punched in a speed dial code. She listened, then looked up. "He's out of town, but expects to be available by noon today."

Marsha looked at her watch. "That's—ten minutes ago. Did he fly?"

"I doubt it. He has properties in Rochester and Duluth. Not so far to drive."

"Do you like Glenn?"

"Actually, amazingly, I do."

"Then you'd better say a prayer." She picked up her phone and called Pen, who answered immediately.

"Yeah, Marsh?"

"Sierra's uncle, Glenn Walsh, owns some rental apartments. Sierra may have gotten him to lend her and Kenny a vacant unit."

"Those mercenaries could probably find that out."

"Absolutely. Glenn is supposed to be home now but doesn't answer his phone, and we're worried about him. He lives in a suburb called Golden Valley."

"That's not far—it borders Minneapolis."

"Should we call the police?"

"Let me call Candiotti," Pen said. "She can have the locals check out the place. Give me the address."

Marsha relayed the address from Susan to Pen. "I'm going over there," Marsha said.

"No!" Pen exclaimed. "Wait for the police."

"All right, I won't approach the house until they get there. But I'm going."

After a brief hesitation, Pen said, "I'll meet you there. But for heaven's sake, keep your distance and be careful."

*   *   *

Glenn Walsh pulled his Lexus into the garage of his townhouse and shut the engine off. He let out a long breath and simply sat behind the wheel. These excursions to Duluth were getting old. He was getting old. He should sell the two small apartment buildings he owned up there. Good properties, but too much hassle. It was fine when he'd been a passive investor and his partner, Dan, had lived up there and could handle plumbing problems and tenant deadbeats. But Dan had retired to Arizona, leaving Glenn with the management responsibility.

It was always something. The unit in northeast Minneapolis was taking longer to rent than it should have. He wondered if he'd done the right thing, lending it to Sierra. He supposed she could just be using it for a tryst, but that didn't seem like Sierra. She was a sweet kid, and when she said she just needed a night or two to get away from her mother, he could understand that. Susan, his former sister-in-law, was a character. She was interesting, and sometimes fun, but she wore on you after a while.

He tapped both hands on the steering wheel. Time to retrieve his suitcase from the trunk and get to work in his home office.

But his garage door was going down. What the hell—had he accidentally hit the button?

He got out of the car. Two people stood facing him inside the now-closed door. Both wore ski masks.

"Who the hell are you?" he demanded.

A female voice responded. "Just a few questions, Glenn. We're looking for Sierra and her boyfriend. And you're going to help us."

*   *   *

Marsha was waiting for me when I pulled up at the townhouse in Golden Valley. I'd gotten lost in Walsh's complex and run into a dead end but eventually found the right address on my navigation app. Marsha got out of her car and came over to the van. I rolled down the window.

"Can you see anything?" I asked.

"No. Everything's closed up, and I haven't seen any movement through the windows."

A police cruiser appeared as we talked, and a young officer rolled down his window. "We got a call for a welfare check at this address from Lieutenant Candiotti in Minneapolis. She said she's coming out—is she here yet?"

We shook our heads.

"The call said there's a possible home invasion here. Do either of you know if Mr. Walsh, the homeowner, is inside?"

More head shakes.

"But you're the ones who called the Minneapolis police?"

"We are," I said. "We're concerned that someone might be trying to harm Mr. Walsh."

"Have you seen anything suspicious? Any vehicles coming or going?"

"No," Marsha answered, "but we've only been here a few minutes."

The cop shrugged and pulled into the driveway. He got out, looked, and warned us to stay back. Then he walked up to the front entrance, put his hand on his holstered gun, and pounded loudly on the door. "Mr. Walsh? Police! Are you all right?"

He turned toward the street. A battered unmarked pulled up to the curb, and Lexi Candiotti jumped out. "Anything?" she called to us as she trotted up to the front door.

We shook our heads again. I was beginning to feel like a bobblehead doll.

She conferred briefly with the patrol officer, and the two cops took turns knocking and calling out. We couldn't hear the officers' conversation that followed, but we could guess its contents from what happened next. Candiotti walked around to the back of the house with the Golden Valley cop walking behind, apparently protesting something. By now I was out of the van, and Marsha and I went halfway up a neighbor's driveway, where we could see the back of Walsh's house. Candiotti was trying to open a back door while the cop argued with her. Finally, she stopped trying the back door, stood up, and snatched the hat off the astonished officer's head.

Candiotti pulled her gun from a shoulder holster under her blazer, turned it around so she was gripping the barrel, and placed the gun inside the hat. Then she punched a hole in a small window next to the back door. After that, she returned the indignant officer's hat and carefully reached through the hole in the window and unlatched the door from the inside. She took her gun by the grip, opened the door, and went in. The officer, after hesitating briefly, followed with his own weapon out.

Candiotti reappeared about three minutes later, talking on her phone. When she finished, she glanced over at us. "Walsh is inside—the place is clear otherwise. He's hurt, but I think he'll be okay. The uniform's giving him first aid, and the ambulance should be here soon. I'm going to check his home office to see if I can find out where the vacant apartment is. Does he have family you can call?"

"I'll call his sister-in-law," Marsha said.

"Fine."

"Did you notice the name of a company he might be using?" I asked.

"I saw a couple of invoices on his desk to GWW Properties." She disappeared inside. Marsha called Susan Bjorklund while I began a new Internet search on my phone. I had already searched for vacant properties owned by Walsh. I hadn't found any, but Walsh might be using other entities, such as GWW Properties.

The ambulance appeared a couple of minutes later. The patrolman met the paramedics at the front door. Five minutes later, with the paramedics still inside, Candiotti reappeared, carrying a ledger book.

"He's apparently not computerized," she said. "Here's a record book. Looks like rent receipts for each of his properties. We can look for units that haven't been getting rent recently. That will take a while."

"Is there a unit on Thirteenth Street Northeast in Minneapolis?"

Candiotti thumbed quickly through the book and finally looked up. "Yes. Here it is."

I checked the address. "That's probably it. GWW Properties has advertised it for rent online on two different sites. I can't find any others."

"Okay. That must be it."

"Do you suppose Glenn gave them anything before he finally lost consciousness? The address on Thirteenth Street, or the name of his company?"

Candiotti glanced toward the house, where the paramedics were bringing a man on a stretcher out to the ambulance. "Absolutely." She pulled out her phone.

*   *   *

Like Pavlov's canine friend, Brit felt the anticipation as she fingered the plastic bag in her pocket like a security blanket. The feeling of excitement came unbidden whenever she faced a situation like this. She had known, since the day she left her mother's burning house, both that she liked the feeling too much, and that she had to experience it again.

She often relived that night, when she had walked away from the burning building with only a backpack filled with a few clothes and other possessions. From a safe distance in the woods outside, she watched the house burn. Since they lived two miles outside of town, no one would see or report the fire until it was too late. A friend in a neighboring town was prepared to give her

168

an alibi, but Brit didn't need it. The fire—and her mother's death—were ruled an accident after a cursory investigation. After all, her mother smoked in bed. Arrangements were made for Brit to live with a local family friend until her eighteenth birthday, only a few months away. But Brit simply took off, and the friend never reported her missing.

The military seemed a natural place for an athletic, resourceful young woman who liked guns and didn't shy away from conflict. More than that, it seemed a good place for a person who knew, perhaps unconsciously, that her skills and her desires came together in a way that was unhealthy—even dangerous, creating the need for oversight by a commanding officer or boss. Brit had advanced rapidly through the ranks and had become one of the first women to train with a Special Forces unit. Deployed to the Middle East, she had come into contact with a number of private military and security contractors, including Security Services International, the company that now employed her and her team. She had found herself assigned to one of the firm's ultra-sensitive covert teams, which occasionally took on domestic operations. She earned the assignment for two reasons: She was good, and she didn't look like an operative.

Sierra's uncle had put up a surprising amount of resistance. He'd been in good shape for an older guy, had fought back hard, and had held out for a long time. But nobody held out forever, and Glenn Walsh finally gave it up. When it came right down to it, tough guys were like anybody else: they wanted to breathe.

Now, in front of a park located a block and a half from the small apartment building in northeast Minneapolis, Brit met with two members of her team in the back of the van. The fourth team member, Oliver, already watched the building from a side street.

"Are you sure you've had it covered?" she asked Oliver, the swarthy farm boy from Mississippi, over the radio.

"Yes. I can see both exits. Nobody in or out since I called you." He had quickly gone in and checked the second-story apartment's door, describing it as a "one-kick wonder," before retreating to his observation post outside.

"Any movement through the window?" Brit asked.

"No."

"Well, we know they're there—the uncle confirmed that. And no security cameras?"

"None."

For the next ten minutes the team discussed the general outlines of their hastily-improvised operational plan for surrounding and entering the supposedly vacant rental apartment. Ten minutes from now, they would have Kenny. And, not long after that, they'd have Z.

"Okay, positions," Brit said. Two team members left the van at staggered intervals.

Brit followed, speaking into a lapel mike. "Carlin, stay in front. Continue to monitor the police channels and watch the street." She spoke into her walkie-talkie. "Ian, you're set?"

"Roger," said the Aussie over the secure channel. He was stationed in the back parking lot of the older twelve-unit building.

She spoke to Oliver. "Let's go. Remember, quiet and low-key."

*   *   *

"We have to move on," Kenny said, peering out the window at the street.

"Where do we go?" Sierra asked.

Kenny sipped from his coffee. "You need to go home."

She rolled her eyes. "We've talked about that. I can't go back."

"You're afraid of your mother?"

"Not afraid. She doesn't care that I took off. I just . . . can't go back to all that."

"You'll be starting college in just a couple of months. Until then, if you're trying to avoid going home, being with me isn't the answer."

"But I want to be with you."

He smiled faintly and squeezed her hand. "And I want to be with you. But it isn't safe. I'm running out of money, and these people will be coming for me. Probably pretty soon."

"How could they find you? They'd have to figure out that my uncle, with a different last name, owns a lot of rental properties, under the name of a company that's not incorporated, and that he has a vacant unit, and—"

"Don't you see? I could do all that in an hour while eating lunch and working crossword puzzles—half an hour if I worked for an employer who subscribed to some private databases. That means they can do it, too. Not only that, but they're willing to hurt people—even to kill. Look what they did to Liam. And Sam. And who knows what they were going to do to you?"

Sierra gave an involuntary shudder. The reference to the attempted attack on her reminded her that their flight was not a game. "For God's sake, Kenny," she said, her voice now shaking. "Who on earth are these people?"

Kenny didn't answer. For several weeks he had thought he knew. Now he wasn't entirely sure. Could Z have been truthful about not employing the blonde woman and her team? But regardless of the who, he still knew the why.

"I shouldn't have gotten involved with . . ." He wouldn't say the name. "I got mixed up with the wrong people. I didn't do very much that was wrong. But now they're doing something bigger. And I wanted out."

"So that's why they're after you?"

"It might be other people who are after them," he said, knowing that using the plural "them" was misleading. It was just as well, he thought. Sierra should know as little as possible.

"Why can't you just go to the police and—"

"Aw, come on," he snapped. "We've been through that a million times. The police don't have a clue what they're dealing with in cyberspace. They can't protect us. I have to figure a way out of this myself."

"How are you going to do that?"

"I don't know yet."

"How about that FBI agent who saved me from those people? Hewitt."

"I tried," he said quietly. "I tried to reach him—called anonymously—and they told me he's awaiting reassignment and has no active cases. They offered to connect me with somebody else. But how can we trust anybody there? You think it's just a coincidence that Hewitt is being abruptly pulled out of Minneapolis?"

"How about your aunt in the wheelchair? You said she's a prosecutor. Maybe she has connections."

"I don't want to involve her. That would mean involving my mother, which would be complicated."

"Then what—"

"Damnit, that's it," Kenny said, springing to his feet. "We have to go. They're here."

*   *   *

Ian listened on the radio as Brit narrated their progress into the building. "First floor landing and hallway clear," she reported.

Ian watched the window of the second-floor unit at the rear corner. Still no movement. "We're on the second floor," Brit said. "The landing is clear."

Her voice became quieter. "Positioning now. All quiet in the unit . . . Let's do it—three, two, one . . ." Ian heard a loud crash. "Living room clear!" Brit shouted.

He heard Oliver's voice for the first time. "Bedroom clear!"

"Bathroom clear!" Brit hollered. A brief pause. "It's empty. Empty. They're not here. Shit! *Shit!*"

*   *   *

Half a block away, through the window of the coffee shop where they'd spent the morning and part of the afternoon, watching the apartment building where they'd stayed the night, Kenny saw them arrive. He had not been pessimistic or cynical when he had predicted the arrival of the operatives. He had been realistic. He counted three of them, though he suspected there was a fourth in the rear. There was a tall woman wearing a base-ball cap, and he figured there was probably blonde hair under-neath. But they didn't wait around to see more. As the mercenar-ies entered the building, he and Sierra grabbed their backpacks, slipped out a back door, and sprinted through an alley. They ran three blocks to a bus stop, where they waited for what seemed an interminable period for a bus. They hid their faces at the stop, standing apart, until the roaring, lumbering vehicle appeared, ready to carry them to . . . Kenny didn't have a clue.

Chapter 32

Marsha and I met back at the condo, having driven separately from Glenn Walsh's house. She returned a few minutes after I got there. "Anything from Candiotti?" she asked.

As the words left her mouth, my phone buzzed. It was Candiotti. They had found the apartment, empty and with the door kicked in. Witnesses had seen what looked like members of the SSI team leaving, but without Kenny or Sierra. Other witnesses had seen a couple fitting their description this morning at a coffee shop down the block. I thanked the lieutenant and clicked off.

"So they escaped," Marsha said.

"Looks that way."

Marsha put her purse down on the kitchen table and sat next to me. "We were so close to finding them," she said.

"The SSI team was even closer."

She just nodded. "It sounds like you and Lieutenant Candiotti have hit it off."

"I guess so, yes." I wasn't about to explain the tragedies that had caused us to form a bond. But I did summarize Candiotti's news about Sierra's visit to a precinct house.

"Interesting," she said. "But I'm not sure it gets us any closer."

"Not at the moment," I agreed. "Did you get anything out of Alec?"

"He didn't tell me much, but I did discern one interesting thing from my visit. Interesting but not surprising. He's living above his means."

"He left his job."

"Not voluntarily. He was fired, about two months ago. I'm surprised it took so long; he's never been much good at holding onto a job. He can't afford that house, or the cars they're driving, or those trips to the casinos."

"Shannon has a job."

"True. And it doesn't sound like a bad job—some sort of executive assistant. But she wouldn't make the kind of money they need to support their current lifestyle."

"So what does that tell us about Kenny?"

"Maybe nothing. But I have the feeling Alec knows more than he's telling us."

"I've sensed that from the beginning."

"Maybe it has something to do with his finances."

"Let's find out." I reached for my phone and called Ben Hewitt.

"Pen," he said, sounding as though my call had really made his day. "What rule-flouting act of insubordination can I perform for you this afternoon?"

"We'd like to check out Alec Sellars's finances," I explained. He sounded uneasy about the request, and I understood. To do it by the book, he'd need a file number and a subpoena. But he agreed to do it.

"Great," I said. "Did Sink ever investigate the local Russian mafia, or the Russian community in general, for links to Z?"

"As far as I can tell, no."

"Thanks, Ben."

I hung up. "He's going to do it," I told Marsha.

"Good."

"Now, here's what I heard at Subway."

She was as baffled and troubled as I had been by Teresa's account of the tattooed older man, and also by the unexpected appearance of a female friend who may have been a girlfriend. "It sounds like it might be the same girl he was seen with in Tampa," she said.

"And the incident at Subway occurred shortly after he moved up here, so the sightings were pretty close together."

"Sierra's mother said she believed Kenny was rebounding from a breakup. Now that might make sense." For several minutes, she recounted her conversation with Susan Bjorklund.

"We need to find the mystery girl," I said.

"I know. And also the gray-haired guy. Sounds like I've got my afternoon's work set. I need to get on the phone to Tampa to see if anybody he knows can tell me about these two mysterious people. I still haven't visited Sam, either—I'll need to do that. What are you going to do?"

"I'm off to do some hacking," I replied.

*   *   *

Emily Radatz's office was located in a trendy older building in the Warehouse District in Minneapolis, not far from the Target Field rail station where Kenny had appeared a couple of nights ago. Emily buzzed me in through the entry door on the street, and I went up in an old-fashioned cage elevator. On the third floor, I waited in a plain outer office, furnished with three chairs and a coffee table. After about ten minutes Emily waddled out, maneuvering her pregnant bulk through the doorway. She looked crisp and professional, wearing a navy blue maternity dress, her perfume a faint, pleasant jasmine scent. We shook, and the perky, caffeinated consultant plopped down in a chair beside me.

"Nice to see you again," she said. "What can I do for you?"

"I'd like to find Z."

"You'd like to . . . *find* him?"

"Yes. This whole thing seems to be about him, somehow. People are apparently trying to find Kenny in order to find Z, or because of what he's doing for Z."

"Why don't you bring me up to date?"

I filled her in on our search for Kenny, including our conclusion that professional contractors or mercenaries were apparently involved.

She sat back, clearly shaken. "It does sound serious. But you have to understand: you don't find Z. The Feds have been looking for him for years."

"Maybe they're not looking that hard." I described the suspicious behavior of Special Agent Gary Sink.

Emily's expression turned skeptical. "Do you know what you're suggesting?"

"I guess I do. Maybe Sink has been bent or co-opted or misled somehow."

"That's a pretty serious charge."

"Maybe there's a better explanation for how he's acting. But none occurs to me right now."

She blew out a breath. "I don't know, Pen."

"Here's another thought: Why is Sink in Minneapolis? His unit is based in Pittsburgh. According to you, Z could be anywhere, and probably in another country. Why would the FBI locate an agent here unless they suspect a physical presence of some kind—if not Z himself, then maybe some family or associates or witnesses?"

Her face wrinkled in concentration. "You might be right."

"Is it possible to find Z online?"

She thought for a long moment, finally appearing to reach a decision. "Come on back."

Emily struggled out of her chair, then walked over to the unmarked door from which she'd emerged a minute earlier. She pressed a button, then placed her thumb on a scanner. A moment later, the door clicked.

"High security," I commented.

"This actually isn't much, especially considering what I do. But I prefer to concentrate most of my resources on preserving computer security. That's my business."

The office suite was surprisingly small, with four work tables, two of them occupied by young men wearing headsets, and two doors. One of the doors was open, and through it I could see a small break room. "My team," she said, gesturing toward the two young men. "Actually I have three other people who work for me, usually from home. But for the really sensitive stuff, I like them to come in here if they're not on the client's premises."

"Do you have anybody working at Columbia Central's premises?"

Emily smiled. "Oh, no. Doogie has the place locked down tight. I do some sensitive things for him, but even so, I have access to only a part of their system. It's very compartmentalized and need-to-know. Lamm's paranoid personality is a perfect fit for the job."

She motioned me over to a table that consisted of a keyboard facing three large monitors. An identical log-in screen was shown on all three displays. She plopped down awkwardly in an armless chair on wheels, and I rolled up beside her. She began typing at lightning speed, and a quick succession of screens appeared on the monitors, none of them displayed long enough for me to really see what was on them. Eventually we ended up on a black screen without graphics, its only content a list of links or files.

"Welcome to the Dark Web," Emily said.

"Is that the same as the Deep Web?"

"Not really. The Deep Web just refers to any page that doesn't have a web address that can be indexed on a search engine. That includes a lot of pages that are perfectly legitimate. The Dark Web is a subset of the Deep Web; its sites also can't be found on any conventional search engines, and some of its content is, well, dark."

"So the Dark Web is all illegal stuff?"

"Not at all. There's plenty of shady stuff here, to be sure. Some of it is illegal; some of it offensive or downright repugnant.

But the Dark Web is basically a place to communicate anony-mously. You'll get a lot of privacy activists, or political activists from totalitarian countries."

"So the anonymity could be used for a valid reason?"

"Absolutely."

"How does the anonymity work?"

"You use an anonymizing browser. Tor is the most com-mon, but I'm using another one called IP2. When I send my re-quest to access one of these links, it will go through somebody else's network, and then another network, and another, and so on, through layers of encryption. For that reason, it often runs more slowly than the regular Internet. It's pretty much untrace-able."

I pointed to the screen. "What are we looking at now?"

"It's a Reddit directory. This one lists advocacy sites—pri-vacy, anti-government, anti-surveillance—that kind of thing."

"None of that sounds very illegal or dangerous."

"It's probably not. Let's see if we can find something a little sketchier." Again, her fingers exploded into action across the keyboard, producing a series of images. We ended up at another menu, this one with a red background and an animated flame around the margins. "Pharmaceuticals," Emily announced.

The triple screens showed sites offering prescription drugs, including morphine, oxycodone, fentanyl, and other powerful opiates, openly for sale, no prescription needed. Other sites ad-vertised illicit chemicals and ingredients for other illegal sub-stances, such as methamphetamine.

Emily manipulated more keys, and another directory ap-peared, this one specializing in weapons. She scrolled through several pages of links to dozens of gun, ammunition, and explo-sives dealers, as well as sites selling various types of body armor, Tasers, stun grenades, night vision goggles, restraints, radios, and other military and police equipment. Appalled, I looked up at her. "Do the police know about these sites?"

She laughed at my naiveté. "Oh, sure. But it's pretty hard to do anything about it. I wouldn't say this anonymity is a hundred percent unbreakable, but it's close. You'd need a sustained, large-scale effort by law enforcement, like they used for Silk Road."

"Silk—what?"

"Silk Road. A large-scale drug marketplace that was busted a few years ago."

"The people who ran it were caught?"

"Some of them were. Who knows if the authorities got all of them? Even if they did, I'm sure other markets were opening up even as Silk Road was being shut down."

"I'm afraid to ask what else you can find here."

"Just about anything. Tons of pornography, including some really sickening stuff. Smuggling. Human trafficking. Fake documents. If it's illegal, immoral, or unethical, you can find it here."

"How about hacking?"

She clicked the keys again, pulling up a directory. "What do you want to see?" she asked.

"I don't know." Obviously we weren't going to search for Z immediately.

"How would you like to buy some stolen credit card numbers?" Without waiting for a response, she clicked one of the links, which took us to a search box. She typed something in the box, too fast for me to see, and soon we were at a site that advertised credit and debit card numbers for sale. You could search by bank, by country, and by credit limit. "What's your pleasure?" Emily asked. "Chase? Bank of America?"

I just shook my head, and she pulled up a directory of Chase credit card numbers for sale, in blocks of one hundred numbers.

"Good Lord," I muttered, still utterly amazed that criminals such as this could operate so openly and brazenly. I imagined some of my fellow prosecutors, who dealt with this type of crime on a daily basis, shaking their heads at my ignorance. "What if I wanted to hire a hacker?"

"No problem." She returned to the menu we'd seen a minute ago and clicked another link. At the destination site, we saw postings by dozens of individuals and groups, offering their services for breaking into almost anything. She clicked on one link. "Here's somebody who will get you into a Gmail account for a hundred bucks."

"Anybody's?"

"Sure."

I felt chilled at the thought that anybody could plunk down a hundred dollars and see all of my personal email.

"What airline do you usually fly?" Emily asked.

"United."

She did another search, and after a few clicks said, "This guy will hack your frequent flyer account for fifty bucks." She continued clicking. "Phony Yelp reviews? Three hundred dollars." More clicks. "Here's somebody who will get into Facebook accounts. He wants three hundred dollars. I think I could find somebody cheaper, but you get the idea."

I was indeed getting the idea, and it was making me nauseous. Somebody could steal all my frequent flyer miles. They could hijack my Facebook page and post hateful rants, or libelous material, or pornography, or whatever, under my name.

"There are also some do-it-yourself tools," Emily said. "Here—you can download a program that allows you to hack Facebook sites yourself—twenty-five dollars for three months." She pointed to a different link. "This person actually gives hacking lessons. They start at twenty bucks."

I sat for a long moment, staring at the screen. "I guess Z must be here somewhere," I said.

Emily nodded and began searching. She soon found an entire discussion group devoted to Z and his exploits. One participant posted: "You're the greatest, Z-ster. Way to stick up Reese Systems." Another: "You're legendary, Z-man!!! Nobody else could have gotten into Gaylord Industries." And another: "Where you been, man? Who's your next target?"

"Stop," I said. "What's the date on that last post?"

"Almost a year ago."

"Even then, people were wondering what he was going to do next. Has he done anything during the past year?"

"Let's see." She spent another five minutes searching the site, along with a couple of others. One posting actually contained a chronology of Z's hacks. Finally Emily turned to me. "As far as I can tell, he hasn't done anything major during that time."

"So he's retired?"

"Unlikely."

"In prison?"

"That's a better possibility. But I doubt it. If the authorities arrested him for something, they would have eventually realized who they had in their jail cell. It would have become public."

"Then the silence probably means he's up to something. Planning the next project."

"And it might be a big project, given the length of time he's been inactive. Everybody's doing ransomware now, anyway. It wouldn't be surprising that he'd want to try something bigger."

"Can we get a message to Z somehow?"

"Sure." The keys clacked, and Emily ended up on a bare black screen with a blinking cursor. "All yours," she said, moving aside and pushing the keyboard toward me. "Z can pick up the message at this site."

I took a breath, exhaled, and reached for the keyboard. Physically finding Z was hopeless. The most I could do was try to persuade him to leave Kenny alone.

Ten minutes later, I read over the three paragraphs I'd written. I'd introduced myself and told Z I had no interest in finding him or getting him into any legal trouble, and that my only priority was my nephew's safety. I told him I assumed he was not the one who had hired professional operatives to track Kenny down. I offered to assist in finding those operatives and whoever hired them, and to either turn them in to the authorities or make a deal with them, depending on what they wanted from Kenny. I urged him to contact me and gave him my phone number, although that seemed unnecessary, given how easy it was for a hacker to find personal information.

I read the message again, and it seemed even lamer the second time. It looked like what it was: a desperate shot in the dark, based mostly on wishful thinking and very little actual information. I could be reading the situation wrong in a dozen ways, possibly making things worse. But I had to try.

"Send it," I said.

Chapter 33

It was close to six by the time I returned to the condo. I had a couple of calls to make and had just rolled up to the kitchen table when my phone rang. I didn't recognize the number or even the area code. I answered anyway.

"This is Pen."

"Pen? My name is Patty Mattison. I'm an FBI special agent in Philadelphia."

"Yes?"

"I got a call from Trey Mathews in LA. He said you're looking for information on Agent Gary Sink."

"That's right. Thanks for calling."

"I can't say no to Trey. I owe him. So do half the country's prosecutors and FBI agents. Trey and I worked on prosecutions for an organized crime task force some years back."

"How well do you know Agent Sink?"

"He was a colleague. We worked on credit card fraud rings here in Philly for about two years. Then he left last year to join one of the FBI cyber-crimes units in Pittsburgh. We weren't particularly close on a personal level, but I worked with him regularly during that two-year period."

"I need to know whether I can trust him," I said. "He's done some things that raise doubts in my mind."

"Really? I always found him to be solid and reliable and competent. He wasn't brilliant, I guess, but few of us are. He developed an interest in cyber-crime when he was working in our unit, and he seemed pretty good at it."

"What was he like on a personal basis?"

"I always found him friendly and reasonable."

"I'm trying to figure out if we're talking about the same person, Agent Mattison."

"Patty, please."

"Sure, Patty. This is a man who, in a routine interview in a missing person case, warned me in very unpleasant terms against withholding information. In fact, I'd have to say he threatened me. He's also been very secretive with his colleagues and has badgered—even bullied—subordinates."

There was a pause. "Wow. That doesn't sound like the Gary Sink I know at all. He was a good guy. He used to go out with a group of us for happy hour on Friday afternoons after work, and we all had a good time. Sometimes his girlfriend, Lindsay, joined us. Lindsay Seiple, her name was. She was nice, too. I know she wouldn't put up with any bullying or abusive behavior, by him or anyone."

"He could be under a lot of stress," I offered.

"I suppose. But he always seemed a pretty cool character to me."

"Do you know how he ended up in Minneapolis?"

"I'm afraid I don't. I pretty much lost track of him and Lindsay after they moved to Pittsburgh."

I'd run out of questions. "You've been a big help, Patty. I appreciate the time."

"I don't feel as though I've been much help at all. I've just made Gary's behavior even more puzzling."

"Thanks again—"

"Wait," she said. "There's something I'd like to try, if you don't mind."

"What's that?"

"I'd like to get hold of Lindsay, just to see how things are going. I regret losing touch with her anyway. Maybe I'll just give her a call to catch up. She might have some explanation for why Gary is acting so strangely."

"That would be great. Just let me know if you find out anything interesting."

"Will do. It was nice talking to you, Pen."

Marsha wasn't back yet, so I took the opportunity to call Lieutenant Candiotti.

"Pen," she said, sounding as if she had nothing better to do at the moment than chat with me. "What can I do for you?"

"First of all, thanks again for all the attention you've given to this case, and for keeping us in the loop."

"You're welcome."

"Second, I wanted to talk to you about Russians."

"Russians?"

"Specifically the Russian mafia or Russian organized crime. I'd like to know what their presence is in this area."

"Why?"

"Z, the hacker, is reputed to be of Russian descent. There are a lot of Russian criminals and gangs who are involved in hacking. We don't know why Z would be physically present in Minnesota, but if he is, it stands to reason that he might have Russian ties here. Even if he isn't here himself, he could have ties to Russian gangsters who could be looking out for his interests."

After a pause the detective said, "There is some logic to that. But I'm not sure where it gets you. There isn't much of a Russian mafia presence here in Minnesota. Most of the gangs we've got are Latin and Asian, as well as the usual homegrown varieties. There have been some isolated problems caused by Russians or groups of Russians, but not much evidence of organized activity. There was an operation a few years ago that ran an insurance scam—staging phony car accidents. The suspects were Russian, but as far as we could tell, they were freelancers. The usual things the Russians are involved in—extortion, gun-running, trafficking, and so on—we can pretty much attribute to somebody else."

"How about hacking?"

"Not really our bailiwick, I'm afraid. Unless the flesh-and-blood bad guys are here in the City of Minneapolis, we don't really get involved."

"Are there Russian neighborhoods in this area?"

"More like enclaves, I'd say. A lot of Russians live in the western Minneapolis suburbs—which is out of my jurisdiction, by the way—with a little pocket in St. Paul. But they're not very concentrated."

I thanked Candiotti and hung up. I hadn't shared with her my chief reason for asking about the local Russians: Sink's lack of interest in investigating them. The more I thought about it, the more I believed that Z or his accomplices had some physical presence in Minnesota. If it was Sink's job to catch Z, it was hard to account for the agent's being here otherwise. If Z was here, that might also account for Kenny's move here from Florida: to serve his shadowy employer. In asking around up here, I'd heard several other explanations for the move, but they were vague, contradictory, and unconvincing. It would be nice to hear Kenny's.

Marsha returned a few minutes later. "The school was a dead end, just as you predicted," she said, sitting down. "Kenny is eighteen. They wouldn't tell me anything. I also struck out trying to find anybody else in Tampa who'd seen Kenny with the dark-haired woman."

"I talked to Lieutenant Candiotti. She had nothing new on either Kenny or Sierra."

"Sort of a good news-bad news situation," Marsha said. "It looks like Sierra and Kenny are both alive. But no information on their whereabouts."

"Candiotti said they were at that apartment at some point. Let's hope they had a fallback—somewhere else to go."

"How did it go with the consultant?"

Marsha's expression darkened as I described what Emily Radatz had shown me on the Dark Web. "And Kenny was mixed up in this kind of stuff?" she asked.

"We don't know exactly what he was doing for Z. We know that Z was involved in ransomware, which seems less tawdry than a lot of the things I saw. In fact, Z is a hero to some people."

"A hero? Why?"

"For standing up to Corporate America."

"What do you think?"

I shook my head. "I'm a jaded prosecutor, Marsha. I've heard every excuse for lawbreaking you can imagine."

"There's no place for principle? For civil disobedience?"

"I guess so, but I don't see it here. Z is extorting money from companies. I see no indication that these targets are unusually evil or deserving, or that they've changed their behavior as a result. It looks like plain old theft to me."

"That brings us back to why he's looking for Kenny."

"I think Kenny might know something about Z's next move." I explained about Z's inaction and near-disappearance from the Dark Web during the past year.

"If Kenny knows something, why doesn't he come forward and tell the authorities?"

"He's probably been involved in some of these illegal ransomware hacks. He might be afraid of implicating himself."

"What if Z could be assured that Kenny won't talk?"

"I tried to do just that. I left Z a message, telling him we have no interest in creating legal trouble for him, and that I was sure Kenny didn't, either. Of course, if Z believed that, he probably wouldn't be after Kenny."

"He wants to make sure. We're running out of leads, Pen. It's only a matter of time before those SSI creeps find Kenny."

I nodded as I pulled up a Google Earth image of Minneapolis on my computer. "I think it's time to shake the tree. And I'll need your help."

Chapter 34

Agent Gary Sink answered on the first ring. "Ms. Wilkinson. Have you heard from your nephew?"

"As a matter of fact, I have."

"Really?" He sounded surprised. "And what was the nature of the contact?"

"He called me. He sounded scared and said he wants to meet me."

"When and where?"

"In an hour. I'd rather not say where."

"You're under an obligation—"

"Agent Sink," I said calmly, "I promised Kenny I wouldn't tell anyone where we'd be meeting. I'm sorry, but that trumps any obligation you may think I have to you. Now, look: I'm dutifully reporting the contact to you. And after I've talked to Kenny and heard his version of the facts, I will pass that along to you as well. If he agrees and I'm convinced it's appropriate, I will persuade him to contact you to arrange an interview. If all that is not enough, all I can say is, arrest me."

There was silence at the other end. Finally he said, "Have you told Hewitt any of this?"

"No."

Another pause. Then, "If you withhold any—"

"Goodbye, Agent Sink." I hung up. He called back immediately, but I didn't pick up the call.

Thirty-five minutes later, I drove out of the garage underneath the condo building and headed south out of downtown. I checked my rearview mirror discreetly but didn't notice anybody following me. Still, I was reasonably sure I'd have a tail. Marsha had left in her rental car ten minutes ahead of me.

I followed Hennepin Avenue south into the congested Uptown area, then turned west into a ritzy residential district. After a few blocks I reached Lake of the Isles, in the heart of the exclusive Kenwood neighborhood. A parkway circled the lake, lined with bike and walking paths next to the water, and seriously expensive mansions on the opposite side. These houses had been built by grain millers, lumber barons, and railroad magnates early in the last century.

I pulled onto the parkway and headed north. When I reached the narrow tip of the lake, I found a parking spot, pulled over, and shut off the engine. I sat and looked at the joggers, bikers, and rollerbladers on a sultry June evening while I waited for Kenny to arrive.

Except that he wouldn't be coming. But I was really interested to see who would.

I waited. I decided to stay in the van, so I'd be able to make a quick getaway if necessary. I looked at my watch. It was a few minutes after seven-thirty, just past the one-hour mark since I'd called Sink.

My phone rang.

"Yes?"

"I see him," Marsha said.

"Who?"

"The tough-looking gray-haired guy. He's in a light blue van with a dent in the passenger-side front door. It's parked on a side street, just across the narrow part of the lake and a little behind you."

I turned and looked across the lake to the other side but couldn't see the van. I couldn't see Marsha, either. Before leaving the apartment, we'd scouted out a vantage point from which she could see me, as well as three side streets from which others might watch my phony meeting with Kenny.

"The world is full of gray-haired guys," I said.

"Who are watching you through binoculars?"

My pulse accelerated. It was the breakthrough I'd been hoping for. With any luck, this would be the man who'd rescued Kenny outside Subway, the man who just might work for Z. His appearance revealed an unpleasant but unavoidable truth: the guy had almost certainly learned of the meeting from Gary Sink, which meant Sink was probably working with or for Z. "We need that license plate, Marsh."

"I already have it. And I'm going to follow him."

"No! Stay away from him. He might be a Russian gang-banger. We'd be in over our heads, trying to follow him."

"At least I can make damn sure he leaves," Marsha said. "We don't need him coming after you. I'm ready to dial 911 at the first sign he moves on you."

"I don't think that will be necessary. I think I'll be getting a visit from law enforcement before that happens."

"All right. I'll stay here and keep watch."

The visit I expected came fifteen minutes later. A face appeared in my window, startling me.

"He's not coming, is he?" said Gary Sink.

"Why, Agent Sink. What a coincidence. Enjoying the nice evening here at the lake?"

"You lied to me."

"You followed me. Did you tail me, or bug my van with a GPS tracker?"

He leaned his head through the car window. "You're in serious—"

"You get out of my face right now!" I snapped. "I've had it up to here with you and your threats." It was all I could do to keep myself from confronting him about the gray-haired man, but I wasn't about to play that card yet.

"You're playing a dangerous game," he said through gritted teeth.

"I'm driving away now, and you're not going to interfere. If you do, you'll be doing it out here in public. I'll file a complaint against you for assault and false imprisonment, and you will lose. You'll be the federal agent who harassed a woman in a wheelchair. Oh, and one more thing: You try to stop me and I'll run your ass down." I pushed a button, and the window slowly closed.

He stood there for a long moment, glaring at me, then stalked away.

I pulled out, drove for several blocks, and pulled over. I sat back and breathed out all the excess tension before calling Marsha.

"I'm about two blocks behind you," she said. "Sink's not following."

"He may not have to, if he's bugged my van. But we're just going to dinner, anyway. And before we do that, let's get our favorite FBI agent to run that license number."

I called Hewitt, who agreed to run the license plate number of the blue van. He sounded shocked when I told him what Gary Sink had done.

"I'll be damned," he said. "Obviously something strange is going on with him, but I never thought he was flat-out bent."

"I don't see another explanation."

"I suppose that depends on who the guy in the blue van is. He wouldn't have to be working for Z."

"Do you have any other ideas?"

"I'll run the plate."

"Thank you."

"By the way, I did some digging on Alec Sellars's finances."

"Do tell."

"I didn't find any current employment."

"There isn't any," I confirmed.

"But he and Shannon are paying the bills. Nothing in arrears, no collection proceedings."

"Marsha says he's got a lot of overhead," I said. "How have they managed to stay current?"

"He's had sizable, regular payments over the past year from a consulting firm, which I'm still in the process of checking out."

"Consulting? Alec?"

"That's what the entity is listed as. The firm appears to be hiding behind a couple of shell corporations. I'm having trouble tracing it, at least without leaving a very large footprint."

"Don't risk getting in trouble."

He chuckled. "You mean more trouble."

Marsha and I sat outside at a fancy pizza restaurant on Hennepin Avenue in Uptown, not far from where we'd encountered Sink and his buddy in the blue van. The sticky weather made it feel more like Tampa than Minneapolis as sunlight forced its way through jagged cracks in the heavy cloud cover. I described my encounter with Sink at the lake.

"We find that van and we just might find Z," she said. "Maybe the driver was Z himself, but he looked more like a thug than a hacker."

"Hewitt told me something else," I said. I repeated what the agent had said about Alec's mysterious income from consulting.

"Please," she scoffed. "He's got the same odds of being an astronaut as a consultant."

"So what's going on?"

"Somebody is paying him secretly to do something secretly. But I don't have a clue what it is."

I didn't, either.

"Hewitt has given us a lot of help," Marsha said. "You think he's just a sucker for a pretty face?"

For a brief moment, I allowed myself to consider the possibility. After all, he had asked if I was dating anyone. And then I just as quickly dismissed the thought. "His career is in the tank, thanks to Gary Sink. His best hope of turning it around is to show that Sink is bent."

"And Sink certainly might be."

"That's a big yes. And digging into his actions on this case might be the best way to prove it."

"Especially if Hewitt is behind the scenes and we're out front, doing the heavy lifting."

"Exactly."

"I forgot to tell you," Marsha said. "I went to visit Sam Fenton. They've moved him to a transitional care facility for another day."

"Did you get in to see him?"

"I met his mother in the hallway outside his room. She said he's improved somewhat and will be going home tomorrow, but they still won't allow visitors other than the immediate family. She didn't tell me anything more."

"Can we talk to him when he feels better?"

"I wouldn't hold my breath. The mother was pretty ticked off at Kenny."

"And by extension, at us," I said. "Do you think either Susan Bjorklund or Mrs. Fenton are holding anything back from us?"

"From us, maybe. But I doubt they'd hold back from the police. If Sam said anything new or significant, I think Lieutenant Candiotti would have heard about it."

"Makes sense. Going back to your meeting with Sierra's mother, I'm still puzzled by her remark that Kenny was on the rebound from a relationship."

"So am I," she said. "Which brings us back to the mystery girl he was seen with at Subway, and the sighting at the coffee shop in Tampa. We can't know for sure they were actually dating in either case. It could have been just a friend from school. And as far as I could tell, he never really dated at all when he lived with me. He went to a couple of school dances with girls, but they went as friends."

"Another mystery." We finished our pepperoni pizza and sipped from our beers, watching the traffic on Hennepin Avenue.

"Mysteries seem to be all we have," Marsha said. "Hardly any facts."

I switched subjects. "Tell me about that doctor you're dating."

She smiled. "I think Nathan's the real deal, Pen. He may not be the flashiest guy around, but he's got character. Kind of quiet, but very sweet." She paused, then said, "We're pretty serious. We're planning on getting married, although we haven't made it official."

I reached across the table and took her hand. "Oh, Marsh. I'm so happy for you. That's wonderful."

Marsha nodded. "I just wish his kids were younger. They're really nice kids, but they'll be done with high school and gone in a couple of years. Nathan will miss them as much as I've missed Kenny over the past year—they both live with him. I'd like to have more kids, but I'm too old."

"You're forty—a little long in the tooth for a baby, but it's not impossible."

"According to the doctor, it's not going to happen for me."

"I'm so sorry." We were silent again, both of us thinking about Tracy and Kenny.

"I love your new look," I said, changing the subject again. "I'd like to check out whoever's doing your hair."

"Well, he does a hell of a lot better job than you ever did." I laughed, just a chuckle at first, then louder. She was recalling the times we played beauty shop when we were girls. I always insisted on being the stylist, while Marsha invariably got stuck with being the luckless customer.

Marsha began laughing, too. "Remember when Dad . . ."

By now, I was in stitches, and so was Marsha. She was referring to an incident when our father had walked into the room and seen Marsha in a chair with a towel around her shoulders. I stood over her with a pair of scissors, and locks of Marsha's brown hair littered the floor. Dad got upset and sternly forbade us from playing beauty shop again, but he wasn't fooling us. We could tell he was suppressing a laugh.

"It was kind of a modernist post-punk sort of style," I said.

Marsha wiped her eyes as her laughter subsided. "I had to wear a baseball cap to school for two weeks after that."

"I'm glad you can finally laugh about it. It's only taken thirty years. For the record, I'm really sorry."

"Apology accepted," she said. We both stopped laughing, and she looked into my eyes for a long moment. It was an acknowledgment of our progress in making a lot of things right. It took us back to a young age, before I'd become arrogant and she'd become bitter. A time when we'd been best friends.

Hewitt still hadn't called when I pulled into the garage underneath the condo building. I extended the van's ramp, swiveled around, and transferred to my wheelchair. Then I started across the garage toward the elevator and froze. Two men stood between me and the elevator lobby. I quickly glanced around the garage, which was deserted except for me and the two men. I fingered the little canister of pepper spray on my keychain.

The men walked toward me. I reached for my phone.

"Stay back," I said, fumbling with the phone as I tried to call 911.

"Good evening, Ms. Wilkinson," one of the men said. He was a tall figure, backlit by the lighting from the elevator lobby, and I couldn't see him clearly. "I'm afraid you'll find there's no cell signal down here."

I started to back up toward the van, but the ramp had already retracted and the door closed.

"There's no reason to be frightened," the man said. I could see him and his partner now. They were young men, athletic and erect, dressed casually. The tall one, who'd done the talking, had thinning hair and no chin. The other guy was muscular and sported a duck-ass haircut.

"Our employer would like to have a chat with you," Chinless said. "Would you come with us, please?"

I had a pretty good idea who the employer was. "What if I don't want to go?"

"We strongly encourage you to come with us."

I hesitated. The man who wanted to see me was, as far as I was concerned, flat-out evil. But I didn't fear him. And my curiosity was getting the better of me.

"How do I know you work for him?" I asked.

"He said to tell you that this time you'll be able to see your route," Chinless replied.

"All right." Only the man I had in mind would know that last time he'd had his guys pick me up, in California, it had been in a closed car, which didn't allow me to see where we were going.

"Give me a minute," I said. I composed a text to Marsha, which would be sent as soon as we left the garage. "Going to meet Osborne Hayes."

Chapter 35

The two guys pulled my wheelchair up so I could transfer into the back seat of an SUV, after which they folded up the chair and put it in the back. We left the garage and headed north through downtown. Last year, I had been driven to another appointment with Osborne Hayes, who at the time served as CEO of North Central Bank. He had been asked to postpone his retirement after James Carter, who was to take over as CEO, had been ousted in the Downfall scandal. At that meeting, we had reached an uneasy agreement, which obligated me to remain silent about things I knew, things that would have trashed Hayes's reputation. In return, Hayes had promised to leave me alone. That concession, coming from a man with his power, influence, and ruthlessness, wasn't trivial.

Since then, a lot had changed. North Central had completed its merger with Texas Columbia Bank and become Columbia Central. Dustin Blount, formerly the head of Texas Columbia, had taken over as CEO. Hayes, now back on the sidelines, was attempting to return to power by convincing shareholders to vote Blount out, and according to Blount, he just might succeed. I didn't know why Hayes wanted to see me now, but his interest raised the possibility that the Columbia Central proxy fight might have something to do with Kenny. I couldn't imagine how, which was why I was now on my way to see what I could learn from the once-again-retired banker.

I watched out the uncovered windows as the SUV crossed the Mississippi over the Hennepin Avenue Bridge. The skies that had threatened all day finally opened up, and big drops of rain began to batter the windshield. On the north bank of the river, we pulled into the garage of an upscale high-rise condo building. I remembered Dustin Blount saying that Hayes had never sold his residence in Minnesota, and this was apparently where he lived.

The guys removed my wheelchair from the back, set it up, rolled it up to the back door, and waited as I transferred to it. I followed them through the garage to the elevators. None of us spoke as we ascended to the top floor. I wiped my hands on my pants as I thought about meeting an immensely wealthy and powerful man who didn't like me at all.

The elevator door opened onto an elegant entryway. I handed Chinless my cell phone while Duck-Ass ran an electronic scanner around my body and wheelchair. Satisfied, the guides took me down a short hallway and began to open a door. They started to walk away, but I held up my hand.

"Not so fast, guys. The phone stays where I can see it." The last thing I needed was Hayes planting some kind of spyware on it.

"Our instructions are to take custody of it," Chinless said.

"Then you can take me back to the car."

The duo exchanged glances, and Chinless disappeared inside the door and returned a minute later, looking unhappy. "Come in," he said. He followed me in and placed the phone on a coffee table.

Osborne Hayes stood up from behind a large desk. A younger man sat in a leather club chair, off to one side. He looked like a younger, thinner version of the banker. Osborne "Skip" Hayes III, I surmised.

"Ms. Wilkinson," Hayes said, nodding briefly. He made no move to shake hands.

"Mr. Hayes."

"My son, Skip."

Skip didn't acknowledge me at all. Not even a grunt. I rolled up closer to the desk, beside the coffee table.

The banker stood for a long moment, hands in pockets, studying me. He was in his late sixties, heavyset, wearing wire-rimmed glasses. He still carried the aristocratic bearing of a scion of a prominent Atlanta family.

"You're making a name for yourself in California," he said in his gentle Southern drawl.

"What can I do for you, Mr. Hayes?"

He sat down slowly while looking out a massive picture window at the rain clouds that crossed over the Mississippi and the darkening Minneapolis skyline beyond. "You and I had an agreement."

"Yes."

"You're breaking it."

"How is that?"

"You met with Blount," the elder Hayes said. "You flaunted it. You didn't even try to keep it secret."

I suppressed the anger I felt at being spied on. "He asked to meet with me. I had nothing to hide. I still don't."

Hayes's courtly Southern geniality finally gave way. "Oh, please. You show up here a week before proxies close, meeting with a man who's trying to defeat us. What am I supposed to think?"

"So I'm supposed to stay away from anybody who dislikes you? Not only was that not our agreement, but it could get awfully lonely."

The little lines around his mouth tightened. "You and Carter are still an item," he said.

"So?"

"Is this about James? He'd love to take me down."

"Blount is a friend of his. But Dustin is his own man. James is busy running his own business. He's had no input at all into what happens at the bank."

"Which brings us to why you're here in Minnesota and why you're meeting with Blount."

I hesitated. None of that was any of his business. But he obviously wasn't going to let it go, and I saw no real reason why I couldn't tell him. "The reason I'm here is no secret," I said. "I'm looking for my eighteen-year-old nephew, who's been missing nearly a week."

"I heard the police were looking for him, too. Is he in trouble?"

"That's none of your business."

"You're right," he said. "I don't really care about your nephew. But then there's the matter of why you met with Blount. That's very much my concern."

"I asked for his help in locating my nephew. Blount is a friend of ours. I see nothing to indicate the Columbia Central dispute has anything to do with Kenny."

"Maybe Blount thinks it does."

"If he did, he didn't tell me. And that's not why the meeting took place."

"And the subject of the proxy never came up? You must think I'm a damned fool, Pen."

I sighed. "Yes, he asked if I could tell him anything that would help his cause. I told him I couldn't."

"And I'm supposed to simply accept your assurance at face value?"

"I'm telling you it's the truth."

"Not good enough." The words came from Skip Hayes, who spoke for the first time, in a high, peevish voice. "Your interests are opposed to ours. We have no reason to accept your word."

"I don't have anything more to give you."

"You should prove your good faith by helping us."

"How could I help you?"

Skip Hayes leaned forward. "You need to tell us what Blount's game is. What eleventh-hour surprise is he going to spring to put himself over the top? How is he going to slander us?"

"You think he would tell me anything like that?"

"Assuming he hasn't already—which I'm not willing to concede—yes, I believe he would. Blount obviously trusts you and Carter. You could go back and talk to him again, if necessary. Or you could pass along information from us."

"You mean misinformation. Lies."

The elder Hayes answered. "Consider this, Pen: We take care of our friends. Your nephew sounds like a very talented young man. Perhaps we could use someone like him at the new Columbia Central. We may even have resources at our disposal that would be useful in locating him."

I wondered if the Hayes "resources" included the mercenaries employed by SSI. "Spare me the carrot-and-shtick," I said. "I am not required to prove anything to you, nor am I interested in being threatened or bought off."

Osborne Hayes, Sr. shook his head in disgust. "Still perched atop your incorruptible, superior high horse. If you come to your senses, give us a call." He slid a card across the desk to me and turned away. I was dismissed.

The door to the study opened. I took my cell phone from the coffee table, collected Hayes's card, and placed both in my purse. Then I turned and rolled out into the hallway, where I was met by the two guys who'd brought me. The three of us proceeded to the elevator and then down to the garage. Once again, I transferred to the SUV's back seat. The door closed, but half a minute later it opened again, and a face appeared in the opening. Skip Hayes.

"Who the hell do you think you are?" he hissed. "You are a little person in the middle of a big, nasty fight, and you'd better figure out whose side you're on, fast."

I didn't respond.

"You think you can just blow us off? I'm here to tell you that's a really bad plan. A terrible idea. If you think Blount can protect you, think again."

I kept my mouth shut, as I'm occasionally able to do.

"Your agreement was made with my father, not me," he said. "I'm not bound by its terms."

"Then neither am I."

He slammed the door shut.

Marsha was waiting up for me when I got home. I filled her in on my conversation with Ozzie and Skip Hayes. Then we called it a night, and I rolled into the bedroom, where I called James.

"Hey," he said. "I've got somebody who wants to talk to you."

A half-minute later, James's thirteen-year-old daughter, Alicia, came on the line. "Pen, you'll never guess what we did today."

"Well, let's see . . . chasing UFOs?"

"Oh, ple-e-e-e-z . . ."

"Okay. I know—hunting for Bigfoot?"

"Pen . . ."

"All right, tell me."

"We went *surfing*."

"Extremely cool. A real California experience."

"Exactly." She went on to tell me how she and James had taken a boat ride to Catalina, played tennis, and hiked in the mountains during the last few days.

Eventually, after I promised I'd be back soon, she gave the phone to her father. "How's it going?" he asked. "Making any progress?"

"Some. It's getting complicated."

I could feel a chill make its way to me over the line from California. "'Complicated'? You'd better explain that."

I filled him in, trying not to go into too much detail, and in particular trying to gloss over any developments that might indicate danger to me. It didn't work.

"Damnit, Pen, you said you weren't going to get yourself into these situations. That you were going to be careful."

"I am being careful. I promise."

"That's BS. You're dealing with hackers, hoodlums, merce-naries. How long before somebody takes a shot at you?"

"You're exaggerating the risk."

"Am I?"

"I'm not doing this for fun. I'm doing it because it's im-portant. Because Marsha and Kenny need my help."

"How about Alicia and me? Don't we get any considera-tion?"

"That's not fair. And give me a little credit. I can take care of myself."

"Right. A guy sticks a gun in your face, and you can just roll over his foot."

"You're patronizing me."

"I'm pointing out that you have physical limitations that come into play, no matter how resourceful and careful you are. And you just had to do this at a time when Alicia is here. Other-wise I'd come out and—"

"I can handle this."

"Like hell. I—"

I hung up, steaming. He was treating me like some incom-petent woman, some helpless cripple.

I glanced at my screen and saw that two voicemail messages had come in while I'd been talking to James. The first was from Patty Mattison, the Philadelphia FBI agent who'd checked out Gary Sink for me. She had tried calling, emailing, and texting Lindsay Seiple, but hadn't gotten a response and was getting a little concerned.

The next message was from Hewitt. The license plate on the blue van had proven to be a dead end, having been registered to a Toyota Camry that had been reported stolen two months ago and had never been recovered.

I stared at the phone, stunned, as he summed up our plight.

"We're nowhere, Pen."

Chapter 36

Friday

Marsha was already at the kitchen table when I rolled out the next morning.

"Did you get any sleep?" I asked.

"Not much, especially after you told me about Hewitt's call."

"Neither did I." I'd been upset not only about Hewitt's news, but about my argument with James.

She got up, went over to the coffee maker, and poured me a cup. Setting it before me, she said, "Bagel?"

"Thanks." For me, it was always nice to be waited on, not having to reach over my head to the counter and fumble precariously with the dishes and utensils.

"What do you think?" I said. "What's our next move?"

She sat down as she waited for the bagel to toast. "I don't know. Without the van, we're out of leads. We have no other way to trace Z. We can't go after SSI. The police have done all they can. So, apparently, has Hewitt."

We sat silently. The bagel popped up in the toaster. Marsha went and got it for me. I began eating, and she sat down again. "Did you have any brilliant ideas while lying awake last night?"

"Not a brilliant idea," I said with my mouth full. "Just a desperate one."

Marsha waited as I chewed my food. "Nothing has resulted from anything the authorities have done," I said. "The only thing I can think of is to concentrate on what they haven't done."

"What's that?"

"The Russian angle. Sink, according to Hewitt, hasn't investigated any local Russian gangsters. It would be a logical place to look for Z."

"Makes sense. If you're Z, and you're coming to this area, and you're from a Russian family, and you're a crook, who would you try to connect with?"

"Maybe a scary-looking gray-haired guy, whom you could also use to babysit Kenny."

"Exactly. But how do we find these Russians?"

"By following the only genuine lead we have," I said.

"Which is?"

"The blue van."

For the next ten minutes, I explained to Marsha how I thought we could look for the van by checking out Russian-owned businesses to find one that might be operating as a front for criminals. Maybe we'd see the van. She couldn't hide her skepticism, but neither could she come up with any better ideas.

I retrieved my purse from the bedroom, saying I had some quick shopping to do, while Marsha got out her laptop and started a search for likely Russian-owned businesses. I left.

Once underway, I drove into south Minneapolis, then pulled over and parked on a side street. I called Ben Hewitt, who sounded as unhappy as I felt. He had received his new assignment, to Spokane, Washington, doing traditional FBI work such as bank robberies and stolen car cases, rather than counter-terrorism. It was a serious career setback, courtesy of Gary Sink. After hearing that, I felt bad about asking him to check out possible ransomware attacks on entities owned by Osborne Hayes and his family.

"Sure," he said. "Right now I've got nothing else to do. Except packing."

Next, I called Alec Sellars, who agreed to meet me at the coffee shop down the road from his house. I had lied when I'd told Marsha I had shopping to do. Instead, I had some confronting to do. I wanted us on equal terms, which meant getting Alec off his home turf, to a place where I didn't have to be pulled up steps. I had nothing specific to go on beyond a feeling that Alec had been lying to me. But it was a really strong feeling.

I waited in the back of the Caribou parking lot until I saw Alec arrive in his shiny Chrysler 300. After he went in, I kept him waiting for ten minutes, then entered the shop myself.

Alec sat at a corner table, a cup of coffee in front of him. I bought myself a caramel cooler at the counter and joined him.

"What can I do for you?" he asked, sporting his easy smile.

"You can stop lying to me."

He gave me a hurt-and-bewildered look. I suspected he used it a lot. "What do you mean?"

"Let's talk about your finances."

"My fi—what does that have to do with Kenny?"

"You didn't tell me you were canned from your job. You told me you were taking vacation time when I found you at home on Monday."

He shrugged. "Sorry. It's a little embarrassing to be unemployed, that's all."

I'd always considered Alec beyond embarrassment. "How are you paying your bills?" I demanded.

"We're managing. Shannon has a decent job, and, well, we're making it."

"Yes, you are. Let's talk about how. You've gotten large payments from an alleged consulting contract from a mysterious entity."

He looked flustered for the first time. "Well, there's nothing wrong with consulting."

"Alec, look at me. Am I wearing a clown suit?"

"You're saying I couldn't be a consultant?"

"Sure, if your clients are interested in how to spend money, gamble, lose jobs, and sit on their asses. Who's paying you?"

"I can't talk about that."

"You can and you will."

He sat up in a defensive posture. "Now, look—"

"You are going to tell me everything, or I'm going to have the FBI tear apart your finances and haul you in for questioning in Kenny's disappearance. You can talk to me or to them."

He gave me a skeptical look. "Come on. The FBI would do that just because you asked them?"

"Without hesitation. I'm a federal prosecutor, Alec. I work with the FBI all the time. How do you think I found out about the consulting payments?"

There was enough truth to my statement that he had to take it seriously. "I promised not to discuss this."

"Promised whom? And why?"

He cradled his coffee cup with a pained expression. "Look, this is sensitive, and it really has nothing to do with Kenny."

"I don't believe you."

After another minute of tortured deliberation, he said, "You have to promise not to tell anybody."

"I promise nothing, except this: If I'm convinced you've told me the truth, I won't tell anybody if I don't have to. But if you've lied about anything, or if I feel Kenny's well-being is at stake, the deal is off."

His expression sank. "All right."

He took his time, working up his courage, considering his phrasing, and drinking from his coffee cup. "The first time the guy called me was a little over a year ago," he said.

"You were still in Tampa then."

He nodded, and I felt chilled. This scheme, whatever it was, had been going on for a long time. "Who was the guy?" I asked.

"I don't know."

"Was it Z?"

"Maybe. He had a Russian accent."

If I'd felt chilled a minute earlier, I was frozen now. "What did he say?"

"He said he'd heard that I was out of work and that maybe a change of pace would do me good. He wanted us to move to Minnesota."

"Why?"

"I asked him, and he said I'd make enough money that I wouldn't want to ask any more questions."

"What did you say to that?"

"I kept listening."

I sipped from my drink, trying to absorb the magnitude of his deception. I'd always sensed that Alec had been lying to me, but I'd had no idea it was this serious. "Did you ever meet the guy?" I asked.

"No. In fact, I only talked to him twice, at least until last week."

"So what happened after the first call?"

"I mentioned the idea to Shannon. She was surprised but was very open to the idea. She didn't care for Tampa all that much, and for her, Minnesota was home. She knew I'd been having trouble finding a job. So I made some calls up to Minnesota and got a line on a job with Southdale Chrysler. After I'd flown up to interview and gotten the job offer, Shannon called her old boss up here—she'd worked for the guy at International Mills, and he said she was welcome back any time. So that pretty much settled it. We were ready to put the house on the market. Then the guy called again."

I waited.

"He asked if I'd thought about his offer, and I told him I was still interested. He asked what Shannon thought about it, and I said she was agreeable, and we were willing to do it if the price was right. So then he talked numbers. Big numbers. He said there'd be ten grand in my account tomorrow, and fifty thousand right after we moved. He'd follow that with a hundred thousand over the next year."

"And you didn't ask why any of this was happening?"

His response was grim and matter-of-fact. "We needed the money, Pen. I didn't ask questions."

"This was the last time you talked to the mystery man?"

"That's right, until Kenny went missing."

I decided to put that subject aside. "Did he say anything else in that second call?"

"Just one thing: Kenny had to move with us."

I felt sick to my stomach. "I don't suppose you asked why."

"Actually I did. It sounded weird; why would anybody want him in Minnesota? The guy said if I asked any more questions, the deal was off."

"But you understood the whole thing was really about Kenny."

"I didn't know for sure. But I couldn't see what else it could be about."

"What did Kenny think about moving?"

"He was torn."

"Was he concerned about missing his senior year in Tampa?"

"Not really. He didn't like school and never really fit in there anyway. He seemed to be making decent money doing programming work for a guy, and I said, 'You can do that in Minnesota, can't you?' He said he probably could. He blew hot and cold on it and argued with Marsha about it and finally decided he'd come."

"Did he know what was going on? That the move was designed to get him up here?"

"I don't know. He might have, but I never told him."

"So what happened after you moved?"

"Things seemed to be going okay," Alec said, studying his cup. "He didn't do great in school, and he didn't like the job at Subway. But he made a couple of friends and he started dating that pretty girl and he spent a lot of time on the computer, so I figured he was working for that guy."

"Was the guy named Z?"

"I don't know. I'd never heard the name until you mentioned it."

"You mean, when I mentioned it after he went missing?"

"Right."

"So tell me about that."

"It happened just the way I told you on Sunday. We came home and he was gone. There'd been a break-in, and the bathroom window was open."

"Then you heard from Z again."

"I told you, I didn't know if the guy was this Z or not. But it was the same man who was paying us, the man with the Russian accent."

"When did he call?"

"Sunday. He said Kenny was in danger and wanted to know where he was. I said I didn't know. So he said if I could find him, it would be worth some money to me."

"For heaven's sake, Alec." I was thoroughly disgusted. He hadn't been at all concerned about finding Kenny when Marsha had called him. Then he'd had a mysterious change in attitude, becoming interested all of a sudden. Now I knew why: He'd seen dollar signs.

"He's called a couple more times," Alec said. "But I haven't been able to tell him anything. He's starting to sound pretty pissed off."

"Did you tell him Marsha and I are looking?"

"Yeah. I couldn't tell whether he was happy about that or not."

Z's ambivalence made sense, I thought. He was happy that more people were looking for Kenny, but unhappy that he couldn't control us.

I took a long minute to collect my thoughts and drink my caramel cooler. "How much does Shannon know?"

He thought about it. "She doesn't know about the Russian. She thinks it was my idea to move up here. She knows

I'm getting money from somewhere, but I told her it was family money."

"And she believes that?"

He shrugged. "She hasn't asked for any details about it."

"All right, Alec. Forget what you know. Tell me what you suspect. It looks as though Z might have wanted Kenny up here. Why would he have wanted that?"

"I figured it was to work on a hacking job of some kind. I mean, that's what Kenny does. Why else would they want him? And I suppose there was no easy way to move him up here without his family. He was a minor."

It seemed like overkill—a huge expenditure—to move an entire family. But maybe the money wasn't a big deal to Z, who'd made a killing in ransomware. "Why here?" I said. "Why couldn't Kenny just work on it from Tampa?"

He shook his head. "Who knows?"

"Have you seen any signs that Kenny has met with Z, or reports to an office or apartment or workplace to do a job?"

"No."

"Do you have any hint or clue whatsoever what Kenny might be working on?"

"No, except that it must be pretty important, considering all the money they've spent."

"There are contractors or mercenaries after him, led by a blonde woman."

"You mean people other than this Z?"

"Yes. They're the ones who broke into your house that night. Do you know anything about them?"

"No."

"Has the Russian guy said anything else?"

"He's promised not to hurt Kenny. But . . ."

"But what?"

"But if we don't find him, he's promised he will hurt me."

"If you lie to me again, I'll be the one hurting you."

"You'll tell the IRS about the payments," he said.

"Tax evasion is just the beginning. I could think of about ten other charges if I felt like it. And believe me, I'd love to do it." I grabbed my purse, turned and rolled toward the door.

I left him staring into his cup, a study in total misery. Meanwhile, I felt as though I needed a shower.

I drove back downtown, furious at Alec's deception. But what made me even angrier was that I had learned so little that I hadn't already known or suspected. I was basically no closer to finding Kenny that I had been before Alec's confession. Hewitt had put it well: I was nowhere.

Chapter 37

Marsha was hard at it when I returned, bent over her laptop. She looked up. "How was Alec?"

I rolled over to the kitchen table. "How did you know?"

"You've never been able to lie to me, Pen. The 'shopping' story didn't make much sense, anyway. So what could you have been doing that you wouldn't want me involved in? Talking to Alec, of course."

"I'm sorry."

She sighed. "It's all right. It's probably better that I wasn't there. Now, what did he say?"

I told her, and I saw her doing a slow burn as I related all of Alec's misdeeds. When I'd finished, she sat silently, shaking her head.

"You seem pretty calm about all the lies," I noted.

"I'm used to it," she said simply.

We looked at each other. "We need to keep trying," I said, "until Kenny is found. We can't give up."

She nodded, and we turned to her laptop screen. "There is a Yellow Pages website for Russian-owned businesses," she said. "Turns out there are quite a few listings—over a hundred."

"The business we're looking for may not be listed."

"If it isn't, we're out of luck. But what can we do about it?"

"So how do we narrow it down?"

"I started by eliminating personal-services listings. Realtors, financial advisors, and so on."

"That makes sense."

"Then I eliminated several nationally franchised businesses. We can always go back to those."

"Okay."

"Then I crossed off those businesses that appear to operate in multi-tenant office buildings. Not multi-tenant strip centers or industrial parks. I think the odds on office buildings would be a lot lower. If you're moving stolen goods, or money laundering, or drug-dealing, or whatever, you'd want some privacy. That means your own entrance and parking. No common areas. No accountants and software guys in the next office."

"That's logical, too."

"That leaves us with about forty places to check out. Dry cleaners, liquor stores, travel agencies, jewelers—lots of different places. They're pretty spread out, too."

The more we got into it, the bigger the haystack seemed, and the smaller the needle. "Let's map it out," I said. We spent the next hour pulling names and addresses from the site and putting them on our phones. We split the metropolitan area roughly in half, divided by Interstate 94. Marsha took the southern half, while I concentrated on the north.

We were still working on our maps when Hewitt called.

"Yes, Ben?"

"You hit pay dirt on this one, Pen. Within the past three years there were serious ransomware attacks on two companies owned by Osborne Hayes and his family: a software outfit in Massachusetts and a real estate development firm based in Atlanta."

"Did they pay the ransom?"

"The real estate company did."

"How much?"

"We don't know. They weren't cooperating with our investigation, so we had to close our file on it."

"What about the other company?"

"The software company refused to pony up, and it cost them. They found all their customer information encrypted, and they couldn't free it. They were nearly driven out of business."

"I'll be damned. Now we have a good suspect for the person or persons who hired SSI to find Z."

"Yes, we do. Hayes has both the wherewithal and a motive to take the law into his own hands, to find Z and take him down."

"Absolutely. But there's a big question that still puzzles me."

"What's that?"

"Why now?"

I thanked Hewitt, and Marsha and I spent a few more minutes mapping our targets and dividing them up. By now it was after one, so we ate a quick lunch and hit the road.

By the time I had checked out a coin-operated laundry, a nail salon, and a used bookstore without finding the van, nearly two hours had elapsed. I realized the job was going to take a lot longer than we'd hoped, and began to feel the first pangs of despair. We were spinning our wheels, consuming valuable time, while Kenny was out there somewhere, on the run from people who were very dangerous—maybe killers. But I couldn't think of anything else to do. I called Marsha, who was going a little faster than I was. She'd checked five places without seeing the van. But I could tell she felt as discouraged as I did. We agreed to keep at it.

I had nearly reached my next destination, a candy shop, when it hit me. The blue van's stolen license plates had come from a Camry, which had never been recovered. Camrys often topped the list of most-stolen cars. I knew that to make a car disappear, professional thieves steal the car and strip it, selling the parts all over, especially overseas. The car loses its identity and disappears.

I called Marsha and explained. "I know what kind of facility we're looking for."

"Okay, what?"

"They're called chop shops," I said. "Usually it's some kind of auto-related facility, most often a garage or body shop."

I could tell she was looking at her list. "I've already looked," I said. "We've got three candidates. A garage in Shakopee, a body shop in Burnsville, and another body shop in Plymouth."

After a few seconds she said, "I see them. I'm in Bloomington now. I'll take that Burnsville location."

"And I'm closest to Plymouth. Let's touch base after we've checked those two."

"All right."

"Be careful, Marsha. Approach the place carefully and stay back. If we see anything, we call Hewitt right away."

"Got it. Good luck."

From north Minneapolis, I swung south to Highway 55, then to Plymouth, a western suburb. Traffic was light as I followed the directions on my phone's navigation app. I turned on County Road 6, crossed I-494, and eventually found my way to Highway 101. The B & A Body Shop was located about half a mile to the north, and then west half a mile on a side street. There were several industrial and older commercial buildings on the north side of the road. I slowed as I reached the address and realized it was a good place for a chop shop. The cinder block building was set well back from the road, surrounded by a high chain-link fence with barbed wire at the top. Cars were parked on three sides of the building and in a separate fenced area in the rear.

Of course, it could be a legitimate body shop, and my theory could be totally wrong. Or the gray-haired guy could have realized he'd been spotted, which meant the van would now be in a hundred pieces, on its way to a dozen destinations. But Sink hadn't known I'd have Marsha watching my back, and with any luck, his Russian buddy hadn't spotted us.

I drove past the building at a normal speed but couldn't see the van. A quarter-mile down the street, I made a U-turn and doubled back, much more slowly this time. There were several cars parked on the side of the street opposite the body shop, in front of a printing business. I pulled up behind one of them. Nobody seemed to be looking, so I pulled out my little binoculars.

I spotted the van almost right away. I felt a catch in my breathing as I stared at it. I couldn't see the license plate, but there was a dent in the front passenger door. It was the right van. It was parked in a row of four vehicles around the corner from what looked like the office door. I fumbled with my phone, ignoring three messages from Wade Hirsch and one from Cassandra, and managed to call Hewitt.

"Hewitt speaking."

"It's Pen. I found Z."

"Come again?"

"Or somebody working for him. We have a vehicle."

"The one I checked out?"

"Right. I found it at a Russian-owned body shop in Plymouth." I explained how we'd set up Gary Sink, identified the van, and found it.

After a pause, he said, "Good grief, Pen. How the hell . . ." His voice trailed off. After another pause he said, "I don't see any probable cause to go busting in there, Pen."

Unfortunately, I couldn't disagree.

"I'll be right there," he said. "I'll talk to the special agent in charge on the way and get clearance for a surveillance team. In the meantime, we'll get some people checking out the body shop and its owners. I'll be there in about half an hour."

"Thanks, Ben."

I hung up and called Marsha. "I found it," I said.

"Hallelujah!"

"How fast can you get up here?"

"It might be a while. I just arrived at the Burnsville location. That's probably forty or fifty minutes away. There's a lot of road construction."

"Hewitt is on the way, too. Just be careful. Pull up at the end of the block."

"Okay. I'll call when I'm about a mile away."

"Good idea."

A pause. "Unbelievable, Pen." She disconnected.

I looked back at the building. There was no sign of activity on the outside, and I couldn't see through the small set of windows next to the office door. To the right of the office were two large garage doors, both closed. Was this it? Would we find the answers we sought inside this dingy building? Was Z inside? Had he captured Kenny? And would Z's scheme be revealed?

I worried about being spotted. I was on the opposite side of the street, trying to blend in with two other parked cars. I was facing toward the highway for a quick getaway, but if I backed up any further away from the driveway, I could be cut off. I couldn't duck down in my seat. I was tempted to keep the engine running but didn't want the exhaust to be seen. All I could do was wait for Hewitt.

After ten minutes had passed, a FedEx truck drove through the gate and delivered a package to the office, but I didn't spot any more activity after the truck left. My heart pounded as I waited. Twenty minutes passed. Twenty-five.

Thirty minutes passed. Still no one going in or out of the facility, although three vehicles had arrived at, and one had left from, the printing business across the road. I was getting worried.

Thirty-five minutes.

Thirty-eight minutes after I'd called Hewitt, a dark, plain sedan cruised slowly down the street from the highway. I exhaled in relief. Hewitt circled, pulled up behind me, and parked. A minute later he was sitting beside me in the van.

"What can you tell me?" he said.

"No one in or out except for a FedEx truck, half an hour ago. I haven't seen any of the people inside."

He took out his own binoculars and scanned the premises. "Yep, there's the van," he said. "And now I can see the plate. It's the plate you had me run."

"So what happens next?"

"I've got people arriving shortly."

"Who will do what?"

He put the binoculars down and said, "They'll start the investigation and hopefully find some basis to raid the place. But we've got to keep this under wraps. Who have you told?"

"Just my sister."

"Good." Just then an SUV turned at the highway and drove down the street toward us.

"Your people?" I asked.

"Yes."

As Hewitt had done, the SUV circled and pulled up behind where we had parked. Instantly, three people got out of the vehicle and sprinted up toward us. A blonde woman and a black guy stood on my side; a middle-aged man stood on Hewitt's side. All were fit, alert, and armed.

"What's going on?" I asked. "I thought you were going to do surveillance."

"I'm sorry, Pen." I looked back at Hewitt. He was pointing a gun at me.

Chapter 38

I gasped, watching Hewitt as he held the gun on me. "Ben. What the . . ."

"Sink shouldn't have hosed me," he said. "He shouldn't have derailed my career. I'm not about to spend years languishing, doing donkey work in some backwater office. I'm better than that."

"And so you—"

"These people made me a much better offer. Working for SSI will mean interesting projects that will use my skills. I'll be based in DC and make a hell of a lot more money."

"All you have to do is betray everything you've ever stood for."

"What I stood for was a lie, Pen. I stood for a system that was fair, that was based on merit. Turns out it was all a sham."

"What about Kenny?"

"I made them promise me they won't kill him."

"They'll just torture him to find out what he knows."

Hewitt didn't respond. He took my phone off the dash. "Open it up," he said. I entered the code, and he grabbed it and checked the call log, verifying that I hadn't called anybody other than Marsha.

"What about me?" I said.

Long hesitation. He wouldn't look me in the eye. "That's not up to me," he said at last. "I'm sorry, Pen."

"And Marsha?"

That didn't even rate a response.

The woman shouted a command, and Hewitt got out of the van. He was instantly replaced by a fourth person from the SUV, a tall, geeky young guy who nonetheless looked at ease holding the automatic pistol on me.

The other three contractors, plus Hewitt, conferred in a huddle a few yards away from the van. I tried to keep my breathing under control. "What's your name?" I asked the guy.

"Carlin."

"Is that a first name or a last name?"

He just stared at me, holding the gun.

The four people outside the car ran back to the SUV. After perhaps half a minute, the vehicle roared to life and shot down the street and through the gate toward the body shop. It stopped about twenty feet from the front door that presumably led to the office. Everybody got out, and three of the people crouched next to the SUV, while the black guy ran in a crouch to the front door. He gave the handle a quick yank, to no avail. Apparently he'd expected this, because he slapped something onto the door jamb, which I assumed was an explosive charge, then ran back to the vehicle. I couldn't see anybody through the body shop windows or around the outside of the building. The four assailants waited, Hewitt in his suit and tie and the three contractors in t-shirts and black pants.

The charge went off, making a loud bang, and the door burst open a few inches, hanging ajar. The white guy was the first in, followed by Hewitt and the blonde woman. I spotted the black guy sprinting down the near side of the building, presumably to cover the rear or side. I glanced down the street; Marsha hadn't yet arrived. But when she did, she'd be driving right into a trap.

Carlin watched the action intently, his eyes darting back and forth, holding the gun in his lap, still pointed at me. I began thinking about making a move, but I had no chance. He had me point-blank. The alternative was to be tortured with a plastic bag, then killed. Was that the decision I now faced? How I wanted to die?

The shooting started almost immediately. There was a lot of gunfire, some of it from automatic weapons, but the sound wasn't as loud as I might have expected—maybe not loud enough to bring the police right away. I risked a quick glance at the printing business behind us, which showed no unusual signs of activity. Even if the police showed up, I wasn't sure how they would react to the situation, or how I would survive the resulting chaos.

The shooting became more sporadic and finally stopped altogether. Then a green van with tinted windows came around from behind the building and raced through the gate and toward the highway. This van, unlike the dented blue minivan, looked modern and powerful, a serious getaway vehicle rather than a surveillance van.

Moments later, three people came racing out of the building through the front door and jumped into the SUV. I looked hard but couldn't see who the people were. The SUV squealed out of the lot, giving pursuit to the van. I glanced at Carlin, who looked apprehensive as he fingered the gun. Perhaps two minutes later, his cell phone rang. He lifted it to his ear as he watched me. I could hear an excited woman's voice clearly over the phone.

"We think there are two people in the green van," she said. "You need to get inside and recover the computers, if there are any left. Are the police responding?"

"No," Carlin said. For the first time, I noticed a jack in his right ear, which was probably connected to a police scanner. "What about the cripple?"

"Just hold her for now. We want to find out what she knows."

I felt a chill make its way hesitantly down my spine as I thought about the plastic bag.

"But if she gives you any trouble, don't hesitate to shoot her," the woman added. "Get her van off the street. We'll dump her body and the vehicle tonight."

Carlin watched me as he listened. He knew I'd heard it all, and he didn't care.

"Oh, and take care of the mother when she shows up," the woman added. "Damn—we've lost the van! Turn here!" After a few seconds she added, apparently to Carlin, "Just get at it." The call ended, and Carlin replaced the phone in his pocket.

"Drive," he said.

"Where?"

"Up to one of the doors."

"Which one?"

"I don't care."

I started the van and drove through the gate. There were two windowless garage doors, and I picked the one closest to the office. I stopped.

"Closer," Carlin said.

I inched up to the door, and to my dismay, it opened. I glanced down at the ground and now saw the electric eye cells for the automatic opener.

"Inside," my captor said.

I drove into a large shop area, where three vehicles sat in various stages of disassembly, including one directly ahead of the space into which I now drove. The office was to the left, barely visible through a small window. I inched forward, trying to memorize as much of the layout of the windowless shop as I could. I put the van into park, and the overhead door closed automatically behind us. I was trapped.

"Get out," Carlin said.

I reached for my clunky keychain and pushed the button that lowered the vehicle's profile, opened the side door, and extended the ramp. When those processes were complete, Carlin got out of the van and watched me through the side door as I pulled my wheelchair off the rack behind the driver's seat, un-folded it, and transferred to it.

I rolled down the ramp, where the geeky operative waited for me, gun in hand. He pointed to my purse and said, "Leave it here." I placed it on the filthy concrete floor and was now without my phone. The place was poorly lit and smelled of dust, grease, and chemicals. "Close it up," he said. I complied, retracting the ramp and closing the door. "Now give me your key."

I gave silent thanks. After a day of facing one grim development after another, I had finally caught a break.

I held the keychain up toward him, and as he reached for it, I stuck it into his face and let him have it with the little canister of pepper spray.

Carlin howled. I sprayed him again for good measure, exhausting the canister. Then, while he clutched at his eyes, I rolled past him, around the front of the van, to the wall bordering the office, where I'd seen a row of light switches. I shut them all off, and the whole windowless place, including the office, went black.

Carlin cursed, and I heard the gun drop and hit the floor, but he'd be back in action within seconds. I didn't bother with the office. Normally it would be the logical place to escape the garage. But the door had looked heavy and metallic and would be a major pain to get myself through. And that's where Carlin would expect me to go.

Instead, I rolled forward along the wall, looking for another exit. I recalled a fairly clear path that went beside a car that was parked ahead of the van. I felt my way in the dark along the wall to my left and the parked car to my right. Carlin's cursing continued, but now a faint light illuminated the garage. The light shifted, waxed, and waned. It was a flashlight.

"Goddamnit, get over here, you little bitch!" he yelled.

I ignored him, continuing to inch forward as quietly as I could in the near-pitch blackness. I also ducked my head as much as I could, which, given my limited abdominal control, wasn't much. But Carlin probably wasn't seeing too clearly yet, and I made it to the front of the parked car and turned right. I immediately ran into something upright—a tray or cart—and made a noise. It wasn't too loud, but Carlin had to have heard it. The rays of the flashlight swung around erratically but were moving generally toward the office wall. The light was weak and diffuse enough that I suspected it came from a cell phone.

I flinched as the sound of a gunshot boomed through the shop. I couldn't tell where it had struck. I tried to extricate myself from the cart, and the whole thing fell over, causing a big metallic racket as it hit the floor. I scooted forward, across the front of the garage, where another vehicle was parked beside the first one. In a brief flash of light from the cell phone, I could see another door on the front wall, but it looked as formidable as the office door.

"You've got about two seconds to get your ass out here!" Carlin roared. "You heard Brit—I can shoot you if I feel like it."

I supposed Brit was the woman I'd heard over the phone. I made it across the front of the second car and turned right against the far wall of the garage. I fought off panic and forced myself to move slowly; despite the flashlight, I couldn't see much and didn't want to hit something and make more noise. I glanced back; the light was now over by the office wall. The rays had stabilized and were sweeping systematically rather than waving around wildly. Carlin had regained at least some vision and was following my path.

I flinched again as another gunshot roared from the direction of the van. Simultaneously, I heard a *clack* as the bullet hit something metallic nearby.

I paused to consider my next move and couldn't think of one. I was trapped in a fairly small area and could hardly see anything. I had no weapon. Carlin was closing in. With no plan in mind, I continued to roll along the far wall, alongside a pickup truck. I hit something and gave a little involuntary yelp. A shot rang out a second later, and I heard a clack as it hit the wall. It sounded as though the bullet had hit behind me, where I'd just been.

I ducked as best I could and tried to move forward, but I hit the unseen obstacle again. The object was below my sight line, toward the floor. A flicker of light swept across the wall behind me, and I could see what the object was: a body. I managed to avoid screaming.

The body blocked any further progress. Carlin would be on my side of the parked vehicle within seconds. I reached down as far as I could and felt the body. There were no signs of movement. I found an arm and tried to grab it. I couldn't. I managed to get hold of some fabric on the sleeve and pulled. The arm seemed heavier than it should have been, for a good reason. The best of reasons, for me.

I felt for the piece of metal that was entangled with the lifeless hand, trying to be careful with it. The light was coming across the front of the garage. In a second or two he'd be on my side of the truck and would have a clear shot. I tugged at the gun in the dead person's hand but couldn't get it loose, and I needed to avoid jerking it violently.

I glanced back. Carlin had reached my side of the car and swung the cell phone flashlight toward me. Now illuminated, I froze like a deer in the headlights. But he couldn't see the body, now behind me, or what I was doing. I waited for him to tell me to put my hands up and come out. But he didn't. He was seriously pissed and didn't care. He leveled the gun at me.

Frantically, I reached up and found the door handle of the pickup truck beside me. I threw the door open, shielding me from Carlin. An instant later, he fired. I felt a bullet hit the door. A second shot shattered the door's window, showering me with glass. I screamed and reached down again for the body's hand. No doubt about Carlin's intentions now.

I saw the light move forward, toward the open pickup door. I continued to try to work the weapon free from the dead fingers. *There.* The gun came loose. As it did, the pickup door slammed shut, revealing Carlin. I swung the pistol up and pulled the trigger, hoping the safety wasn't on. Hoping there was a bullet in the chamber. Hoping it wouldn't jam. Hoping . . .

Boom! The pistol was heavy, the sound deafening, and the recoil caused me to drop the weapon. It landed back on top of the body . . . and bounced underneath the car, where I had no chance of reaching it.

Carlin froze, and the arm holding the phone dropped to his side, pointing the light at the floor. He staggered backward slightly, bracing himself on the bed of the truck. Then he went down to one knee. Maybe I'd hit him.

"Drop it!" I yelled, hoping he hadn't noticed me drop the gun.

From a kneeling position, Carlin swung the gun up at me again but couldn't hold it steady.

Then he fell over backwards and lay there, motionless.

Despite my ringing ears, I heard a faint thumping sound from across the garage. I couldn't identify it and didn't have time to think about it now. I couldn't get around the body and had nowhere to go except back toward Carlin. I spent a minute carefully plucking as much glass as I could off my shoulders and legs. Then I took a deep breath and started toward him. He thrashed a bit, slowly, but didn't make any sound. His left hand lay over his chest, holding the cell phone. His right hand, still holding the gun, was on the floor. I wiped my hands on my pants and noticed my right hand was sticky. It was apparently bloody from touching the body.

"Carlin. Give me your phone and I'll call an ambulance."

He moaned but made no move to comply. I turned sideways as best I could, reached over, and managed to take the cell phone from him. Although the flashlight app was on, the phone itself was still protected by a PIN. I managed to make my way around him and behind the pickup truck, back to the van, and after a minute of searching, found my own phone in my purse, sitting on a fender. Carlin remained motionless as I called 911 and asked for an ambulance and police, watching his gun hand for any sign of activity. I told the dispatcher I was a federal prosecutor and asked that Lieutenant Candiotti be notified of the call. I asked her to speak up, since the gunshot still had my ears ringing.

"I show units already called to this location," the dispatcher repeated. "Has someone else called?"

I realized Marsha was probably outside and had wisely called 911 rather than trying to come in and find me. But I had to tell the dispatcher I wasn't sure. In response to her questioning, I told her there were probably no active shooters at the location.

I hung up, swung the cell phone light around, and saw the still-motionless Carlin. I felt uneasy, leaving him there with the gun in his hand, but I couldn't reach the weapon, so I retraced my route back toward the office door with the thought of getting out that way. For all I knew there could be other shooters—wounded or not—still on the premises, although everything seemed quiet. I found the row of light switches and turned them on. As I'd feared, the office door was heavy. I got hold of the knob, and after several tries managed to get the door open, brace it with one hand, and roll myself through with the other.

There was an outer office with two desks, a couple of extra chairs, and a filing cabinet. Disconnected cables were splayed across both desktops; the computers had apparently been taken away. An open door led to another office, which contained only one desk, a larger one. I rolled in and saw that a computer had been removed in here, too. I looked around. Was this Z's office? I couldn't tell. There were no personal trappings, but there was a lot of disarray, presumably from a hasty departure.

I rifled through a couple of drawers in the desk, and in one I found a cell phone. It looked like a prepaid disposable. I turned it on and noticed that it didn't seem to be password protected. I flipped through the call log and pulled up the number of the last call received. The caller wasn't identified, and on impulse, I pressed the Send button, returning the call. The phone rang twice before a male voice answered. A familiar voice. "Doug Lamm speaking."

I gasped and hung up. Why would a phone in Z's place of business be receiving calls from Doogie Lamm? I couldn't think of any innocent explanation, and I didn't have time to sort out the guilty ones.

Without really knowing why, I shut the phone off, wiped my fingerprints off the phone, and left it in the drawer where I'd found it. I'd let the police, or more likely the FBI, figure out the significance of the call when they got around to it. I left, and as I went through the door caught a hint of a smell that seemed familiar, but that I couldn't identify. There was no time to think about it.

I headed back toward the shop. And then I remembered the sound I'd heard in the shop area. I hesitated; I doubted that Carlin or any other shooters posed a threat, but there was always that possibility. Every instinct told me to get out, except a most powerful one: the need to help someone in trouble.

Back in the garage, Carlin still lay motionless. He might be dying, but there was nothing more I could do for him. Once again, I heard a faint thumping from the front of the shop area. I rolled toward the sound, which appeared to come from behind the door I had seen earlier. I rolled up to the door, which was secured by a latch.

I knew it was foolish to proceed any further, but I couldn't help myself. I rolled over, lifted the latch, and opened the door a crack. "Lindsay?"

A face appeared in the crack. It belonged to a terrified-looking, red-haired woman. "Who—are you?"

"I'm a friend of Gary's." It was a lie, but easier than explaining. "You're safe."

"You're sure?"

I could see Carlin's arm behind the car, still motionless. "Yes." I hoped I was right.

She pushed the door open slowly and came out, looking around. Behind her I could see a small room, heavily insulated, with a cot and sink. Lindsay Seiple looked disheveled and haggard. She glanced around, her face full of fear. "Where are the guys who run this place? The Russians?"

"Gone or dead." I hoped I was right about that, too. I hadn't looked outside. "The police are on their way."

"I need to call Gary."

I knew that might not be a great idea. But this woman had suffered enough. And so, it now seemed clear, had Agent Gary Sink. I handed her the phone.

Chapter 39

When the police arrived, I was briefly reunited with Marsha, who had been waiting outside, had in fact called 911, and was now disappointed that no clues to Kenny's whereabouts had yet been found. Before long, personnel from Plymouth, Hennepin County, and the state were fanning out over the crime scene. After a brief medical check, crime-scene officers tested my hands for gunshot residue. Then the questioning from Plymouth police detectives began, first at the shop and then at Plymouth police headquarters. They first had me run through the shooting in the chop shop. That process was straightforward, but reconstructing what had happened before I entered the shop was going to be a lot harder. I soon learned that the dead body I'd taken the gun from was Ben Hewitt. My stomach gave a lurch, but I managed to hold it together.

I wondered if I'd ever be able to process the incredible treachery Hewitt had engaged in, the twisted worldview that had allowed ambition to hijack his principles and sworn duty. By all appearances, he'd been a decent, helpful guy who cared about his family, and about misguided Somali youths, and who I'd thought might have even cared a little bit about me. But he obviously cared even more about himself. *What a colossal waste*, I thought.

Outside, behind the shop, police found the bodies of two armed men wearing work clothes. Z's soldiers, I supposed. There was, however, no sign of the gray-haired guy who'd appeared at Lake of the Isles. Carlin, whom I'd shot in the shoulder or chest area, was still alive and had been rushed to the hospital. A BOLO had been put out for the green van and the pursuing SUV, but I hadn't seen the license plate numbers on either vehicle. One of the techs mentioned that they'd found blood not accounted for by the bodies at the scene.

Lindsay Seiple was pulled aside for medical attention and questioning. I found out later that she'd been kidnapped and held for more than three weeks. Periodically, pictures of her would be texted to Sink, along with reminders to cooperate in finding Kenny while thwarting the search for Z. Medical personnel took Lindsay to the hospital for a more thorough examination.

Lieutenant Lexi Candiotti arrived shortly after questioning started, and after twenty minutes, she left to call the FBI's Minneapolis special agent in charge to tell him Ben Hewitt was dead and Gary Sink compromised. The local officers braced themselves; they knew a massive FBI presence would soon descend on the chop shop. I wasn't thrilled, either. I knew I'd have to repeat my entire story to Bureau agents. Ben Hewitt may have been a turncoat, but he'd been an FBI agent, and the Bureau would spare no effort in tracking down his killers, including, no doubt, a visit in force to SSI's headquarters in Virginia.

After several hours, I was taken to FBI headquarters in Brooklyn Center, a northern suburb, for further questioning. I told FBI agents everything I knew about the mercenaries and about Z, whom I believed to be using the body shop as a secure base, in cooperation with local Russian criminals. I just kept talking, trying to delay the time when, inevitably, the enormity of what had happened would sink in. The Bureau moved immediately to find the SSI contractors, knowing that they might well try to flee the country. They hoped Carlin would recover and give them more information on his accomplices. And, in an it's-about-time move, both police and the FBI agreed to mount a more serious search for Kenny.

The gray-haired man who'd watched us at Lake of the Isles and driven the blue van was identified as Stefan Fedorenko. He and an accomplice had fled in the green van, chased by the mercenaries. He was known to authorities in New Jersey as a Russian immigrant who'd been suspected of mob activities. He was also known to Minnesota authorities, who'd been puzzled as to what he'd been up to during the year and a half he'd been here. The police believed the other dead guys worked for Fedorenko. The FBI was doubtful, based on what they knew of Fedorenko, that he was Z.

And now I wondered, What *was* Z up to? I'd had time to think about the cell phone in Z's office, which had received at least one call from Doogie Lamm. I'd been afraid that Z, maybe with Kenny's help, was trying to attack Columbia Central. If he had, he'd hardly be receiving calls from Lamm. So now I had to consider the possibility Z had been working with the bank. If so, why hadn't Blount mentioned it? Or what if Z was working for the bank against Hayes somehow? And there was always the most disturbing possibility: that Doogie Lamm was secretly working with Z against his own bank. The police and FBI, who had found the phone, had asked me factual questions, not inviting me to theorize, and I had been happy to comply.

Marsha waited for me in the hallway when I finally rolled out of the interview room a little before midnight. She reached down soundlessly and embraced me for a long time. When we disengaged, she said, "Somebody else has been waiting for you." She gestured toward a nearby bench, where Gary Sink sat patiently.

He walked over, eyeing me warily.

"How's Lindsay?" I asked.

"Tired. Shaken up and stressed out, but no serious physical injuries. The doctors wanted to keep her overnight in the hospital. Eventually, she'll have to answer more questions."

"How did the Russians treat her?"

"It could have been worse, I guess. They slapped her around in front of the camera a couple of times, the bastards. They recorded it and sent it to me. I don't know what they planned to do with her when it was over. I suppose they would have killed her."

He nodded toward the bench where Marsha sat. I followed him over, and he took a seat next to her. He leaned over, elbows on knees. "I need to apologize," he began. "I said some things. I threatened you. I was—well, I guess 'out of line' doesn't describe it adequately. It sounds lame, I know, but I'm sorry."

I gave him the briefest of nods.

"We've been trying to trace Z for years," Sink said. "We'd been getting some faint indications that Z might have some kind of operation here in Minnesota, so the Bureau sent me out here for a few months to see what I could find out. I'd only been here a couple of weeks when the Russians took Lindsay. They told me to stop looking for Z. I did stop, but they told me to declare failure and go back to Pittsburgh. I tried, but it wasn't something I could pull off right away, so they held onto Lindsay."

"And then they told you to find Kenny," I said.

"Yes. They said there were contractors—mercs—looking for Kenny, and I needed to find him first."

"Kenny would have given up Z," Marsha said.

"Yes, he would have," Sink replied. "So would you, and so would I. When you're being suffocated with a plastic bag, you talk. Period."

Marsha and I looked at each other, fighting off panic and despair. Kenny was still out there. And so, as far as we knew, was Z.

"I got desperate," Sink said. "They were threatening to kill Lindsay and . . . to rape her. That's why I had to call Z when you said you were going to meet Kenny."

"Even though you knew he'd send a goon to snatch Kenny."

He exhaled slowly. "Yes. I'm sorry."

We didn't respond.

"And the whole time," he continued, "I couldn't tell anybody what was going on, and I had to risk using Bureau resources."

"You mean Hewitt."

"Yes. I didn't treat Ben right."

"No, you didn't. But that didn't justify his defecting to the criminals."

He nodded awkwardly. "I just wanted to say I'm sorry, and to thank you for finding Lindsay."

I wasn't sure I really deserved the thanks. It was Sink's own weird behavior that had allowed me to find Z in the first place. Because he'd told Z about the phony meeting at the lake, I'd been able to spot and trace Fedorenko, the guy Z had sent.

"I've tendered my resignation," Sink said. "But of course, it's not over. They've let me go pending the investigation."

"Your career . . ." Marsha said.

He smiled weakly. "Maybe my freedom, too. It was nice while it lasted. Of course, I had a duty to report everything right away. But I did what I had to do for Lindsay, and I'd do it again in a minute. I'm sorry, Pen. But thank you."

I wasn't sure what to say. "There are mitigating circumstances."

"Right. Mitigating." He got up and walked away.

I thought about the dilemma Sink had been faced with and wondered what I would have done in the same situation. What if someone had kidnapped James, put a gun to his head, and ordered me to throw a case? I honestly couldn't say what I'd do, but I hoped I'd be able to resist the path Sink had taken and avoid giving in to the extortionists. By complying with their demands, he'd let the situation spiral out of control. He'd alienated Hewitt, causing the young agent to cast his lot with SSI. And that had resulted in a bloodbath, instead of a properly managed SWAT situation, at the chop shop. Sink's motives were entirely understandable, but he'd been a fool to think he could trust the kidnappers, or manage the situation at all.

Still, what would I have done in his place?

Chapter 40

Somehow the authorities had brought my van to FBI headquarters—not an easy thing to do with the hand controls. Eventually we'd have to drive back out to Plymouth to retrieve Marsha's rental car, since she'd ridden over with FBI agents.

We got in. "Are you okay to drive?" Marsha asked.

I knew I was due for some serious downtime and recovery when I got home. It was now past one in the morning. "I'm okay."

"The guy you shot is going to make it, Pen."

"I know." I'd been lucky in several ways. I'd shot Carlin in the shoulder, missing most of the major organs and arteries. I was glad that one shot had been enough to take him down, since that was all I'd been able to get off. But given that, I was also glad that I'd dropped the gun; I'd have emptied the entire clip into him otherwise. And, of course, I was glad the gun had contained at least one bullet and had been ready to fire.

I started the engine, put the van in gear, and pulled away. We were about halfway back to the condo, headed south on I-94, when I slowed down abruptly.

Marsha looked at me with a worried expression. "What?"

I didn't respond right away. Instead, I pulled off an exit and into a parking place on the street, not far from Sam Fenton's house.

"What if Z were a woman?" I said at last.

She gave me a startled look. "Where the hell is that coming from?"

"Just humor me. What if Z were a woman?"

"But you were told he's a man."

"Who told us that?"

Marsha thought about it. "A woman."

"That's right." *But who really knows?* she'd added.

"But what makes you think it's a woman?"

"Perfume. A jasmine scent I caught on my way out of the chop shop. I just remembered where I'd smelled it before."

I pulled out my phone and called Dustin Blount. I wasn't surprised to find him awake and working during this frantic time leading up to the proxy vote. I asked him to track down a home address for me, and he obliged.

With Marsha navigating, we found the address Blount had given us in an exclusive neighborhood north of Lake of the Isles. I paused down the block from the address, looking up and down the dark, empty street. "Shouldn't we take the police along?" Marsha said.

"I think we need to talk alone. I don't think there will be any danger."

"What if there is?"

"I don't think our friend will talk to the police. Even if we wanted to bring the police, who would we call? I'm not sure who has jurisdiction. We'd have to explain everything, and we have no probable cause. This is between us and Z. We might have a chance. And we need to try now."

"This is awfully thin, Pen. It's all based on a momentary whiff of perfume."

"Then let's see if we can do better." I put the van in gear and inched along toward the house.

"That's it, up on the right," said Marsha. The house was a 1950s glass-and-brick structure, built in Prairie style. Lights were on in the lower level.

I pulled up in front of the driveway. A car had been parked haphazardly, its front end buried in a hedge. "It's green," I said.

"A green BMW. Good God, that's it."

It was indeed the same memorable color and make as the car that had been used to pick up Kenny from the Subway restaurant by the mysterious, tall, dark-haired woman who was somewhat older than Kenny. Who, I reflected, might be the same woman he'd been seen with in a Tampa coffee shop. Who might account for Susan Bjorklund's belief that Kenny was recovering from a breakup. Who: a) was a hacker; b) lived in Minnesota; c) had access to Columbia Central's systems; and d) had previously been in trouble with the law. And who had made a call from Z's office to Doogie Lamm.

Who *was* Z.

It had literally been in front of me all along.

I backed the van up, out of sight, and began the laborious process of getting out. Marsha helped me up the steep driveway and then up the short sidewalk to the front door.

"What's that?" I asked, pointing to a dark spot on the sidewalk.

Marsha leaned down, touched it, and looked at her finger. "Blood."

"Are you sure?"

"I'm a damned nurse, Pen."

We continued up the sidewalk, finding more dark spots. "There was blood at the body shop. They didn't know whom it belonged to."

We made it up to the front door. Marsha took a breath and pushed the doorbell. We could hear the chimes inside, but sensed no signs of movement. Marsha pushed the bell again. We waited.

"Try the door," I said. Marsha turned the knob and pushed it ajar.

I rolled closer. "Emily! It's Pen. Are you hurt?"

No response.

"Should I call 911?" Marsha asked.

"Let's check first."

I did a little wheelie up over the threshold, following Marsha inside to a dark entryway. A faint light came from around a corner to the right. I could see more dark spots on the hardwood floor in the entry. We proceeded slowly forward and looked around the corner to the right.

"Don't come any closer," said Emily Radatz, who lay propped up on a sofa, covered by a bloodstained blanket, pointing a gun at us.

"Emily," I said. "You've been shot. Let us call for help."

"No," she said, her voice faint but firm. Then her face grimaced in pain, but not from being shot.

It was a contraction.

Chapter 41

"You have to get help," Marsha said, phone in hand. "You've obviously lost some blood. The baby could be in distress."

"Put the phone on the floor," Emily said. "Do it now."

Marsha obeyed.

"Now kick it away."

Again, Marsha complied. The lighting was dim, and Emily had a blanket over her, but based on the location of the blood, it looked as though she had been shot in the abdomen, and possibly in the leg. I wondered if the baby had been hit.

Marsha glanced at the door.

"Don't," Emily said. "Stay where you are. Sit down on the floor."

Again, Marsha obeyed. I wasn't going anywhere, either, not without help.

"You must be Kenny's mom," Emily said to Marsha.

"Yes."

No one said anything for a moment. "Is Emily Radatz your real name?" I asked.

"No, but it will do."

"You said Z was a man named Mishkin."

"And the FBI bought it. I had no idea when I set up the Mishkin identity that it would keep them on a false trail for so long. That was the nice thing about being a woman—I could hide in plain sight. Nobody thought to look for a female Z."

It had in fact been Z who had received Doogie Lamm's call on the cell phone at the body shop. It had also been Emily Radatz, who'd regularly had occasion to talk to Lamm.

I said, "The part about being born in New Jersey, of Russian parents—is that true?"

She nodded, coughed, and winced as she experienced another contraction.

"Where is Kenny?" Marsha demanded.

"I don't know. I've tried calling him. He won't answer."

"Is he safe?"

"I hope so."

"Who are those people—those SSI contractors—who are looking for him?"

"Hired guns who are trying to stop me."

"From doing what?"

She coughed again, then managed a faint smile. "That's what everybody would love to know. It's my last project. I made a very nice living doing ransomware, but I needed one big score before hanging it up. And then a nice opportunity came along." Her features contorted from another contraction, accompanied by an involuntary grunt of pain.

"And you got Kenny to help you?" Marsha said.

"Not right away. I'd been working with Liam on ransomware for several years, although I never actually met him, of course. He told me I should hire Kenny, so I did. Your son was very helpful."

"You should have left it at that," I said.

"I know. But I didn't. From our interaction online, he seemed like an interesting kid. So after a few months, I Googled Kenny and saw a picture of him." She smiled again. "That's when I decided I wanted to meet him."

"Where did you meet him?"

"In Tampa. I finally decided I had to see the kid in that picture, so I went down there. I approached Kenny at a coffee shop. I didn't tell him who I was. I was just Emily, cyber security consultant. We hit it off, just as we had online. We were both interested in hacking, of course."

Marsha shook her head, her expression combining curiosity, dread, and disgust.

Emily ignored her. "For the first month I didn't tell him I was Z. By then I'd fallen hard for him. But I needed to get back to Minnesota. I had my consulting business here, in a nice out-of-the-way city, and had set up my hacking out in Plymouth at the body shop, hired Stefan and his men for security. That's when I got the idea to move Kenny and his family up here. By then, he was smitten with me, too. So I moved everybody up here, and everything went peachy until he dumped me for some high school girl. He dumped *me*."

"He recognized what you were—what you were capable of," Marsha said. "That you're a thief. Maybe a murderer, too."

"Yeah, I'm bad. You don't want to hear how I got that way—all the BS about my immigrant childhood, growing up around mafia types . . ." Her expression contorted again, and she gasped.

"Emily, for God's sake," I said. "You need help now. Think of the baby."

"Kenny is gentle," Emily continued after recovering. "He's decent. All the things I can't be. That's what I love about him. I couldn't let him go. And when he started dating that high school girl . . ."

"You got him involved in something dangerous," I said. "It got the mercenaries from SSI looking for him."

"He's not involved with the project," Emily said. "I could have used his help, but I didn't want to involve him. SSI just wants to use him to find me. I tried to bring Kenny in where my guys could protect him. I had Stefan looking for him. We had a guy go down and talk to Liam."

"Your guy—Waddle—did a lot more than just talk to Liam," I said. "He killed him."

"He wasn't supposed to. Just found Liam sort of semi-conscious—couldn't answer questions. Hard to find good help . . ." She winced and gasped again from another contraction. They were coming closer together, I noted. Marsha began to get up, but Emily waved the gun. "Stay," she ordered. She was fighting to remain conscious.

"Why is SSI trying to find you?" I said. "What are you up to? What is this big project?"

She didn't respond, so I stated the obvious. "It involves Columbia Central Bank somehow, doesn't it?"

Emily muttered something unintelligible, then, ". . . take them down Sunday . . . wipe them out . . . can't stop it."

"Why?" I said. "What is this about?"

Her eyes rolled back, and she dropped the gun.

Marsha got up and ran over to her while I called 911.

Chapter 42

I explained our emergency to the 911 operator while Marsha pulled antiseptic hand cleaner from her purse and approached Emily.

"They shouldn't be long," I said after I'd hung up.

"We don't have any time at all."

"What can I do?"

"Get some light over here. Then find some towels and scissors. Bandages if you can."

I found light switches near the front door and turned them on. Then I went over to a lamp on an end table next to the couch and pushed it over so it illuminated Marsha and Emily. The light revealed a horrifying sight: blood everywhere, and Emily lying semi-conscious, groaning in pain. Marsha had moved her sideways on the couch, gotten some of her clothes off, and was inspecting the situation.

I rolled frantically down the hall, looking behind two doors before locating a bathroom. I found a pile of towels under the sink and managed to maneuver myself around so I could pick them up. I didn't see any bandages. There might have been some in the medicine cabinet above the sink, but I couldn't reach it. I put the towels on my lap, rolled back to the living room, and placed them next to Marsha on a coffee table.

Marsha took a towel and tried to stop the bleeding from the abdominal wound. She felt Emily's belly. "The gunshot might have caused an abruption," she said, inspecting and maneuvering.

"A—what?"

"Abruption. The placenta separating from the uterine wall. That would account for some of the bleeding. Move that lamp around this way, will you?"

I moved the lamp forward on the end table so Marsha could see better.

"There's no way to know for sure if there's an abruption. We'll just have to assume there is." Emily let out a little shriek as she experienced another contraction.

"We can't wait any longer," Marsha said. "She's fully dilated, and the contractions are right on top of each other. Emily, you have to push."

Emily, lying motionless with her eyes closed, didn't respond.

Marsha shook her, slapped her once. "Emily! You have to push now!" She turned to me. "Find those scissors."

I took off for the kitchen. There were knives stored in a wooden block on the counter, and I could see the handles of a pair of scissors sticking out of the block, but I couldn't reach them. I looked around frantically, rummaging through drawers, without success. I glanced around the kitchen and spotted several garments in a dry cleaning bag draped over a chair back.

From the next room I could hear Marsha yelling at Emily. "That's it!"

Emily shrieked.

"Again! You can do it!"

I grabbed one of the wire hangers from the dry cleaning and tore it from the plastic, then slipped off the sweater it held. Then I took the hanger back to the counter, held it up, and after a couple of tries managed to yank the scissors from the block and slide them across the counter. I took the scissors into the living room, where Emily was screaming and pushing again.

"We'll need blankets right away," Marsha said, glancing over to me. "Just use those thick towels you brought."

"Got it."

"Do you have the scissors?"

"Yes."

"Okay. Just sit tight."

I waited. There wasn't anything for me to do now.

Or was there? I rolled over to the end table and grabbed an object I'd seen earlier: a cell phone. After a little maneuvering, using Emily's thumbprint, I got it unlocked and scrolled through the contacts. I quickly found the information I was looking for and emailed it to myself.

"It's breech." I looked up, startled. Marsha was leaning down toward Emily, covered in blood.

I peered over and saw the baby's bottom. "Oh, no. That's bad, right?"

"It's not great," Marsha replied calmly. She moved forward on her knees and reached inside.

"What are you doing?"

"The head is stuck. I'm feeling for the baby's mouth, to pull the head downward. Where the hell is that ambulance?" She continued to feel around. "Now," she said.

Emily moaned, managed to push.

"Again!"

"Be ready," Marsha said to me. I moved to the side and spread towels out across my lap.

Emily screamed and pushed again. I could see more of the baby.

"Again!" Marsha ordered. Emily's scream came out as an anguished moan.

And then it was over. The baby appeared, along with a gush of blood. Marsha quickly examined the infant, which had blue fingers and toes. Marsha tilted the baby over, checking its airway. "We're good," she said, massaging the baby's back. The baby sputtered, then let out a brief cry. She handed it to me, cord still attached. I glanced down; the baby was a girl. I wrapped her up tightly as she squawked some more.

"The placenta could come pretty quick," Marsha said as she reached over and expertly cut the umbilical cord and tied it off.

Sure enough—a few seconds later the new mother expelled a bloody mass. I looked away; I'd never seen so much blood in my life. Marsha went to work on Emily, trying to stop the bleeding.

I could hear the slamming of vehicle doors outside, and a few seconds later there was loud pounding on the front door. We both yelled at the paramedics to come in. When they entered, Marsha quickly filled them in as they took charge. One of them reached for the baby.

I looked down at the infant— pink, puckered, and still a little bloody and slimy.

And unimaginably beautiful.

I found I didn't want to give her up.

Chapter 43

When we arrived at the hospital, Marsha, still blood-spattered, went to talk to the doctors and nurses in the ER. I found a spot in the waiting room, where the universal hospital smell of burnt coffee invaded my nostrils. I pulled out my cell phone to call Dustin Blount. This time, he was sleeping.

"Yes, Pen?"

"Are you sitting down?"

"Lying down, actually. It's four in the morning."

"You'd better get all of your IT systems locked down, because Emily Radatz has been trying to pick your pocket."

"Why?"

"She's Z."

"You're absolutely sure?" He was incredulous.

"No doubt whatsoever."

"It was her all along? Holy . . . But I thought . . . Never mind, I've got to get Doogie on the line."

Less than a minute later Doogie Lamm joined our conversation. I explained how we'd identified Emily as Z.

"Unbelievable," Lamm said.

"No kidding." I felt like an idiot, and more than a little creeped out, knowing I'd been sitting right next to Z, telling her everything.

"Doogs, where does that leave us?" Blount asked.

"We'll have to do a damage assessment."

"There may not be time," I said. "She said it's going to happen Sunday."

"What's going to happen?" Blount demanded.

"She said she's going to 'take down' the bank, to 'wipe it out.'"

"How?"

"I don't know. That's all she said."

"Did she mean Sunday as in midnight, or some other time during the day?"

"I don't know."

"Are the police questioning her?"

"No. She was shot and is unconscious. Her baby has been delivered and is okay, but Emily may not survive."

After a brief silence, Lamm said, "I had her pretty well compartmentalized. Her access was limited."

"You didn't trust her?" I asked.

"I did trust her, as much as I trust anyone."

That would be *not much*, I thought.

"I was careful," Lamm continued. "When you give somebody access to our systems, you're trusting everybody who has access to their systems. Everybody they're working with or who may have infiltrated them. Mainly, we had her doing penetration testing."

"Trying to break in?"

"Right. She was doing it as an outsider. She gave us some valuable insights."

"But did she gain some insights as well?"

"I'm afraid so."

Blount cut in. "All right, Doogs. Assemble the emergency team right away. I've got to warn the Federal Reserve, Treasury, and the other banking regulators. If we go down, we might take the entire banking system with us. The stock market would tank for sure. Hell, the entire economy could go into freefall."

I hung up, went over to the desk, and checked on Emily. She was unconscious and in critical condition, having lost a large amount of blood. I was sipping from a cup of the burnt coffee when the police arrived. There were three officers—Lieutenant

Candiotti and two fellow detectives. In a family waiting room down the hall, I spent half an hour recounting what had happened at Emily Radatz's house and explaining the threat to Columbia Central. The detectives had recovered a computer from the house but found it encrypted and thus unreadable. They had also raided the offices of Emily's consulting firm and questioned the employees, whom they concluded were not involved in illegal hacking. At least one of Emily's accomplices—probably Fedorenko—was still at large.

I asked Candiotti if she could cut through the red tape to get the seized computer released from Evidence and taken over to Columbia Central. She turned to the other detective, a younger woman, who nodded and got up. "I'll get on it, Lieutenant." She left the room.

We continued for another half hour as Candiotti and her colleague asked detailed questions, trying to figure out where Emily fit into the cases they needed to solve. I noticed that the remaining detective, an older guy, seemed to defer to the lieutenant, who handled most of the interview. The questioning wrapped up at about 5:30 AM. The older detective excused himself, and I was left with Candiotti.

"How are you holding up?" she asked.

"Okay so far. I'm set for a major crash when we get back." I paused. "Those cops—I noticed how they treated you. They really respect you."

"I'm a lieutenant."

"It was more than that. It wasn't the rank. It was you."

She shrugged. "Most cops around town thought I got a raw deal. They can imagine themselves in the same situation I was in." She stood up, gathered up her notes and purse, and grabbed the door handle. "It's nice of them," she said. "But they don't get it."

"Get what?"

"I killed a kid."

I nodded. I did get it.

She left, and I rolled back out into the waiting area, hoping that the burnt-coffee smell would somehow revive me.

Ten minutes later, Marsha came out, wearing a set of clean scrubs that the nurses had thoughtfully lent her. She sank into a chair next to me.

"How are the patients doing?" I asked.

"The baby is in neonatal intensive care but is doing well. We believe she's about a month premature—not so bad."

"Thank God. How about Emily?"

"Touch-and-go. She's unconscious. One problem is that we don't know who she is—not even a real name."

"Both Emily and the baby would have died if you hadn't saved them."

"It was the trickiest delivery I've had in a while."

"So congratulations, Grandma."

"I suspect tests will show you're right." She leaned forward, elbows on knees. "You knew, didn't you? That's why you didn't want to bring the police to Emily's house."

"I suspected it, yes. That's why we needed a low-key, non-threatening conversation with her. We didn't need a big confrontation with a SWAT team. Somebody could have gotten trigger-happy and endangered the baby."

"Thank you."

"You're the one who really deserves a shout-out," I said, "and I see there's somebody here who wants to give it to you." I motioned with my head toward the ER door, where Kenny and Sierra were entering.

Marsha shrieked, jumped up, and sprinted for the door, enveloping her son in her arms. Sierra, too, received an embrace. Eventually, the trio made its way over to me, and Kenny gave me a hug, too. "How did you know to come here?" Marsha asked Kenny.

"Aunt Pen texted me."

"How did you do that?" Marsha demanded.

"I found the number on Emily's phone when we were at her house."

"Why don't you and Sierra sit down?" I said to Kenny. "We need to know what you know, and vice versa."

Kenny looked uncomfortable. "Maybe first I could see . . ." He motioned vaguely toward the ER door.

Marsha stood up. "They've been moved upstairs. I'll show you where they are." They started off to see Emily and the baby, leaving Sierra standing awkwardly next to me. I convinced her to call her mother to let her know she was safe.

Sierra walked outside and returned five minutes later. In response to my inquiring look, she said, "Mom is going to come down and pick me up. She was really worried about me. I hadn't expected that. I'm glad I called." Tears began to form in her eyes.

Sierra sat down next to me. "Did you know about the baby?" I asked gently.

"Yes. I know about Emily, and the baby. Kenny told me everything."

"Where have you guys been the last couple of days?"

"Kenny went online and found a homeowner offering his place for rent. It's one of those sites like Airbnb. Anyway, he got hold of the owner and made a deal directly with him, instead of booking through the site, so the transaction didn't show up online. We had to leave there today, because we'd run out of money."

We chatted for a few more minutes before Marsha and Kenny returned. Both looked excited from seeing the baby, but apprehensive about Emily and about what would happen next. They sat down across from us. "Kenny," Marsha said, "did you have any idea who you were dealing with?"

"Not at first. I thought Emily was just a nice girl who was into hacking."

"You'd never met her before that encounter in the coffee shop in Tampa?"

"Not in person. I'd been working with Liam and with Z for more than a year on some hacks. The hacks weren't really that big a deal . . ."

"Don't worry about what you've done," Marsha said. "Be honest, and we'll deal with it later. This is critical."

"Yeah, we held up some companies. Ransomware. Liam told me we were working for a guy named Z. When Emily dropped the bomb on me, told me she's Z, I'd never been that shocked in my life. I was spooked. But by then, well . . ."

"You were in love."

He flushed. "I thought so, I guess." He couldn't look at Sierra, and neither could I.

"What happened next?" I asked.

"We moved up here. But before long, I could see that living with Dad was a mistake, and that being with her was an even bigger mistake." He shifted uncomfortably in the hard hospital chair. "I was attracted to her because she was pretty, and she was strong, and confident—older, you know. I was flattered. I was confused. I didn't realize until too late what she was. She was mixed up with bad people. She hired bad people. She had Stefan, that scary Russian goon, trailing me around."

"That would be Stefan Fedorenko, the gray-haired guy?"

"Right. Anyway, early this year Emily told me about the baby and said she was going to keep it. I said I'd take my share of responsibility for it, somehow. But I couldn't go on with her. And I'd met Sierra—she understood about the baby. She understands a lot of things."

Sierra grabbed his hand but didn't say anything.

"That's when Emily turned nasty," he continued. "She kept calling me, had Stefan watching me, and hassled me online. And then last week Liam told me that people were watching him. He warned me to get away somewhere, so I got ready to run. Then they killed him. I thought it was probably Emily who had him killed and was after me, but now I'm not so sure. I don't know who it was."

"Both sides were after you," Marsha said. "Both Emily and the people who were after *her*. Emily's guy killed Liam, but Emily may not have wanted that to happen."

"Kenny," I said, "what was Emily up to? We know she's trying to take down Columbia Central Bank somehow."

His face registered nothing but surprise and confusion. "Really? That's a lot bigger company than she normally goes after. Banks are tough to hack. And she usually just plants ransomware. She doesn't try to cripple the company unless they won't pay."

Marsha and I looked at each other. Kenny obviously didn't know about Z's last, biggest project. "Do you know anything about how she operates?" I asked. "Anything that might be useful in figuring out what she's done?"

"Sure. Like I said, I did quite a bit of work on ransomware projects for her. Nothing like taking down a bank, but I know a lot of her favorite tricks, and I'd know where to look for malware."

"Get over to Columbia Central right away," I said. "I'll call the CTO over there and let him know you're on the way and will help if you can. Tell them you're there to see Mr. Lamm on the thirty-seventh floor."

"Got it. It would be nice to be able to help." He and Sierra left.

I called Doogie Lamm, got his voicemail, and told him Kenny was on the way to help. Then I turned to Marsha. "We should get going."

"Sure. Just give me a couple of minutes."

She disappeared, and I smiled to myself. She wanted another look at the baby.

Chapter 44

It was evening by the time we reached the Columbia Central building. Marsha and I had been able to get a shower, a meal, and a few hours' sleep, but Kenny had spent the entire day with Doogie Lamm and his team, working frantically to find the malware planted by Emily Radatz. It felt strange to enter the building where I'd once worked. A tsunami of bad memories hit me as I ascended in the elevator toward the executive floor. On impulse, I hit the elevator button for the thirty-fourth floor. As the doors slid open, I glanced through the opening onto the area where I'd once worked. It was here that I'd been torpedoed by the corporate sabotage scheme called Downfall a year and a half ago. I took a long look at the big cubicle farm, quiet and dark on a Saturday evening. I swallowed my bad memories and retreated into the elevator.

Marsha and I proceeded to the executive level on thirty-seven. In the main reception area, Dustin Blount's assistant intercepted us and ushered us down the hall toward a conference room. Blount came outside to talk to us in the hallway, looking as though he hadn't slept in days. He probably hadn't. "We've been hunting everywhere for this bomb Emily planted in the system," he said, "but we've gotten nowhere. We've patched in a second team, located at our IT-Ops Center."

"That's that big building down by the University of Minnesota?" I asked.

"Correct. You said this was supposed to hit on Sunday, right?"

"That's what Emily told me."

"That's about right. The voting takes place at the annual meeting on Friday. And four days is about right for the bad publicity about our systems breach to really take hold and sway the votes." He lowered his voice. "After the merger, we flunked the government's financial stress test for large banks. We don't have enough capital to withstand this kind of hit. The shareholders could be wiped out. And the rest of the economy . . ." He sighed heavily. "Come on in."

In the conference room a disheveled team, led by Doogie Lamm, was working feverishly. A video screen on the opposite wall displayed another conference table, at which the second team was seated. Also seated at our table was a detective from the Minneapolis police. And seated next to him was Kenny, who gave us a quick wave. All the participants had at least one computer on the table in front of them. Papers, coffee cups, food wrappers, and soda cans were strewn everywhere. Marsha and I sat along a back wall, away from the table.

Lamm saw us, came over, and sat down.

"How is it going?" I asked.

"We haven't found it yet," he said in a quiet voice. "As you know, we're facing the ultimate nightmare: an inside job. The threat is also somewhat different from what we expected. We've always concentrated our defenses against thieves trying to steal money. This attack may involve more than that. We've put less emphasis on the threat of somebody trying to just trash the bank. Z's specialty was ransomware, which mostly targets companies a lot smaller than ours, with defenses less sophisticated than ours. But we shouldn't underestimate her—she's good."

"Who's the detective?" I asked.

"His name is Shriver. He and his team have been able to partially decrypt the laptop they seized at Emily Radatz's house. We're still analyzing it." He paused. "Pen, can you tell us anything more about the timing of the threat?"

"She said it would happen Sunday."

"But she didn't give any indication of what time specifically?" I shook my head.

He nodded. "Thanks." He returned to the table and announced, "Okay, people. As far as the deadline goes, we know it's Sunday, but we still don't know anything more. So, theoretically, it could go off at 12:01 AM Sunday. That's five hours and twenty-six minutes from now."

"Or," somebody from the remote center said, "it might activate at 11:59 PM tomorrow, just before the beginning of the workweek."

"Or anytime in between," Dustin Blount pointed out.

"We'll have to assume the worst," Lamm said. "We'll have to work flat-out and hope to hell our deadline isn't midnight." He turned to a woman at the table. "Nancy, has your team come up with anything from analyzing Emily Radatz's penetration testing for us?"

"Not so far," the woman replied. "She basically learned where we're weakest."

Lamm gestured toward a young man at the table. "Ray, we might as well start re-analyzing all of Emily's accesses."

"Already on it, Doogs."

"We can do that for what it's worth," said a man on the remote screen. "But that's not the answer, Doogie."

"Hell, I know that," Lamm said testily. "Once the hacker is in, it's hard to believe anything the system tells you. You can't trust the access logs."

An older woman said, "That's why nobody detected the exploit. Once she was in, she erased any record of her entry—covered her tracks."

"She programmed the system to lie to us," Lamm agreed. "But we have to start somewhere." He turned to Kenny. "You're up, young man. We know Z got in. Now, where did she go?"

I looked at Marsha, and she nodded. Our presence didn't seem to be needed; apparently Blount had admitted us as a courtesy. We'd be unlikely to understand much of what we would see and hear. We headed for the door, telling Blount on the way out that we'd be nearby if we were needed. We waited in the reception area, saying little.

Marsha's voice woke me up. I opened my eyes; she was talking to Kenny, who was apparently taking a break. It was 11:06 PM.

"How's it going?" I asked.

"Nothing yet," he said, rubbing his eyes.

"What if it's set to go off at midnight?" Marsha asked.

"Then we're screwed, because there's no way we'll find it and get it safely removed by then." He sipped an energy drink from a tall can.

"When you find it, how much time will you need?"

He sighed and swallowed the rest of his drink. "I guess we'll find out." He stood up. "I have to get back in there."

Chapter 45

Sunday

There was no going to sleep now. We sat silently. My right foot, which I couldn't actually feel, was doing a furious phantom fidget. I tried to avoid checking my watch too often. Dustin Blount went in and out of the room frequently, spending a lot of time on the phone in an adjacent office. Coffee had been brought in.

Midnight came and went. At 12:20 AM, Kenny came out. "It wasn't midnight," he said and returned to the conference room. I dozed a couple of times during the next few hours, but I was awake when Kenny returned at 5:31.

"We found it," he announced, sitting down next to us.

We sat up. "Just now?" I asked.

"No, about an hour and a half ago. It was set to go live at 5:00 AM. It was slipped in with a routine batch of tasks relating to new accounts."

"What would it have done?"

"We're still analyzing it," he said. "But it was a multi-pronged bug. It would have transferred millions of dollars out of the bank. It would have encrypted thousands of data files, including customer information. It would have erased thousands of other files and spread to the backup sites to erase them there, too. It would have disabled servers and switched off dozens of processes needed to run the system, with no easy way of turning them back on."

"What a mess," Marsha exclaimed.

"Mess" didn't adequately describe it, I thought. The bank could have been bankrupted, its reputation trashed, thousands of employees laid off, its management disgraced, its stock worthless, with the risk of taking the rest of the banking system down with it. Everything associated with Columbia Central Bancorp would have gone into freefall. And the cleanup would have been presided over by its new chairman and savior, Osborne Hayes.

"So you've got it all removed?" I asked.

"No, no. We think we've managed to deactivate it. But it will take a lot of time to remove everything and get it totally out of the system. We still haven't found every place the code was inserted, or everything it was supposed to do. We'll need to run a lot of tests." He looked at his mother. "I have to go back in."

Marsha nodded, and we both exhaled in relief.

At 5:54 AM, Dustin Blount, in shirtsleeves with tie askew, walked out and sat down across from us. "It's over."

"Kenny told us," I said.

"Kenny pointed us in several possible directions for the search. Fortunately, one of them panned out. Emily was right; it would have destroyed us."

"I'm glad Kenny was able to help," Marsha said.

Blount, stubbly with bloodshot eyes, responded with a faint smile. "Doogie offered him a job on the spot. But Kenny politely declined—said he's going to college." He stood up and shook both our hands. "I can't thank you enough."

"Dustin," I said, "could we talk privately for a minute?"

"Sure." Marsha gave me a quizzical look as I left, following Blount to a conference room down the hall from his office.

He sat down. "What can I do for you?"

"First of all, congratulations. You're going to win the proxy fight. With less than a week left, Hayes hasn't gotten the boost he needs."

"Thank you for helping to make it happen."

"Here's what I'd like you to do, Dustin: After the vote at the annual meeting, I'd like you, within a week, to line up a competent, trustworthy successor, and then resign."

His expression didn't change. He didn't try to act bewildered or outraged. He knew I knew.

"You hired the SSI mercenaries," I continued. "You didn't trust your own people or the authorities to thwart Z. You took the law into your own hands. The FBI will be investigating the entire incident, and eventually they should be able to prove your involvement. Your motive is obvious. But the investigation could take a while."

Blount leaned forward, clasping his hands together on the conference table. "I was desperate, Pen. I knew Hayes was coming after us."

"Whoa—wait a minute. *Hayes* hired Z?"

Blount nodded.

"But Z attacked two of his companies—almost sent one of them into bankruptcy."

"True. But he saw what she could do. He admired her work. And he hired her to go after us."

"It would have ruined the bank."

"True, but it would have ruined me, too. And elected him. He was on a mission, Pen. He didn't mind inheriting the *Titanic* as long as he was captain."

What kind of man, I wondered, would be willing to ruin a company so that he could run it?

"He'd blame it all on me, anyway," Blount continued. "And I knew how he'd come after us. Our IT systems are fragile. They're still coming together after the merger of North Central and Texas Columbia. We had to use a lot of patches and workarounds to make them function. Doogie was working like hell, trying to plug all the holes, but there just wasn't enough time. I was desperate. What I did was in the interest of shareholders. It was self-defense."

"It was criminal. By hiring those thugs, you became an accessory to Liam Blankenship's murder, and to the attacks on Sam Fenton, Sierra Bjorklund, and Glenn Walsh, in addition to the shooting of Emily Radatz and killing of the two Russians at the body shop. You're an accessory to the bribery and death of Special Agent Ben Hewitt. You also put my nephew in danger. You crossed the line. You should have left it to the authorities."

He didn't respond.

"There's one thing I don't understand, though," I said. "Tell me how you knew it was Z."

He hesitated, then said, "It began four months ago. We knew Hayes was going to make a run at us, and we were nearly certain it would be through our IT systems. I hired SSI to do a threat assessment. Nothing more. After looking at it for a couple of weeks, they agreed we were vulnerable. But they didn't know who Hayes had hired to do the job. I told them to investigate and find out. Two months ago, they came back with the conclusion that it was almost certainly a hacker named Z, who had the capabilities, was known to Hayes, and had been out of public sight for a year. I told them to find Z and put him out of business."

"Why didn't you just go to the authorities?"

"We have our sources. We knew the FBI wasn't doing its job to find Z. That FBI agent—Sink—was inactive and incompetent to the point of criminality. We were running out of time. We had to take matters into our own hands."

"What did SSI do next?"

"They kept working on it. It didn't look like they were going to succeed. But then, two weeks ago, they got a break. They told me they'd identified Z's former right-hand man in Florida and knew approximately where he was."

"Liam Blankenship."

"If you say so. SSI said that to confirm Z was working against us, and to actually locate him, they'd have to move the case from their cyber department to their operational wing."

"You knew what that meant?"

"I could guess. Operatives. Strong-arm people of some type."

"Strong-arm—" I sputtered. "They *tortured* people. They got Liam killed. They would have done the same to Kenny, and to me."

"We never guessed they'd be so violent. But they did the job. They confirmed Z was working for Hayes, and they traced him—her—up here to Minnesota. And for all the money I paid them, it was you, not SSI, who found her."

"Dustin, you are so far out of line . . . you have to resign."

His features hardened. "None of this is for you to decide. It's not your business."

"It became my business when you put my nephew in the line of fire, and when I saved you from being thrown out of here on your ass."

"Don't be rash, Pen. If you try to take me down, I'll take Kenny with me."

"Kenny has no exposure. He was not involved in this scheme. He may have worked with Z on prior ransomware projects, but there's no proof. The only witnesses would be Liam and Emily."

He stood up. "I think we're done here, Pen. I'm not going anywhere, and there's nothing you can do to change that."

I didn't move. "You're used to giving orders, Dustin. Now, I know it's inconvenient as hell, but I don't work for you. Here's the deal: You give me your word right now that you'll resign. If you don't, I'll leave here and call a press conference. I'll start by telling everybody about this near-miss with your systems, which will raise questions about your competence. I'll bet you were hoping to keep that under wraps, at least until the election is over, weren't you? But, as I said, I don't work for you, and I haven't signed any confidentiality agreement. I'm free to tell anybody anything. And when I do, the proxy fight just might get a little more interesting."

He didn't respond.

"And then I'll tell everybody you're under investigation for hiring SSI, after which I'll detail all the havoc they've caused. I think that will throw the outcome of the proxy contest back into doubt, whatever comes out about Hayes in the next few days."

"So I get the axe and Hayes gets off scot-free?"

"He hired Z to sabotage the bank, and for that, the Feds should get him eventually, just as they'll get you. By the way, if you double-cross me and don't resign, I'll call my press conference next week. After that, there would be lawsuits to overturn the proxy vote and throw you out, but I suspect your own board would take care of that. You're going to have to answer for this, Dustin. But you're an old friend and ally of James, and, God help me, I'm giving you the chance to resign now."

He sat for perhaps two minutes, staring alternately at me and at the wall, his face giving away nothing. Then he got up. "Have it your way. But if I were you, I'd watch my back in the years to come. For both Hayes and me. We don't forget."

Chapter 46

Marsha decided to wait with Kenny to clear up some final details, so I headed back to the condo for some desperately-needed sleep. After rolling across 7th Street, where I'd parked in a ramp, I retrieved the van and wound my way down to the exit, paid, and left. It took me less than five minutes in light Sunday morning traffic to reach the south end of Nicollet Mall, where I entered the condo building's underground garage. I pulled into a handicapped spot, shut the engine off, and sat for a long moment, collecting my thoughts. It was finally over. Now I had to go back to LA and try to salvage my career. My relationship with James also needed some mending.

I had opened the side door, unbuckled my seatbelt, and swiveled around, reaching for my wheelchair, when I was stopped cold. I gasped, frantically searching around for my phone, but it was too late. Stefan Fedorenko had stepped in through the side door and was pointing a pistol at me.

"What do you want?" I managed to ask.

"Money."

"I don't have any money."

"But Osborne Hayes does. He has my money. And you're going to help me get it." Fedorenko spoke calmly, in a heavy Russian accent. "Let's go."

With Fedorenko crouching behind me, holding the gun, I fastened my seatbelt, restarted the engine, and backed out of the parking space. Then I drove through the garage to the exit.

"Where do you want me to go?" I asked.

"Turn left." We headed for Hennepin Avenue, where he instructed me to turn right. He continued to give directions as we wove north through downtown, past Target Field. Finally we pulled into an alley in the North Loop, near the river.

"Stop here."

I put the van back in gear.

"Shut the engine off."

I obeyed. I glanced out the windows; the alley was empty.

"Here's what's going to happen," Fedorenko said.

I started to turn around. "Look—"

"Shut up and turn around."

I did.

"Here's the deal," he continued. "Mr. Osborne Hayes has stiffed us. He claims we didn't hold up our end of the deal. We got everything set up to do the job. The things that happened along the way—the mercenaries, the kid escaping—nobody could predict any of that. It wasn't our fault. Emily did the work. She deserved to get paid. I deserve to get my share. And I will."

I gripped the steering wheel with shaking hands. "What does any of it have to do with me?"

"*You* . . ." I felt the gun barrel on the back of my neck. "You are lucky I haven't just shot you. I was planning on it. But then I realized I could use you." He leaned closer, his breath hot on my neck. "You set me up, you little bitch. You led Sink and me into a trap at Lake of the Isles. You brought the mercs to my shop. *My* shop. Where they shot Emily and killed my men." He punched me in the side of the face. Pain exploded in my head as it banged against the side window.

I tried to clear my throbbing head and focus as he continued in an angry voice. "Don't play stupid. It's all about you. Emily and I knew you were trouble the day you came here. I was going to shoot you. But Hayes told us no. He said he wanted you alive. We knew why, of course. You have something on him. Hayes was afraid you had it buried somewhere and it would come out if you died."

So that's why I was still alive. Emily, with her formidable brainpower, had figured it out.

"Guess what?" Fedorenko said. "I don't give a shit if more stuff comes out about Hayes. But he does. And so you can talk to him, to convince him."

"Convince him to do what?"

"To send his son out of his condo building and get into this vehicle with you."

"Why?"

"Because I'm going to snatch the son until I get paid."

"Why would Skip agree to come out and get into a vehicle with me?"

"Because you're you, not me. They don't fear you—only what you know."

"But how do I—"

"That's your problem. You'll think of something. Be creative."

"Why don't you just wait for him to come out and then grab him?"

"I don't have time. They're holed up in that building, dodging the media. Meanwhile, the police are looking for me. I need to get paid and leave. You can get him out of that building and into a vehicle."

It was a simple plan, bold and desperate. I took deep breaths. "Why should I help you? You're going to kill me anyway."

I saw him smile in the rearview mirror. "Now, why would I do that? I'm a good guy. I've just got a thing about getting paid, that's all."

He hadn't actually denied an intent to kill me, I noticed. I'd been listening for any reassurance, however unconvincing. I hadn't gotten it.

"Where's your cell phone?" he demanded.

"In my purse."

He grabbed the purse from the seat beside me, reached inside, and found the phone. "Unlock it," he said, handing it to me. After I'd done that, he took the phone back, entered Hayes's number, and returned the phone to me.

"Don't give him any extra time," Fedorenko said. "No more than twenty minutes. Now do it."

I took a deep breath as I tried to think of a convincing spiel for Hayes. I pressed the Send button.

Hayes answered. "Yes?"

"Pen Wilkinson."

A pause. Then, "Ms. Wilkinson. What can I do for you?" His tone was neutral and professional.

"We need to talk."

"About what?"

"About Downfall."

"Downfall was terrible. I experienced the effects of it on my bank. But I see no reason why you and I would have occasion to converse about it."

"Things have changed, Mr. Hayes. As you know, I'm sitting on some information you would not want to see publicized."

"I'm quite sure I have no idea what you're talking about."

"It would be in your interest to talk to me."

"I hate to be impolite, Ms. Wilkinson, but I'm rather busy at the moment. Now, if you'll excuse me . . ."

I felt panicky. He was blowing me off. He was also talking in a way that was stilted and formal, even for a pompous ass like him. What was he—?

Then I understood.

"I'm not recording you, Mr. Hayes. I have no interest in entrapping you for the authorities. But know this: Any agreements I've made with you are null and void, as far as I'm concerned. The price of my silence has gone up after everything you put me and my family through with this latest fiasco."

He didn't respond, so I pressed on.

"I'm going to be in my van in front of your building in twenty minutes," I said. "I want you to send your son down to talk. If he's not there, everything is off, and I'll be releasing a full account of Downfall to the media this afternoon."

After a long silence, he said, "Why do you want Skip?"

I knew I had him.

"I have a few things to say to him after he threatened me in your parking garage. He's also less likely to be recognized. You have twenty minutes." I hung up.

Fedorenko ripped the phone from my hand. "Very good," he said. He squeezed between the two front seats, sat down in the passenger seat, and fastened his seatbelt. He looked at his watch. "We have about ten minutes before we have to leave."

We sat awkwardly for a couple of minutes before I decided to break the silence. "How are you connected with Emily?"

"I go back with her family to the old country. Her uncle and I served time together. We settled in New Jersey in the nineties."

"And you worked for the Russian mafia."

He shrugged. "I made a living."

"What is Emily's real name?"

"Natalia." He said it with real affection. "She was a computer genius as a child. We encouraged her to find ways to make money with her skills, and she did. Soon she was in business for herself. Her father and uncle made her hire me to watch her back. A few years ago, the FBI got close and she had to disappear. She set up the Mishkin identity, changed her name to Emily, and moved a couple of times. That's when she set up a legitimate consulting business. We ended up in Minnesota to work on the Columbia Central project. I set up the body shop and helped her."

"She became obsessed with Kenny."

"Yes. I disapproved. It was a schoolgirl crush. Kenny, he's a nice boy. And smart. But he was a distraction."

"Emily will have to go to prison."

He leaned over in my direction. "Yes, she will. Thanks to you." He lowered his voice. "She is like a daughter to me. I promised her father I would protect her. I couldn't, because of your meddling." For a moment, he looked like he was going to hit me again. Instead, he glanced at his watch. "It's time."

I had only been half-listening to Fedorenko. I'd been stalling, thinking of ways to get out of this situation, ways to survive. And I couldn't think of any. He was going to kill me. When he got his money, he'd probably kill Skip, too. My head and jaw throbbed as the adrenaline in my bloodstream fought the exhaustion.

I started the van and pulled out of the alley. After a couple of blocks, I turned east onto Fourth Street. When we reached Hennepin Avenue, he said, "Turn here."

"We need to take the Central Avenue Bridge."

"Take this one instead."

I turned. A possible plan had gone down the drain.

"Do you think I'm an idiot?" he demanded. "Don't you think I know Central Avenue goes past police headquarters?"

We drove through the traffic to the Hennepin Avenue Bridge. We'd have to circle and come back to Hayes's building on the river.

Except that I wasn't going to do it.

An odd sense of peace descended over me as I neared the bridge. I had seen two people, Alec Sellars and Gary Sink, give in to coercion. They had survived. Their loved ones had survived. I wouldn't. And I saw no reason to facilitate a kidnapping before I was killed. This crime spree had to end somewhere. I could do my part to see that it ended here, even if the effect was to protect a man—Skip Hayes—whom I detested. I could give my life to something worthwhile. I wouldn't be bullied or coerced just to extend my life by a couple of minutes or hours. I'd go on my own terms.

Traffic loosened and sped up when we reached the bridge. I increased my speed, too.

Thoughts and images—random or maybe not so random— flooded my consciousness at high speed. Thoughts about my life, and about Marsha, and James, and Kenny, and Tracy. Thoughts about all the experiences I'd had—all the conflicts, all the hits and near-misses, and a couple of times when maybe I'd done something worthwhile.

It had all been okay, I concluded.

As we neared the far end of the bridge, by Nicollet Island, I hit the brakes.

"What are you doing?" Fedorenko yelled.

I continued to brake.

"Speed up!" He stuck the gun in my face.

We slid to a halt. Horns honked, brakes screeched, and cars swerved around us.

"Get going or I'll kill you!"

I didn't respond.

He struck me in the face with the gun. I gasped in pain. But I opened my door, yanked the keys out of the ignition, and threw them out onto the street.

"You stupid bitch!" He wound up to hit me again. I flinched, but there was no way to escape or avoid the blow.

And then everything exploded. I was hurled forward, and a few seconds later, sideways, and then back against the seat.

I found out later that throwing my door open was what had distracted one of the drivers behind us, causing him to panic, freeze, and ram us in the right rear end. The impact shoved us into the adjacent lane, where a second car T-boned us. An airbag blew up in my face. I lost consciousness, but apparently for only a few seconds. When I came to, Fedorenko was wrestling with his own air bag. He didn't seem to be holding the gun, I noticed. My own airbag had mostly deflated.

People appeared outside the vehicle.

"Are you all right?"

"Hang on—I've called 911!"

I had to brush off a woman who wanted to help me out of the van and didn't realize how much help I actually needed. Only my seatbelt prevented her from yanking me out into the street, where I would have collapsed like a rag doll.

Fedorenko's door opened. "Hang on, buddy!" a man said. Fedorenko disengaged himself from the air bag and his seatbelt. Now he started searching the floor of the van for his gun.

A second man—a young fellow—appeared in Fedorenko's doorway. "I'm an off-duty paramedic," he said. "Let's check you over."

"He's got a gun," I managed to shout. "He's kidnapping me."

The paramedic froze. "What the hell—"

"The gun is on the floor or in the back," I said, my head spinning from the effort of talking. Now I could hear sirens.

The paramedic and Fedorenko seemed to have spotted the gun at the same time. Both lunged for it. Fedorenko punched the young man. A struggle ensued. The gun went off. I was groggy, barely able to follow the action.

I saw the paramedic reel backward onto the sidewalk, and Fedorenko followed him, lunging unsteadily out of the vehicle.

People screamed. There were shouts. The young paramedic stood back, apparently unharmed. The sirens grew louder. Fedorenko, I could now see, had the gun. He looked around, apparently trying to decide whom to shoot. Then he decided to run.

He didn't get far. The reports of a gun, and now of shots fired, had apparently reached the police responding to the accident, and units had blocked both ends of the bridge. Fedorenko fled down a side street to Nicollet Island. But Nicollet Island is, well, an island, and was easy for the police to seal off. He surrendered within minutes.

I bent over and rested my head against the steering wheel. My last thought, before consciousness left the building, was that the van rental company was going to be pissed.

Epilogue

My first few hours in the hospital were fuzzy, with bouts of confusion interspersed with police questioning. Finally, I was left in peace to sleep off the exhaustion and painkiller. I was drifting in and out of awareness late that night when James Carter walked in. He held me silently for a long time. And even though he quickly became satisfied that my injuries were not serious, he didn't leave my bedside until I was released the following afternoon.

Stefan Fedorenko was being held in the Hennepin County Jail. He would plead innocent to kidnapping and assault charges, but the investigation into his activities, by both state and federal authorities, was just beginning. Emily Radatz, born Natalia Zubkhov, regained consciousness and was moved to the secure wing of the hospital.

Brit and the other two members of the SSI team were detained at an airstrip in New Mexico, trying to leave the country. They would undoubtedly call upon their friends in the federal government to intervene on their behalf. There seemed to be, however, a general feeling that by attacking US citizens on US soil, the contractors had crossed a line that would make it impossible for their spook buddies to get them off the hook. Carlin remained in the hospital in Minneapolis under tight security; I'd warned Lieutenant Candiotti that the contractor's colleagues might try to bust him out.

Dustin Blount won his proxy fight, having secured enough votes to clinch the election of his slate of directors. His victory was aided by the stunning news about the investigation of Osborne

Hayes for malicious cyber-hacking, and even a link to a murder in Florida. The day after his victory, Blount resigned, in an action analysts were at a loss to explain.

Sam Fenton was home now, largely recovered from his attack, but would need therapy for post-traumatic stress disorder. Sierra's uncle, Glenn Walsh, was released from the hospital and seemed to be doing fine. Sierra returned to her job at the boutique. Kenny began the process of finishing two high school classes and enrolling at the University of Minnesota in the fall. Alec seemed likely to be prosecuted for tax evasion, since he'd failed to report the large sums Z had paid him. But he'd need to find emotional support elsewhere, since Shannon was filing for divorce.

I didn't win the Vargas case, because there was no trial, the defendants having decided to plead guilty, accepting the same deal I'd been offering them for months. That was most fortunate for me, since I was in no shape, mentally or physically, to try a case.

The news media ran extensive coverage of my encounter with Fedorenko, portraying me as a hero for thwarting the kidnapping. The publicity made me cringe. The news reports were an in-your-face rebuke to Osborne Hayes and Dustin Blount, the two powerful bankers who were already decidedly unhappy with me. It got worse when California media picked up the story a day later. My already-furious boss could now watch me on TV in a faraway state, doing something totally unrelated to my job—and getting acclaim for it. Worse, the publicity might make it harder for him to mete out the punishment he undoubtedly thought I deserved. You can't, as James put it, "fire a damn hero." I wasn't so sure about that. But Wade Hirsch could, in any event, continue to make my life miserable.

I'd refused all requests for interviews, but when the paramedic who'd helped me on the bridge appeared at my bedside with a TV news crew, James and I reluctantly concluded that we couldn't say no to the brave passerby who'd probably saved my life. And so my face appeared on TV, sporting big bruises from the airbag and the blow from Fedorenko. When the time came for my discharge from the hospital, the nurse, who hadn't seen me out of bed, said she'd order me a wheelchair to take me out to the curb. I laughed and told her not to bother.

After driving me from the hospital back to the condo, James stayed with me for an extra day before preparing to head home and leave me in Marsha's care. He'd left Alicia in Santa Monica with his brother, Eric. Marsha and James had never met each other and were decidedly wary at first, but to my relief, they were chatting easily by the time James left.

With typically colorful language, James noted that "Your leg may not work great, but you gave my pal Ozzie a hell of an ass-kicking." His buddy Dustin had gotten one, too, but James understood. As for my simultaneously alienating both bankers, he observed drily, "You've always had that talent." The levity of these comments, however, masked a deep-seated fear and dismay, reopening longstanding, recurring disagreements. James was, in fact, deeply disturbed by my exploits, occasionally expressing admiration but gravitating inevitably back toward fear.

We said little on the day of his departure. I was propped up in bed when James walked in, his bag packed, ready to leave for the airport. He sat down on the bed and held my hand, his face a mask of doubt and turmoil. I wondered if we were going to talk about the subject we'd been avoiding, the new Elephant.

He stared out the window for a long time, not voicing the uncomfortable truths we already knew: that my latest escapade wouldn't be my last; that sooner rather than later, I'd be drawn into another situation, another non-coincidence, that would put me in conflict with powerful interests; and that ultimately, these episodes were not the result of bad luck.

They were who I was.

He knew, as I did, that my entire path—from a trial lawyer representing the underdog, to an accident victim trying to survive, to a wronged employee fighting back, to a prosecutor righting injustice, to an aunt and a sister who couldn't ignore a call for help—all of it had led inexorably to encounters that weren't just traumatic events. They were my life—maybe not the life I wanted, exactly, but seemingly the one I was destined for.

James and I sat in silence, contemplating the costs of living this way. What if it meant losing each other?

"What are we going to do?" he said at last, voicing my thoughts.

I didn't answer.

"I don't know if I can handle any more of this," he said. "I don't know if Alicia can take it, either."

"Maybe we need to take a break from each other while we think about it." I could scarcely believe I had said it. I took deep breaths, trying to keep from sobbing.

"I don't know, Pen."

"We'll have to talk about it when I get home," I said.

And then he left.

Now, two days later—five days after the Columbia Central crisis had come to a head—I shrugged off my gloom and anxiety about James and drove across downtown on a beautiful June afternoon. My destination was the hospital, where I would visit Marsha and her new granddaughter. It was probably a little early for me to drive, since I still had some mild concussion symptoms, from the car crash and from Fedorenko slugging me. But I was recovering, and I had optimistically ordered a replacement rental van delivered to the condo.

I parked in a handicapped spot in the ramp and rolled across the skyway to the hospital. On an upper floor, I found Marsha in the waiting area for the neonatal intensive care unit, seated next to a man with thinning hair and glasses. Both stood up as I approached.

Marsha beamed as she presented her fiancé. "Pen, meet Dr. Nathan Schuler."

His smile was shy but genuine as we shook, then hugged. "So glad to finally meet you, Pen."

After a brief exchange of pleasantries, I asked, "Did you get a chance to talk to Emily?"

"We did," Marsha said, "and she was very agreeable."

"Oh, Marsh, I'm so happy for you two." She leaned down and hugged me, tears in her eyes. Neither Kenny nor Emily, who faced a difficult recovery followed by jail time, were equipped to raise a child. Accordingly, after consultations with both parents, everybody had now agreed to the adoption of their baby girl by Marsha and Nathan. Given her pedigree, the baby was likely to be very smart indeed.

"Do you have a name yet?" I asked.

"Yes, we do. All four of us agreed on Christine." Now Marsha and I felt our tears change to full-blown blubbering. Christine had been our mother's name.

After we'd regained our composure, Marsha and Nathan sat down again. "I've taken a leave of absence from the hospital," Marsha said. "We should be able to bring the baby down to Florida in a month or so. And don't make any plans for mid-August. We need you in Tampa."

"Why?"

"Because we can't get married without our maid of honor."

I almost broke down again.

"Pen," she said, "I feel incredibly guilty about getting you involved in all this. But thank God you did help."

"And I'm glad I did."

I thought about the road ahead. The challenges I'd faced last week—my troubled relationship with James, my hostile boss, and the daily grind of living as a paraplegic—looked pretty much the same as they did today. But now, it felt different.

When you have a family, everything is different.

AN INVITATION TO READING GROUPS/BOOK CLUBS

I would like to extend an invitation to reading groups/book clubs across the country. Invite me to your group and I'll be happy to participate in your discussion. I'm available to join your discussion either in person or via the telephone. (Reading groups should have a speakerphone.) You can arrange a date and time by e-mailing me at brian@brianlutterman.com. I look forward to hearing from you.

Not Sure What to Read Next?
Try these authors from Conquill Press

Jenifer LeClair

The Windjammer Mystery Series
Rigged for Murder
Danger Sector
Cold Coast
Apparition Island
Dead Astern
www.windjammermysteries.com

Chuck Logan

Fallen Angel
Broker
www.chucklogan.org

Brian Lutterman

The Pen Wilkinson Mystery Series
Downfall
Windfall
www.brianlutterman.com

Steve Thayer

Ithaca Falls
The Wheat Field
www.stevethayer.com

Christopher Valen

The John Santana Mystery Series
White Tombs
The Black Minute
Bad Weed Never Die
Bone Shadows
Death's Way
The Darkness Hunter
www.christophervalen.com

For more information on all these titles go to:
www.conquillpress.com

CPSIA information can be obtained
at www.ICGtesting.com
Printed in the USA
LVOW11s0521140317
527066LV00001B/4/P